THE BADDEST CHICK

Also by Alastair J. Hatter

It's On and Poppin'

THE BADDEST CHICK

Alastair J. Hatter

URBAN BOOKS
www.urbanbooks.net

Urban Books
10 Brennan Place
Deer Park, NY 11729

ISBN-13: 978-1-60162-009-5
ISBN-10: 1-60162-009-8

First Printing July 2007
Printed in the United States of America

10 9 8 7 6 5 4 3 2 1

Submit Wholesale Orders to:
Kensington Publishing Corp.
C/O Penguin Group (USA) Inc.
Attention: Order Processing
405 Murray Hill Parkway
East Rutherford, NJ 07073-2316
Phone: 1-800-526-0275
Fax: 1-800-227-9604

This book is dedicated to the ones who are supporting me. The ones who spent their hard earned money to get both the sequel and It's On And Poppin'. The ones who always gave me a word of encouragement in my time of need. To the ones who saw the capability that I possess in writing knock out stories. I just wanted y'all to know that I am truly grateful cuz y'all played a great part in my success. I will never forget y'all, be-lev-dat!

This book is also dedicated to all the men and women who are locked up doing time, especially my peeps (Vernon "Cool V" Smith—Toledo, Ohio) doing life. Y'all hold your head up, cuz y'all may be gone but you're not forgotten. Word Up! Stay Strong!

Acknowledgment

Dear Heavenly Father, I speak to you often even though I don't abide by all your rules like you ask of me. I feel guilty and ashamed at times for not doing so. Why? Well look at all that you have done for a brothah (your child). You have given so much. My career has begun because of you. But Father, I see that you are working on me slowly but surely cuz in the past when I tried to do things on my own I failed. But when I realized that nothing is possible without you and started asking you to grant me ideas, things changed. I'm glad I wised up and starting asking before acting. Thank you. I Luv U.

To my moms and pops. Bertha "Tot" Hatter and Herbert "Big Duke' Hatter, y'all are the best parents that a son could ever have. Because y'all were entrepreneurs your kids inherited the gift. Y'all did a great job, I just thought I would tell you that and let the world know also.

To my brothers and sister. Marvin (Willie) Jobe, Bobby Jobe, Danny Jobe, Herbert (Len) Hatter, Albert Hatter, Rutha (Rudy) Jobe-Kitchen, Marcella (Sally Ann) Jobe-Dickerson, Tina (Teen Bean) Jobe, Yvette Jobe, Diane Jobe, Karen Jobe, Samantha (Sammy) Hatter, Greg Dickerson, Linda Hatter and all my brother-in-laws and sister-in-laws. I love y'all!

ACKNOWLEDGMENT

To my nieces and nephews. It's crazy how a lot of y'all have the names of one of your uncles or aunts. Hey, if the shit works why not keep passing it down the family tree no matter who gots the name. I love y'all. Hatters and Jobe are running sh*t!

To the big man Mark Anthony. Man Mark. God really gots his hand on you. Feel truly blessed brother. Your last book Lady's Night was like that. I still hear cats saying that book was a good read. You're not only a talented brother but you're showing your ability to lead and manage a company. The moves you made are commendable. The future shows prosperity so don't slow down but keep focus cuz the hard work is showing and paying off. Oh yeah, I notice something about your personal character. In other authors acknowledgements from various companies I peeped they gave you shout outs. The impressive thing about it was how they spoke of you, which was humbly respectful. Just wanted you to know that if that many people speak that way about you then that confirms what I already felt and knew. Glad to be a friend.

To Linda (Super Mom) Williams, you are something else. I am so proud to see that our bond has gotten close. You handle me just the way you should. Your leadership and guidance has kept me on track and focus. You have showed me while you are at work on other author's books there is still room for a pleasant conversation. Trust me when I say this, I am glad that I made the choice to call you Super Mom, I know in my heart it was the fitting title for you. I love you, MOM.

ACKNOWLEDGMENT

To Dolly Lopez, hey girl. Did you think I forgot about you this go around? Come On Now. This is me. You have spoken honestly and openly. I can tell you this from the bottom of my heart. Thank you for being kind and honest.

To my kids' mothers. Jada Price (Mercedes, Alexus & Alonte), I'm glad to see you happy. Kia Jones (Alil), you have been a friend, I owe you, girl. Tiffany Nelson (Ashly-Tot), I thank you for keeping me and Tot close. Christiana Yager (Aubrianna), thank you for a beautiful daughter. Enidina Benivides (Anthony), I'm stepping up to the plate. He and I need each other and now is the time. Ladies y'all are the most respected ladies I know. I take my hat off to y'all. Thank you for keeping it real.

To Christina (Shorty Momma), you have made a move that took a lot of faith. I love you for that. I hope I'm able to show you the same in return. Your kids are in good hands especially Lil'Momma. I love you.

T Dianna (Dreamy), you have always been in my mind. You showed me something that I can never forget. Where I thought there was no hope, you proved it to be false. Past is the past. I love you.

To Latosha (PYT), why is all of this feeling so good? You show up and brighten a brothah's day. Your words is real I can feel your words are real. What you went through in the past is over with. Let yourself now explore a new life of happiness from here on out. Your hero is not a myth. I'm in the flesh.

ACKNOWLEDGMENT

To the Hensley family. Curtis and Karen—what can I say, but thanks a lot for helping me through the dark times. Cedric, I will never forget the force you sent through my body through that punching bag. Good luck up North in the cold. Find married older people to give you and your wife wisdom on how to keep a family together. Take that tip. Lil'Bro. Shelly, Shelly, Shelly. What's this about another child? Why didn't you tell me? I'm your big brother. Now I wanna yell at you, but what is done is done. Don't sit on your butt, do you, take control like Hensely women do. Get your degree. I love ya, Lil'Sis. To the rest of the Hensely family. Y'all have been a pleasure to know and I will love to be part of your family, but I guess y'all knew that already, huh?

Chapter One

"Your Honor, we, the State, respectfully request that the defendant, Deondra Davis, be held without bond due to the nature and severity of the crime she's been charged with. The State also feels the defendant is a potential flight risk," the tall, fake blonde prosecutor said sternly.

"That's bullshit! The whole charge is some bullshit! Y'all always harassing black folks instead of helping us out," Ronshay shouted, standing up and pointing her finger at the prosecutor, as if she were shooting her words with her hand.

"Young lady, let's get this straight once and for all. This nameplate right here"—The judge jumped up and slid her finger across her name— "says Judge Ruby Jones, which is me, not you or anybody else in this courtroom. So one more outburst like that and I will show you just how much power God has vested in me, a black woman like yourself."

The courtroom was so quiet at the end of her statement that if a penny dropped on the floor and rolled, everybody would've known exactly where it stopped.

The judge kept her eyes focused right on Ronshay.

Finally, Miya, who was seated next to Ronshay, tugged on her blue blouse, and Ronshay gave in and sat down. Miya quickly put her arms around Ronshay's neck and brought her in for a hug. Both had tears coming from their eyes, and the affection between the two was evident to the judge and everybody else present in the courtroom.

Ronshay couldn't help the outburst, which was just a way of relieving the monstrous weight of hurt and sadness that had built up inside of her since Bee and his brother Jay were gunned down and killed. After all, she too had just lost the love of her life, Bee, to yet another tragic ghetto mishap.

The judge had already heard about the death of Dee Dee's two brothers, Jay and Bee, because the newspaper had a field day plastering an article about the shooting all over the front page of the *Memphis Herald*. The headline read: "Two Suspected Drug Dealers Beat Case In Court, Only to Be Gunned Down in the Streets."

The judge ordered the proceedings to continue, and once again, Ms. Laureen Cole, the prosecutor, picked her argument as to why she thought Dee Dee shouldn't receive any type of bail. "Your Honor, the defendant should be denied bail. This is a case that the State feels it can win, but if the defendant is granted bail, then who knows if she will return to court, since the State will seek the death penalty when—"

"Objection, Your Honor! The prosecutor, Ms. Cole, is out of line." Mr. Cee leapt to his feet, adopting a serious look for the lump sum of money he was being paid to handle Dee Dee's case. "For one thing, Your Honor, the State doesn't have a strong case against my client, and, two, they should never have charged my client with what little evidence they presented. Your Honor, Deondra Davis is no more of a flight risk than she is guilty of the State's accusations against her. I respectfully ask that my client be granted bail on her own recognizance. Thank you, Your Honor."

Dee Dee was looking out of the window the whole time her lawyer was pleading her case, at the humming bird that kept flying around the outside, capturing her attention, and taking her far away from the melee that was taking place inside the courtroom.

"Ms. Davis!" The judge aimed her words directly at Dee Dee herself, who was oblivious to the proceedings.

Mr. Cee nudged her leg under the table, out of sight of the judge.

Dee Dee made eye contact with him. "I'm sorry, Mr. Cee. You were talking to me?"

"You need to be paying attention in here, Deondra," he said in a deep, serious tone. "This is your life we're fighting to preserve. By the way, it wasn't me talking to you, it was the judge."

Dee Dee swung her attention straight to the judge, who was already looking dead at her with a look that said, "Get your head outta the clouds."

"Young lady, I'm going to give you an opportunity to tell me why I should grant you bail when the State is surely opposed to granting such. Isn't that right, Ms. Cole?"

The prosecutor stood and spoke, looking at both the judge and Dee Dee. "That is correct, Your Honor."

Mr. Cee looked at Dee Dee then whispered softly to her, "This is your one shot to make the judge see and hear why you should be set free." He placed his hand under Dee Dee's elbow, which was resting on the dark brown wooden table at which they were seated, and lightly signaled for her to rise to her feet, the proper way to address someone controlling your fate.

Dee Dee placed her hand over her face and took a deep breath. She really wasn't too concerned with getting released from jail like she once was, since her brothers weren't around anymore. Life didn't mean as much to her as it once did. Jay and Bee were gone, and she knew nothing could bring them back.

Another nudge from Mr. Cee brought Dee Dee back out of her thoughts. She removed her hand from her face to reveal teary eyes.

"You okay?" Mr. Cee asked.

Dee Dee didn't look Mr. Cee's way, but she was able to muster a nod of her head.

"Young lady, do you wish to address this court on why you should be granted bail?" the judge asked again, leaning back in her seat and rocking.

Dee Dee, dressed in her blue issue county jail jumpsuit with the initials MCG stamped on the back in big letters, rose out of her light brown wooden chair. Even with her eyes puffy and dressed in something so tacky, she still looked good. She wiped her eyes then raised her head to face the judge, who was waiting patiently to hear what she had to say.

"Your Honor . . ." Dee Dee didn't mean for her words to come out incorrect or muffled, but her throat was dry.

Her lawyer quickly handed her a glass of water.

She took a couple of sips and cleared her throat with a cough. "I'm sorry. I guess I needed that drink." Then she continued, "Your Honor, I am not guilty of what they got me sitting in that nasty jail for. All I know is that life is taking me through some changes that I feel no one should have to go through. I can remember having two brothers who were always trying to run my life by keeping boys away from me. Now they're gone and I'm all alone. I realize that they weren't just doing that to be mean or to make my life hard, but in fact, all they were doing was looking out for their little sister. Now, how can I tell them how grateful I am for having them as brothers who went out of their way to show that kind of love and affection?" The tears began flowing once again, only harder this time, and when Mr. Cee tried to give Dee Dee a tissue, she lightly pushed his hand back. Her feelings were coming out and she didn't want anything to stop them. She wanted to talk and remember her brothers because, for the first time in her life, she liked talking about them.

"If it is your wish, Your Honor, to keep me in that place, then I guess I will have to stay there. And if it is, then I guess I'll probably be better off in jail, seeing as how I'm all alone now.

Ronshay leapt to her feet and shouted, "Don't say that, Dee Dee. You're not alone."

"That's right, Dee Dee." Miya stood and clasped her hand in Ronshay's. "We're here for you."

Dee Dee turned around and saw both Miya and Ronshay looking her way with tears in their own eyes. Dee Dee knew in her heart and mind that those two were gonna be there for her, no matter what.

"Order in the court!" The judge slammed her gavel repeatedly on the sound block.

Dee Dee's head quickly whipped back around to face the judge, and Miya and Ronshay sat down just as quickly, like they were little girls in church being scolded for not paying attention.

"Young lady, it seems that you are not alone like you thought, judging from those two in the back that I have to keep telling to be quiet in my courtroom." The judge looked dead at Miya and Ronshay with a heated stare. "Now, back to the matter at hand. Ms. Davis, I want to ask you a question." The judge waited until she got the look she wanted from Dee Dee that would show her that she understood. "Ms. Davis, do you believe in God?"

Dee Dee wasn't sure where the question was leading, but it did arouse her curiosity. Dee Dee did believe in God. In fact her mother was a strict Christian, which was exactly why she'd moved out of her mom's house and in with her brothers in the first place. Now she began to wonder if there really was a God. She felt that for her to lose both of her brothers at once was some straight bullshit, and if God would let something like that happen, then there was no God.

The judge leaned forward. "Ms. Davis, I'm waiting for your response."

Dee Dee straightened up. "Your Honor, that's a tough one. I mean, I was raised in a church, and so were my brothers, and looked what happened to them. Now I'm sitting in jail for something that I didn't do. My brothers are never coming back. I find it kind of hard for a merciful God to let anything like that happen when I believed in him. Now I just don't know."

The judge leaned back in her chair once again. She looked Dee Dee over, asking herself whether she could've committed the crime she was being charged with. She couldn't see a girl as cute as Dee Dee committing a crime as bad as murder, but she knew all too well from experience that looks could be deceiving.

The judge closed her eyes and flashed back in time to when black women were strong. When they held a family together through thick and thin, no matter how many kids they had or how unhappy they were in their relationship with the kids' father. She fast-forwarded to the present, to a time when black women were being locked up at a rate that was catching up with rate black men were being imprisoned at.

The judge felt that if Dee Dee was going to connect with God again, then she was going to have to be released, to see the meaning of what was good in her life and what wasn't. Her decision to release Dee Dee was also due to the fact that she'd had lost two people who were very close to her. The judge started writing something down on a paper that rested in front of her.

Everyone was watching, except for Dee Dee, whose focus was now back on the hummingbird flying outside the window.

The prosecutor, Ms. Cole, was damn near breaking her neck trying to see what Judge Jones was writing down, until the judge raised her head and looked toward the courtroom, which made Ms. Cole snap her body back into her seat.

"May the defendant please rise," Judge Jones said.

Dee Dee and her lawyer rose at the same time.

"I feel you need to take some time and find God again.

I don't believe that you left Him, and I know that He has not left you. My granting you bail is a certain sign that He is still there for you. I hereby—"

Ms. Cole, sure that the judge was about to go against the grain and grant bail, interjected quickly, "Your Honor, I object! You can't be serious about granting this defendant bail. She will skip court. I can see it in her eyes."

Judge Jones was already expecting Ms. Cole to react in such a defensive manner. That's why she let her speak her mind. It was just one of Judge Jones's tactics to let someone sink their own ship before she blew it up herself.

"Ms. Cole, this is my courtroom. This nameplate bears my name. When you're in a position to make the final decisions, then you will not have to object," she stated in a tone that said she was the H.B.I.C. (Head Bitch In Charge).

"Your Honor, since that is your final decision, then the State respectfully asks that the defendant's bail be set at one million dollars to ensure that she doesn't skip town." Ms. Cole flicked her hair over her shoulder in a bold and cocky manner.

Judge Jones looked at Ms. Cole as if she'd lost her mind. She knew that she hated black people and felt they all needed to be locked up. And since Dee Dee didn't look like she had a hundred dollars, let alone one million, she ignored Ms. Cole's recommendation.

"I hereby set bail at one hundred thousand dollars—"

Ms. Cole jumped to her feet when she heard that.

"With ten percent of that being paid by either funds or property."

Ms. Cole damn near shit on herself when she heard the rest. She knew not to say another word, so she sat down in her chair and leaned back like she was home drinking wine.

Miya and Ronshay ran up to Dee Dee and leaned over the waist-high dark brown wooden rail that separated the gallery from the court officers.

Dee Dee was a millionaire forty times over, so one hundred thousand was nothing.

The judge walked out of the courtroom through the door behind her bench, feeling good about her decision, and went into her chambers and prayed for peace of mind for Deondra Davis, and for her to keep the faith that she would find God once again.

The day was gloomy, and the clouds in the sky were dark. Today was truly a sad day for all who were connected to the two brothers who lay in their caskets, ready to be buried six feet deep.

Dee sat next to her mother outside in the front row seats in front of her brothers' open caskets, as all who were present at the funeral were crying and holding on to each other for comfort. Miya and Ronshay, both crying away, sat opposite Dee Dee.

Pastor Troy went on with his sermon, stressing that Jay and Bee had been called back home to the sky above to be with God. As he preached, the ten-person choir sang softly. The whole service was beautiful, but it was all too much for Dee Dee to bear. Memories of her brothers started bombarding her mind. She thought of their over-protective ways, and how they would catch an attitude with any guy who got caught looking at her wrong, said something to her, or tried to touch her. Though it pissed her off so much back then, she wished she had them now.

Dee Dee stood up, tears falling from her eyes. The black dress she had on with her women's cashmere trench coat was swaying from the stormy wind. Her hair was laid down straight and covered the side of her face. She walked over to Jay's oak casket, decorated with assorted flower arrangements and different-sized wreathes, and draped inside with red silk. Jay didn't look like he was dead at all, but more like he was asleep. The mortuary had done a lovely job on their faces to make them look that way. After all, they were shot at point-blank range.

Dee Dee leaned over and kissed Jay on his forehead then told him that she would see him again, promising she would get the bitch-ass muthafucka that got them before she met back up with him and Bee, no matter what. Then she laid three roses on his chest and patted them, telling him to look out for her when she couldn't for herself.

Next, she went to Bee's oak casket. The black Gucci suits that she had picked out for them to be buried in did both true justice. They looked like they were ready to step out on the town.

Dee Dee looked back when she heard Ronshay cry out. No longer the happy-go-lucky female Dee Dee once knew, Ronshay seemed to be taking it hard. Since the incident, all she did was mope around as if she were dying herself. She had had big dreams for her and Bee, but now she couldn't see anything without him being around.

Dee Dee took the last three roses and placed them in the same place on Bee as she did with Jay. She then leaned her head into his casket and gave him a kiss, telling him that whoever did this to them would pay with their life, and that she meant it.

As Dee Dee walked away crying while the service was

still going on, her mother looked at her and wondered what fate would befall her only child. She wanted to go after her, but she remained stern, like always, since Dee Dee chose to be a grown woman and move out. Behind the sheer black veil hanging from her bonnet down in front of her face, she just closed her eyes and let her tears fall, saying a silent prayer for all of her children to be kept safe in God Almighty's hands.

After leaving the funeral, Dee Dee drove around on the expressway in her H2, zoned out and not knowing exactly where she was headed. For a moment her tears had taken a break. God knows, her eyes needed it. They were already bloodshot, not to mention the bags under her eyes, which were becoming quite noticeable. As she was driving, the blaring sirens of the police car that just flew past her broke her train of thoughts and made her think about what she was going to do with all the dope she had.

Before Jay and Bee were killed, they'd told Dee Dee, the sole beneficiary of their estate, all about Tony and Don Valdez getting killed, meaning she now had no one to pay back, making her a rich muthafucka, even though she didn't feel like it.

Dee Dee whipped her Hummer H2 around in the middle of traffic and busted a U-turn. She wanted to head back to the safe house, where she hadn't been since her release, to check things out. She figured if she was gonna find out who killed her brothers then she would have to become one with the streets again. Her mission was to get back in the game, shake shit up, pumping the dope. While doing that, she would seek out her brothers' killer or killers. She knew that she had to step her game up and take it to the next level, which was the only way that she could become the baddest bitch to ever hit the streets of Memphis.

Dee Dee pulled in front of the apartment building and parked, opened the driver's door, and stepped out and just stood there looking on at what her brothers had started. The two-story building with six apartments on each floor was impressive. Jay and Bee were two of the smartest guys she ever knew. No one suspected that five thousand kilos of coke and over forty million dollars in cold, hard cash was hidden behind a wall inside one of the apartments.

Dee Dee headed for the building. As she made it to the entrance door leading into the hallway, a car horn blew. She whipped her head around just in time to see stankin'-ass Mieka waving at her, and with that bitch-ass nigga who used to be her brothers' homeboy, until what was in the dark came to light. Dee Dee didn't know why Mieka was blowing at her, especially after that fight they'd had at the house when Mieka showed up at the front door and threw paint all up in her face. That was a for-sure indicator that they would never been on good terms again. Actually, just seeing Mieka sparked the fire in Dee Dee to want to just whup that ass again.

Dee Dee shook Mieka out of her thoughts, like a pimp be poppin' his collar, then went inside. She finally realized how cold it was outside when she felt the heat coming from the electric heater that lined the walls in the hallways.

Dee Dee unlocked the door to the stash apartment that held the dope and the money, closed the door, and put all the locks on, making sure it was as secure as a bank vault. She kicked her heels off and walked over to the security monitors to make sure no one was outside looking around, playing sneaky.

Everything was cool from what she could see, so she walked over to the wall and turned the thermostat. Turning the thermostat this way and that was like turning the dial on one of those combination locks where a person had to stop on the right numbers to open the lock. With the right combination entered, the wall cracked open. Dee Dee opened both sides all the way open and stood back and looked at all that was on the shelves. She had plenty of work to do, if she wanted to get rid of all that product.

She was now the real boss, and now she had to start acting the part. No longer did she have her girls, the RBM Clique, to have her back anymore, or her brothers to give her guidance. It was just her from here on out, which meant she had no time to fuck anything up or play around.

Dee Dee walked over to the dark brown desk and pulled the black cushioned chair out so she could get to the upper drawer. She reached her hand out and slid the drawer open. Her eyes were now fixed on two chrome 9mm Beretta pistols. Dee Dee raised her head up and looked around the apartment as if someone was there with her, even though she knew she was alone. It was just that she didn't put the guns there where she found them. There was only one possible way the guns could've gotten there. It had to be that Jay or Bee bought them. Both guns were new, as there wasn't a scratch or blemish anywhere on the chrome, four hollow-point bullets in each clip.

Dee Dee reached down and gripped both guns in each hand. The power and feeling of the steel impressed her. She raised the guns up and pointed toward an imaginary target in front of her, pretending she had the punk muthafucka who killed her brothers cornered, pinned up against

a wall, his bitch ass begging for his life as she dumped bullets into him. The urge to pop somebody took Dee Dee's
body over, and she instinctively pulled the triggers, not
knowing whether the guns were loaded, or if there were
bullets in the chambers.

Two loud BOOOMMMs startled Dee Dee, making her
jump back and drop the guns to the floor. She looked at
the shelf where the bullets had struck two kilo packages,
piercing one and lodging in the other. The cloud of smoke
coming from the bricks was streaming out like somebody
just blew a whole bunch of weed smoke out of their mouth
after inhaling.

Dee Dee covered her mouth as she giggled. She was
hoping that none of the tenants who occupied the apartments downstairs heard the shooting, and fearing for their
lives, thought about calling the police. She walked to the
desk and placed the guns back where she found them. Then
before closing back the fake wall, she reached in and
grabbed a hundred-thousand-dollar stack, just to do a little
shopping.

Once the wall was secured, she walked out of the front
door of the apartment, then went to all the other apartments, telling the tenants that she had somehow blown up
her microwave, which would explain the loud blast they
might've heard earlier. Dee Dee also told them that she
was having an electrician come by to check the wiring,
and that they should tell him if they suspected their own
wiring to be faulty. Which they wouldn't, 'cuz she wasn't
really gonna call one.

Chapter Two

Dee Dee walked through the crowded lobby of the mall with lots of bags filled with designer clothes and shoes. The shopping spree was exactly what she needed to relieve some of the stress plaguing her.

She had been trying to locate Lil' Man since deciding to jump back in the game, but when she asked around, no one seemed to have any knowledge of his whereabouts. Lil' Man was one of few people she felt she could trust, at least to a certain extent. After her own cousins crossed her by tying her up and jacking her, she trusted no one fully.

As she kept walking through the mall, a little white kid shot past her screaming like a spoiled little brat. Dee Dee wondered just where the boy's mother was, with his little ass doing all that acting up. Dee Dee was glad she didn't have any kids. Just seeing his little ass acting like he done lost his mind caused her to want to commit "child abuse in the right way," 'cuz his ass needed a sho' nuff ass-whuppin'.

Dee Dee cast her eyes into the store from where the little kid ran out, and there she saw a black female who was doing a white lady's hair point at the child. Dee Dee quickly figured the boy had to be hers. She didn't understand how the white lady could sit there and get her hair done in the mall salon, but not get her little rug rat and stop his little ass from making her and him look like some fools. But Dee Dee didn't bother with their problems. She had too much of her own shit to worry about and concentrate on.

As she started to walk off, she halted her forward progress. Something told her to stop and look back, which she did. She raised her hand to her head and touched her ponytail. She wondered just how she would look with her hair chopped off and fixed in a new style. Right then, she made up her mind to get her wig chopped, and she knew just the person for the job. Janelle.

Dee Dee walked out of the mall and headed to her ride. After piling her shopping bags on the back seat, she turned her head as she heard a cute black female say, "Love that ride." Dee Dee smiled politely as she got in.

As she drove on the expressway, she thought back to the day when she surprised the RBM Clique, her homegirls, Tricksy, Diamond, and Chills, with their own Hummer H2's. It made Dee Dee feel good that particular day to present them each with a gift like that. She wished that Chills an' 'em didn't rob that bank in the first place, especially when they could've gotten anything they wanted from Dee Dee . . . besides pushing up on her, 'cuz they all liked women. Except Diamond, who went both ways. Now they were sitting in a federal holding facility waiting to be sentenced for a long time.

Dee Dee turned onto her street and headed for her house. As she drove, she could see the person she was looking for sweeping the porch. Dee Dee had to laugh when she parked in front of Janelle's crib and saw those same old mismatched rollers. She could never understand why she put rollers in her shit if she never took them out to style her hair.

Janelle leapt off the porch, like a little kid spotting their momma getting outta the car with bags of groceries in her hands. Janelle was just happy to see Dee Dee, who hadn't been staying in the hood since getting out of jail. The last time Janelle had seen her was at the funeral when Jay and Bee got laid to rest.

As Dee Dee got out of her metallic pink H2, Janelle wrapped her arms around her like crazy and gave her a big-ass hug. "You know you wrong for not comin' home sooner than this. The neighborhood been dead"—Janelle broke her embrace to look at Dee Dee's face as the word, *dead*, escaped her mouth. "I'm so sorry, girl. Me and my big mouth is always saying something jacked up."

Dee Dee knew Janelle meant no harm by the remark. "Janelle, ain't nobody trippin' on that shit anymore. What's done is done." She then gave her a hug.

"So, you back now? I mean, ain't no more of this disappearin' shit?"

"Come on now, I ain't never left. A bitch just needed to get her mind right, you know." Dee Dee smiled.

"I feel that. Hell, God knows if anybody needed to take some time out for herself then it was you, with all the stuff you been through." Janelle looked at Dee Dee from head to toe. "So, let me get this straight, 'cuz if I'm right, you parked on my side of the street, not yours, so that's telling me you want something. Don't tell me, let me guess—You came over so I can fix you a plate of my good cooking."

"That's not why I stopped, but since you're offering, I'm ready to eat then."

"Then, what you waitin' on? My kitchen ain't open for everybody, like Rodney ol' beggin' ass. He think I'm supposed to feed his ass every time he look around." Janelle started walking toward the house.

"Where is Rodney, anyways?" Dee Dee looked at Janelle as they walked.

"I don't know where his ass is at, and frankly, he can stay wherever his little-dick-havin' ass is at." Janelle made two snaps to the right and one to the left.

"What you mean, 'his little-dick-havin' ass'? The only way you can know is if you done sample it, and the way you said it made me think that y'all done did something."

"Well, I did give him some. The nigga came to my house late one night drunk, knocking on my door. So when I went to answer it, he got to telling me how much he really been liking me, and of course he slipped in there how much he liked my cooking too. I fell for the shit, but it ain't like I didn't know him and Teonna had just broke up. But before he went back to her ass, I drained his ass. I don't see what that girl see in his ass, anyways, 'cuz that nigga dick is really small." She smirked. "But his tongue is a different story."

Dee Dee had already figured out a long time ago that the two had something going on because of them fighting all the time. She laughed on the inside. Just looking at how Janelle carried herself, looking like a scrub, or better yet, a hood rat, made her know why a nigga would just want to hit it and quit it. "Mmm-mmm," Dee Dee said to herself as she pictured those two doing the nasty.

While they were inside eating, Dee Dee asked Janelle to hook her hair up, so right after they got through eating, Janelle went and got all of her hair stuff to do the job. As Janelle combed through Dee Dee's long, thick, shoulder-length hair, and got ready to put the hot iron in it, Dee Dee grabbed her hand.

"What's up, Dee Dee? I thought you wanted me to do your hair?" Janelle leaned forward and looked Dee Dee in the eyes.

"I do. It's just that I want you to cut it. I want something different, you know."

"You mean cut all this beautiful hair off? Girl, you must be crazy. I won't have no part of that shit. Hoes always want something new, but when they get it, two days later their asses be cryin' the blues, talking 'bout, 'I can't believe I cut all my hair off.' Don't get me wrong, though, Dee Dee. Those hoes don't mean shit to me but cash in hand, so I cut their shit off as quick as the light man will cut my electricity off for not paying my bill. But you, now that's a different story. You're my girl. Hell, you're like family. To cut all this off"—Janelle flipped Dee Dee's hair up in the air from the back and side—"would be crazy, that is unless you came to me two times a week so I can keep it looking good."

Dee Dee turned her head around to look at Janelle. She realized Janelle was dead serious, which was the only way that Dee Dee wanted to have it. "You got yourself a deal, Janelle. Two times a week it is. Now this should take care of a month's worth of doing my do." Dee Dee pulled out a stack of money that was wrapped in a thousand-dollar wrapper.

"Dee Dee, this is a thousand dollars." Janelle gasped, her eyes bugged the fuck out from seeing that much money in her own hands.

"Yep, and it's all yours, homegirl. But if it ain't enough, I can pay you more."

"Is you crazy? Not enough? Girl, you gave me more than Uncle Sam's cheap ass be givin' me in a month, and they asses know how many kids I gotta feed, just like everybody else around here knows. Hell yeah, this is enough, only if it ain't hurtin' your pocket, 'cuz I know I can do your wig for way less than this right here."

What Janelle said to Dee Dee made her think. Janelle was right. She did have a lot of kids, and Dee Dee knew that they needed more than just their bellies filled up. There weren't a lot of toys around, and Janelle didn't have a car to get to the places she needed to go. The house she was staying in was nice, but it wasn't hers. The people who owned the house before Janelle got it through Section 8 wouldn't sell it to Jay or Bee, who wanted to buy it. Now Janelle's dream was going to come true.

After Janelle was through chopping Dee Dee's hair and Marcelle curled it, she put the handheld mirror in Dee Dee's hand.

Dee Dee took a deep breath before looking into the mirror. She didn't know what she was gonna see or if she would like her new look. As Dee Dee raised the mirror, she was praying that her forehead didn't look big like so many other females' who'd got low cuts. She put the mirror in front of her face and opened her eyes. A big smile leapt onto her face at what she was looking at. Halle Berry three times better-looking was the only way to describe it. The long curled bangs in the front just added that extra pizzazz to her fineness. Dee Dee was happy with what Janelle had created, and for that, she pulled out four more thousand-dollar wraps, just for GP, so Janelle could get her and the kids something nice.

The stunned look on Janelle's face told Dee Dee that Janelle didn't know what to say. Dee Dee just told her not to say thank you, just pack her shit, 'cuz the house across the street that she and her brothers once lived in would soon be rebuilt, and would be Janelle's to live in rent-free.

"Girl, quit playing," Janelle said, sounding unconvinced.

"Janelle, look at me."

Janelle looked on like Dee Dee said.

"I'm not playing. I'm giving you the house. I can't stay in that big ol' thang by myself. Besides, it won't be the same without my brothers there with me. When it's done being worked on, you can move in. All that I ask is that you keep a room for me, so from time to time I can stay over and kick it with family. Deal?"

Janelle was flabbergasted, but she could tell from the look on Dee Dee's face that she wasn't bullshitting. She didn't know whether to smile or cry, cuz it was all too un-real, but what she did know was that if Dee Dee ever needed anything, she would try her damnedest to lend a hand.

As Dee Dee and Janelle walked out of the house and stood on the porch, she gripped Janelle's hand and turned it palm side up and dropped the house keys in it. "I gotta get going. A bitch got a lot to take care of." Dee Dee smiled and headed for her H2.

Just as Dee Dee was about to get in and take off, Janelle yelled out, "But where you gonna stay now, Dee Dee?"

Dee Dee just closed her door and started her ride and rolled off slowly, telling Janelle, "I got plenty of spots to lay my head."

As Dee Dee rolled down her street, there was one person outside leaning back in the seat of his black 2002 GMC Jimmy, waiting the whole time, smoking on some fire-ass weed laced with that crack shit. Junior hadn't forgotten a muthafuckin' thang. He wanted that pussy, just like he wanted that bitch-ass nigga Mikey. In his early search Junior couldn't find Mikey for nothing in the world, that was until Mikey crossed his path. He beat Mikey so bad, and didn't stop until he cracked Mikey's head wide the fuck open, to where the yellow shit seeped out. Mikey's body was placed in an old rundown crackhouse, where now the crackheads didn't bother going into to get high. By now the rats, roaches, and other insects probably had the body to the bone.

As Dee Dee rolled, listening to the radio, Junior was right behind her, still getting high as a kite. He had serious plans for Dee Dee. Only, this time he wasn't planning on getting interrupted by anyone. He figured if someone wanted to be Superman, then the snub-nosed .38 between his legs on the seat would be the kryptonite.

Not suspecting she was being followed by a sick nigga with a vendetta against her, Dee Dee headed for Ronshay's crib. She turned onto the street that led to Farmingdale Apartments, then pulled into the parking lot and parked. Dee Dee opened the door, but before she stepped out, she took a minute to grab the stuff that she'd bought from the mall. As she closed the door with a bump from

her butt, she made her way to Ronshay's door, two shopping bags in each hand.

Junior pulled his black Jimmy into a parking spot not
too far from where Dee Dee had parked her H2. He took
one more toke from the blunt then broke the fire off. His
driver's door swung open, then he emerged out dressed
in an RP55 blue jean outfit with a blue hoody underneath
it. He pulled his hoody over his head then stepped with pep
to catch up with Dee Dee as she made her way through the
courtyard.

If Dee Dee's sixth sense had only been working right
now, she would have known to turn around. Then she
would have seen the nigga coming up from behind her.

Ronshay's apartment was located on the bottom floor.
She had recently changed apartments after Bee and Jay
were buried. Just living in the same apartment that she
and her boo shared so many good times in was just too
much for her. The apartment building's manager didn't
have a problem with Ronshay's request to move, because
she thought Bee was a nice guy, and she knew that Ronshay's request was a reasonable one.

Dee Dee reached the door then knocked on it. She
wanted to wait for a few seconds before putting the bags
down to open it herself. Dee Dee did have a key, but she
wanted Ronshay to open the door, to avoid putting the
bags down then picking them up.

Ronshay heard the knock, but she was too busy puking
in the toilet. Since Bee's death, she'd been going through
some changes. She was lost without her boo. She finally
got herself together and went to answer the door.

* * *

"Perkins, I don't think anybody lives here anymore," Gary stated, as his partner continued to knock on the door.

"How can you say that? We just visited this apartment before we arrested her." Detective Perkins pulled his note-pad out of his shirt pocket. "You see?" He held the paper smack dead in front of Gary's eyes. "Apartment number 245, just like on the freaking door."

"All right, smarty pants. Go ahead and keep knocking so your damn knuckles can bust open."

"Listen, Gary, if you know something that I don't, then I wish you would spit it out instead of beating round the got-darn bush."

"Well, I don't see any curtains or blinds on the windows up there. That's why I don't think anybody is living there."

"Hell, Gary, you could have said all of that earlier."

"Where to now?"

"To the manager's office. They should know why she moved out so abruptly, and if we're lucky then just maybe they have a new address. You know other apartment complexes want reference checks from a last known address."

Gary liked his partner, and sometimes his tactics. It was just that he felt that, at times, his partner took his job too seriously for all the wrong reasons. They were on a mission to find Deondra so they could give her some news, hoping to stir her up a little, to get her to confess to the crime, because the bottom line was, their case against her was weak. They'd heard from the prosecutor, Ms. Cole, that Judge Ruby Jones seemed to take a liking to the girl, which was another strike against their case.

* * *

Ronshay opened the door.

Dee Dee stood there with her hand held high and a big smile on her face. "Look what I got for us," she said, hoping to cheer Ronshay up.

Ronshay broke into a light smile then turned around and headed for her room.

"What! You don't want to see what I—"

THUMMMMPPP! was all Dee Dee felt as she was pushed to the ground.

"Oh yeah, bitch, I do wanna to see what you got, but only inside your pants, not in those damn bags." Junior slammed the door closed.

Ronshay turned around quickly when she heard the unfamiliar voice in her home. She tried to rush to Dee Dee's aid.

Junior pointed his gun straight at her head. "Bitch, you better back the fuck up and sit your ass down on the couch before I floor you too." He nudged her in her forehead with the nose of the gun barrel.

"Why you doin' this, Junior?" Dee Dee pleaded. "We ain't did shit to you."

"Bitch, you forgot? Naw, you ain't forgot. You remember that bullshit that went down. And just for the record, so that you know, Mikey's crackhead ass won't be saving that pussy this go-around 'cuz I already dealt with him. Now it's our turn."

Dee Dee knew that they were in a fucked-up situation. She wondered how she was gonna get her and Ronshay out of the jam that they were in, without getting either of them hurt or killed in the process. She also wondered what he did to Mikey.

"Bitch, I said sit your monkey ass on the couch! I

promise you I won't tell you again. Naw, better yet, start taking those clothes off. You too, bitch."

Dee Dee knew the nigga was trying to finish what he'd started, until Mikey had come out of nowhere and beat the would-be rapist damn near to death. Dee Dee didn't know what to do. "Look, Junior, let Ronshay go and you can do whatever you want with me, okay?"

"Bitch, who the fuck do I look like? That bitch ain't goin' nowhere, just like you ain't, and if y'all don't get undressed like I told you, then I'ma just start lettin' off right here and now."

Dee Dee knew the nigga was serious. She thought that if she undressed slowly, then maybe she could buy some time for a miracle to happen.

"That's right, take that shit off just like that," he said as he watched Dee Dee start to get undressed.

Ronshay sat there crying, scared to death. She clinched her shirt as tight as she could, not making a move.

"You got a problem with what I said to do? 'Cuz if you do, then maybe this will help your ass outta those goddamned clothes." Junior swung the gun in her direction, a mean look on his face.

"JUNIOR!" Dee Dee shouted to get his attention. "She's just scared, that's all. She been through a lot, you know that."

"Bitch, she ain't been through nothing until I go through her ass." Junior now pointed the gun at Dee Dee.

Dee Dee asked Junior if she could go over and talk to Ronshay for a sec, and he agreed, telling her to get buttnaked before she moved an inch from where she was. Dee Dee, more concerned about Ronshay not getting shot, wasn't ashamed about showing off her body under the circumstances.

As she took off her socks, the last piece of clothing she had on, Junior started massaging his dick through his pants at the sight of her nakedness. The ass had him going, and the blunt mixed with the crack had him beaming up to Scottie.

Dee Dee sat next to Ronshay and told her that their life depended on them doing what the crazy bastard told them to do, but Ronshay still didn't budge.

"Fuck that bitch. I ain't here for her ass, anyways. She's just a bonus. Who knows, if your shit ain't good like I think, then she's next up."

Junior yanked the plug to the lamp from the wall socket, then ripped the cord right out of the lamp. He commanded Dee Dee to lay on the floor face down while he tied Ronshay up. He wasn't going for anybody sneaking up on him again and giving him the one-two lump. Naw, Junior played it safe, tying Ronshay's hands tight as hell behind her back, then her feet, connecting it all together so she couldn't move at all. Then he dragged her to the closet, rolled her inside, and closed the door behind her.

"Now get your ass up," he ordered Dee Dee. "Now move it." He didn't know exactly where the bedroom was, but in an apartment it wasn't hard to find, seeing as all apartments are basically laid out the same way, one hallway, a couple of rooms, and a kitchen usually connected to the living room.

As they walked, he looked behind him just out of instinct. Of course, when a person just tied someone up and stuck their ass in a closet, that's the type of feeling they'd usually get, so he was just following up on what he felt in his bones. As he turned his head back around, he saw the open door to Ronshay's bedroom. With a pat on Dee Dee's ass, he told her, "Get in there."

Even though her tears had dried up a long time ago, the fear of what was to come was fully present in her body.

Once inside the room he pushed Dee Dee down on the bed and moved in.

She tried to back up, but the headboard stopped her from moving anywhere else. She wished her brothers Jay and Bee were around to deal with this sick bastard.

Junior gripped one of Dee Dee's ankles and yanked her toward him.

She kicked and tussled, but the nigga was too strong, and his grip on her leg was too tight.

"Keep fighting me and I swear I'll knock your head off and that face won't be so pretty no more." Junior took off his clothes. "Don't move an inch."

Dee Dee couldn't believe she had escaped this sick muthafucka's clutches once, and now the shit was happening all over again. And it looked like there was no way out this time. Once his clothes were off and she realized there was no way out of the jam she was in, not wanting to make things worse for herself, and to save Ronshay from that fool-ass rapist, she closed her eyes and let the nigga have his way.

Junior mounted Dee Dee with the gun still clutched in his hand. As he humped, Dee Dee felt sick as a dog. She kept her head turned away from his body, gagging the whole time. She wanted to cry, but something inside her wouldn't let a single tear fall from her eyes. She was taking this one for the team. Her legs were already spread, but Junior acted like that wasn't enough, splitting them open like the Grand Canyon. The worst was to come of her feeling used and abused when the nigga heaved then exploded all inside of her as he lay on top of her, the gun pressed against her head, talking crazy in her right ear.

* * *

"You see, Gary? It's always good to talk with a manager when you need a little assistance. I think she said apartment number 413 is this way," Perkins said as they started to walk.

They headed towards Ronshay's new apartment, not knowing what was taking place. As they walked, Perkins thought, *What if Deondra Davis wasn't the one to pull the trigger-man?*

It was such thoughts that had Gary saying that his partner took his job a little too seriously. To Gary you were either guilty or innocent, no exceptions, and with a little help, he would make an iffy case a certainty, if he believed the person was guilty.

Perkins wasn't that type. He had a conscience that would eat the shit out of him, and sending someone to jail to get the death penalty just wasn't his thing, if there was reasonable doubt.

* * *

Ronshay had managed to free herself, but not without deep bruises on her wrists and ankles from the electric cord. Her only thought was getting out of that closet and getting Dee Dee out of there. The whole time she was in the closet trying to get free, she could hear Junior moaning as he raped Dee Dee. The sound drove her to the point where she didn't give a fuck about how her body would look. All she knew was, she needed to get free and help her sister-in-law-slash-homegirl.

She opened the closet door as quietly as she could, then paused for a moment. She could still hear him talking, telling Dee Dee that he was almost ready for round two. *Over my dead body,* Ronshay thought. She reached her hand up on the top shelf of the closet and felt around. Her hand finally touched what she was feeling for. Now she had in her hand Bee's 9mm Smith & Wesson handgun. Thinking only about how this nigga wasn't going to harm Dee Dee anymore, she didn't wait a second to move towards the room.

* * *

"Hell, the shit must be downstairs, Perkins," Gary hissed after they hit every floor except the bottom. He couldn't believe how jokers could start numbering shit as far down as what he didn't even consider the first floor, but more like a basement, now that he knew the apartment was downstairs underneath the steps.

At first they thought they were in the wrong building, until they saw the number board telling them that there was an apartment 413 in the building.

"Here we are, number 413." Gary pointed to the apartment number and looked at his short, stocky, out of breath partner. "You wanna do the honors, or shall I?"

Perkins gasped as he leaned up against the wall. "Give me a second to catch my wind, and then it will be my pleasure."

* * *

Ronshay walked in to the open bedroom door and stood looking on at Junior's stinking rapist ass lying on top of Dee Dee's butt-naked body. "Get off of her, you filthy rapist, before I kill you!" Ronshay shouted, startling both Dee Dee and Junior.

Junior decided to make his move and flip over, hoping to catch her before she caught him with a hot one.

As quick as he rolled over, Ronshay pulled the trigger, but nothing happened. And she kept pulling the trigger.

Junior started laughing, while Dee Dee was frozen with fear. He told Ronshay, "Next time, try taking the safety off before you pull the trigger." Then his gun exploded, ejecting a bullet out of it that smacked right into Ronshay's chest and slammed her out of the doorway and into the wall behind her.

"RONSHAY!!! NOOOO!!!" Dee Dee's words echoed throughout the whole apartment.

"Gary, what the Sam Hill!" Perkins quickly raised himself off the wall then drew his gun out of its holster at his waist.

"Vest on?" Gary patted his chest as he stood against the wall on one side of the door. Gary signaled to his partner, who was on the other side holding his gun up with both hands. "On the count of three."

"Gary, wait. If for some reason I don't make it back to—"

Gary cut Perkins off, knowing what he was about to say. "Look, we're both going home. Just keep your head up and eyes open." Gary put two fingers in front of his eyes, then pointed them at Perkins's eyes, telling him to be alert.

"On three, okay."

"Got it," Perkins replied, sweat now visible on his forehead.

"One, two—"

"Hold up, Gary. Let me try." Perkins reached across his body with his left hand, gripped the doorknob, and turned. He smiled at his partner when the door swung open. The element of surprise was now on their side, since they didn't have to ram or kick the door, and alert the shooter.

They moved with their veteran skills, trying to preserve their lives as they entered the apartment. The first thing they saw was Ronshay's body slumped over in a sitting position and blood everywhere. They could hear the noise of someone shouting from down the hallway, where the door to a room was open. They crept down with guns drawn, pointing in every direction, not knowing how many perps were in the apartment or what to expect from around each crack and crevice.

"Bitch, she made me do it!" Junior shouted, standing over Dee Dee's naked body.

"She didn't make you shoot her! You shot her for nothing when you knew that she had the safety on. Wasn't it enough that you raped me? I hope you get yours, you bastard!" Dee Dee vented, tears now streaming down her face.

"Damn! You know what? I wasted my time raping your stinkin' ass. The pussy wasn't all that, anyways. Maybe I shouldn't have shot the bitch, cuz maybe her pussy was better than your shit. Damn! Why I had to shoot her and not you?" he said laughing. "Well, I guess I may as well give you one too. So tell me, where you want it—in the head or the chest, bitch?" Junior pointed the gun from her head to her chest, back and forth repeatedly.

Gary signaled his partner on when to move in. They heard everything and knew that the guy who was talking had forced his way in the apartment and raped at least one of the girls, who, from what they could hear, was still alive.

On the silent count of three, they jumped into the room and yelled, "FREEZE! MEMPHIS POLICE! DROP YOUR GUN AND PUT YOUR HANDS UP!"

Junior knew the words were coming from real cops, but he wasn't having that. As he turned around, Gary and Perkins let loose, making his body shake, rattle, and roll as their bullets sank into his body.

Junior managed to get off a couple of shots, not because he was quick on the draw, but mainly because of muscle spasms caused by being hit with so many bullets. His body fell backward on Ronshay's bed, and he lay there butt-ass naked, his arms and legs spread wide, and his feet touching the floor.

When Perkins and Gary had announced themselves and Junior took his eyes off of her, Dee Dee had quickly rolled off the bed, taking the blanket with her, and took cover underneath the other side of the bed, knowing what was about to come.

Perkins and Garry couldn't believe what had just happened. It had been a long time since either of them had been in a firefight with an assailant. They both walked towards the bed with their guns still drawn and pointed as they moved in on Junior. As they stood over him, they were able to see him take his last breath as his eyes rolled into the back of his head, then closed for good. Only after Gary checked for a pulse at Junior's neck did they holster their guns.

Unnoticed by the two detectives, Dee Dee came out from under the bed and went to check on Ronshay. Knowing Ronshay was gone, she grabbed the gun, crept up and stood behind them, and let off two rounds into Junior's groin, blowing his dick completely off to where there was no more bat or balls where they used to be. "Now, mutha-fucka, I only wish you could have been alive to see me shoot your dick off, you fuckin' rapist." Dee Dee then hawked a lugie (a wad of saliva) on his body.

Two detectives, hearing the gunfire, dove to the ground and drew their weapons again.

"Deondra, take it easy. Just put the gun down and every-thing will be okay, I promise," Perkins pleaded.

"Put the damn gun down like my partner said. NOW!" Gary shouted, lying on the floor on his back, his weapon aimed at Dee Dee.

"Gary, please, let me do the talking. I can handle this." Then to Dee Dee, he said, "Now, Deondra, please lower the gun so we can work this all out."

Dee Dee still had the gun pointed at Junior's lifeless body. She then turned her back to Junior and slowly low-ered her arm until it touched her side. Then her grip on the gun loosened, and it fell out of her hand onto the floor.

Chapter Three

Don Ruiz was swimming laps in the indoor pool of his mansion estate in Veracruz, California. Up in age, swimming was his way of staying in shape. His other passion was soccer, which he'd watch either live at the stadiums or on TV.

As a youngster, there were two things he couldn't stand while growing up, competition with others, and running errands.

Ever since they were little kids, before everybody started calling him Don Ruiz instead of Angelo, there was bad blood between himself and Ricardo Valdez. As they got older, and money and power became a big factor in the struggle for complete control, the competition heated up and both men moved up in the ranks quickly by impressing all the families, erasing problems when rival families seemed to be trying to muscle in on their territory. Many men had to be assassinated in order to maintain order in their region.

When the time came for them to become bosses, they were both ordered to go to the States. Angelo Ruiz would take sunny California, and Ricardo Valdez would take the Lone Star State, Texas. There were other dons in other states, like Illinois, New York, Florida, and Washington, but to the big bosses in Costa Rica, the two states that mattered most were those bordering Mexico, Texas and California.

Angelo's feelings about Ricardo never went unnoticed by the head of the family. So when they heard about one of their own being killed, they just swept it under the table, leaving family matters to be resolved and dealt with when they felt the time was right. It was never good to hit another don without permission from "the Heads."

Don Ruiz finally finished his last lap and headed for the shallow part of the pool. His bodyguards quickly moved to assist him out of the water as they took hold of his extended hand. One of the maids stood patiently by the pool with a silver tray in her hand containing Don Ruiz's hundred-thousand-dollar diamond and gold Swiss watch, and two gold rings that were bigger than his puffy knuckles. His gold necklace with the family's emblem embedded on a triangle medallion also rested on the tray, and of course, his prescription Mafioso shades.

After putting on all his jewelry, Don Ruiz took the towel from his bodyguard and placed it around his neck, holding on to both ends with his hands. He walked back toward his mansion and stood on the big wooden patio. He raised his arms in the air and stretched, taking in a breath of the warm September air.

Don Ruiz then walked over to one of the many padded chaise-lounge lawn chairs, his bodyguard assisting him down as he moved to get comfortable. Once the maid saw that he was seated, she brought over on a silver tray a pitcher of ice water and a cognac glass filled with the finest imported brandy. She sat the tray down on the table next to Don Ruiz's elbow and solemnly bowed her head and backed away.

Don Ruiz took the glass of brandy and sipped. He found it to be to his liking, as always. Good help was hard to find, but Don Ruiz didn't really seem to have a problem in that department. For one, if a person took a position working for "the Boss," they would find it in their best interest to "come to work with their game," like a good hooker, or get their head knocked off, like a pimp would do. Only, a pimp wouldn't go as far as to kill his help without batting an eye, unlike Don Ruiz.

Don Ruiz's bodyguard saw that his boss was pleased with his drink, so he took it upon himself to clap his hands together twice. At the sound of the claps, ten beautiful Costa Rican females came running from out of the guesthouse barefoot and dressed in the skimpiest string bikinis.

Don Ruiz, accustomed to having them around at his beck and call, ignored the women, as if they weren't there. The women, all of Costa Rican descent, came in all colors, black, white, and brown. As the girls ran to the volleyball court to start a game of "titties jumping and ass bouncing" while playing volleyball, two other females went to ease Don Ruiz's tension. One performed a body massage, and the other, a manicure and a pedicure.

His bodyguard, dressed in all-black combat attire, stood

and watched the sculptured feminine bodies doing their thing as they laughed out loud and played.

Don Ruiz's whole estate was being patrolled and protected by other heavily armed bodyguards who were all under the command of the one standing watch over Don Ruiz on the patio.

Don Ruiz lay relaxed, thinking of the day he'd wiped out Don Valdez. It was a sweet victory for him, but now he wondered if his personal dislike for Don Valdez and the way he'd handled the Texas region would put him on bad terms with the Heads back home. He was sure that the incident wouldn't go unaddressed because his hit was without the family's blessing.

Don Ruiz's bodyguard reached his hand up to the headset resting in his ear. Somebody from the outpost up front was saying something to him. Once he received the message loud and clear, he gave them the okay to let the guy in. The bodyguard then patted the female on the ass who was giving Don Ruiz a massage, to get her out of his way so he could relay the message that company was coming. When she moved to the side, he leaned over and whispered into Don Ruiz's ear, telling him what was up.

Don Ruiz clapped his hands together, and the two attending females ran to join the others in the volleyball game.

When the bodyguard saw that Don Ruiz was about to rise, he clapped his hands together, and the maid flew out of the house with his white robe. The bodyguard helped him up, and the maid placed the robe on Don Ruiz when he held out and extended his arms. Don Ruiz then tied the belt, to keep the robe closed.

They walked into the mansion and went to the lounge. He then took a seat on the couch. His bodyguard opened the big wooden humidor that lay on the cracked glass table and reached in and took out one of the Cuban cigars (illegal in the United States). He then took the snipper, clipped the end, and handed it to Don Ruiz, who then looked it over before waving it slowly underneath his nose and inhaling the sweet aroma of the expensive cigar.

With a flick of his 14k solid gold lighter with the Costa Rican family crest embedded on it, Don Ruiz watched the flame fire his cigar, and puffed contentedly with half-closed eyes. As he smoked and sipped his glass of brandy, his attention was drawn toward the door and his visitor. Dressed in a blue suit and black shoes, and looking more like a nerd than a person affiliated with the cartel, the man stood in the hallway, where the bodyguards patted him down. Once the other bodyguards were through searching him, one of them looked toward Don Ruiz and signaled that the man was clean. Don Ruiz then waved the man to enter as he took another sip of brandy.

"*Señor* Ruiz, once again, it's a pleasure." The man then bowed his head as Don Ruiz stood.

"Johnny Rogers, it's nice to see you too. When you show up, it usually means that you have some information for me, which is usually good for my ears." Don Ruiz blew a cloud of smoke right into the man's face.

Johnny didn't dare fan the smoke out of his face or make any unpleasant faces, no matter how much the smoke grossed him out. He took a seat as he was instructed. He then went on with why he came to see Don Ruiz. He was Don Ruiz's accountant, and his job mostly consisted of keeping records of who got what and who owed what, along with laundering a lot of money in the States.

"*Señor* Ruiz, all the product that was recovered from Texas has arrived with no problems." With a cautious eye Johnny looked Don Ruiz's way.

"Johnny, Johnny, Johnny, you came all the way out here to tell me that? Haven't you heard of a phone? Mondo!" he said out loud, "get this man two cell phones, *pronto!*" Don Ruiz laughed all by himself.

Johnny's head turned to Mondo, the bodyguard, who was standing at attention and looking very serious in his dark shades and all-black combat uniform. Then he whipped his head back to Don Ruiz, who had just slapped him roughly on his back.

"I made a joke, Johnny! Quite funny, don't you think?"

"Quite funny, *señor*. You could be a comedian, who knows?" Johnny replied, trying his own hand at humor.

"Johnny, do I look like a fuckin' comedian to you? I'm Don Ruiz, and don't you fuckin' forget it either. Now, what brings you out here? And make it quick, because my time is valuable."

Johnny went from comfortable to a scared white guy. He knew the power that Don Ruiz possessed and he didn't want to feel the wrath of it either. All he wanted to do was notify him of his discovery and get the hell out of the powerful man's eyesight as quickly as his feet could carry him to his Maserati and burn rubber. He raised his black briefcase from the floor then rested it in his lap.

"*Señor*, upon going over the inventory that was confiscated from Don Valdez's barn, the men found his black book. It contains something that I think you should see." He popped the latches to open up the briefcase and pulled out a black ledger then handed it over to Don Ruiz.

Don Ruiz began reading the contents. "What the hell is this?" He looked over at Johnny.

"*Señor*, the places where I highlighted in yellow are now the people who owe you a substantial amount of money. It seems Don Valdez was quite generous with the people he did business with." Johnny pointed out the names of the people in the ledger who owed big money, names including Bee and Jay.

"That piece of shit, Ricardo! This is how he handled business? That's why the *maricón* is now out of business. Fuckin' *puta*!" Don Ruiz shouted. "Mondo, get Picasso on these *culos*. Who the fuck are these two *putas* Jay and Bee that he shipped five thousand kilos of coca to in Memphis, fuckin' Tennessee?"

A deadly man for hire who always satisfied his employees, Picasso was the special hitman that most cartels used.

When Don Ruiz didn't see anybody move, he grabbed his chrome 45 semi-automatic with the pearl handle and blasted two shots that rang out like thunder.

Chapter Four

It had been a month since Dee Dee attended her brothers' funeral. Now Junior had succeeded in raping her. Dee Dee had been in shock since then. The probability of God really existing, in her head, was now slim to almost none because of what she'd been through. She had no idea that the world could be so cruel, no idea where she fitted in the big ol' world she was living in.

The crisis counselor carefully touched Dee Dee's arm. "Deondra, are you still with us?"

Dee Dee was in a zone as she looked out the window. Her legs were crossed tighter than a pair of vise grips, and her arms were folded across her chest. When Mr. Washington, the counselor holding the twelve-woman session, touched Dee Dee's arm, she jumped into a defensive mode, throwing her dukes up from being startled.

"Hold up, Deondra!" He held up his hands to stop an incoming fist. "I should have spoken from a distance. I didn't mean to startle you. Are you feeling okay? You can take ten if you need to." He spoke quick as fuck, trying to calm her down.

A *ten* was a time-out available to the session members for when they felt the stress coming on.

Dee Dee just looked at the white counselor. "You know what, instead of taking ten, I think I'll just skip the whole session."

"Sometimes we need to do that. I'm sure you will be more focused at tomorrow's session. Now remember if you need to talk to someone you got all our numbers. Right, class?" He looked on as everybody held up the pink laminated name cards that hung on their necks, looking like a backstage VIP pass or something.

"No, Mr. Washington. I mean I'm gonna just skip the whole thang. It's just not working for me. I know this class is for people dealing with issues, but so far my issues haven't gotten any better at all since I've been attending these sessions. I'm not knocking it or nothing, so don't get me wrong. Actually the session has helped me, 'cuz I was truly fucked up when I first started coming here. I got raped and my best friend got shot and died before my very own eyes. I wish all of y'all the best of luck in getting over whatever happened to you. This is something that I know I got to handle on my own, and I don't need another session for me to figure that out." Dee Dee stood up and plucked her brown leather jacket off the back of the chair that she was sitting in.

"Deondra, we all gotta deal with our problems in one fashion or another, so I wish you the very best of luck. But, like I said, if you need us, we're just a phone call away.

Now can we have a group hug?" He smiled big and held his arms open wide.

Water flooded Dee Dee's eyes, then tears started dripping out as she embraced him.

All the other women were touched by what Dee Dee had said and what they were now seeing. Most got a sense that in order to get over their problems, they first had to make a stand and empower themselves, kinda how Dee Dee just did. They all rushed in to join the hugging session with tears falling outta their own eyes.

After saying their goodbyes, Dee Dee opened the wooden white door with the large square glass pane. As she exited the room, she closed the door behind her. Now she stood on the other side, her back against the wall. She then took the time to clear her eyes free of the remaining tears. She now felt that she needed something to calm her nerves. The class was cool and all, but it was also a drag. Time seemed to go as slow as it did for a muthafucka who's locked up and counting the last few days left to do before returning back to the world they once knew. She felt nothing in the class was of any importance to her, but actually it was.

Dee Dee only knew that she had been raped, but the class taught her that in time of need there should always be someone around that you can trust and count on to give support, whether physical, mental, or verbal. In Dee Dee's case she needed it all. The hugs showed her that it was okay to let someone touch her again without fear that they would harm her, like that bitch-ass nigga Junior did. She also learned in the session that as long as she could talk about what was bothering her, she could find a way to get over the hurdle. Dee Dee knew that she couldn't feel sad for herself, recognizing that it could hold her down to where she wouldn't be able to accomplish a damn thing. That helped her to build her self-esteem back up and empower herself once again. She now felt her game had to be stepped up.

She sat in her H2 for a second outside the apartment building. Her mind was wandering here and there as she sat thinking. The sudden knock on her rolled up window made her react in such a way that the person who knocked hit the street pavement with the quickness when she drew her black 9mm and pointed it. Dee Dee vowed to herself that other niggas who thought they was slick and smooth would never ever catch her slipping for nothing in the world.

She got out her H2, still clutching her heater tight, and walked around to the passenger side where the guy had knocked on the window.

"DEE DEE, DON'T SHOOT! It's me," the person shouted as he lay on the ground, his hands covering his head.

"Lil' Man, is that you?" Dee Dee asked, unable to see his face.

"Yeah, it's me. Don't shoot."

"Lil' Man, if you don't get your little black ass up off the ground, I just may leave you down there permanently!" Dee Dee lightly nudged him with her white Lotto cross-trainer shoe.

"Shit, Dee Dee. Why you pullin' a heater on your boy? If you're not careful you gonna plug somebody, and I ain't aimin' for it to be me, feel me?" Lil' Man stood and dusted off the debris of his clothes.

"My bad. Boy, where you been? I been lookin' for you all over town." Dee Dee hopped back in the driver's seat.

"I been outta town handlin' some business."

"Outta town handlin' some business? Get the fuck outta here, nigga. You ain't even old enough to have any business to take care of."

"I can push your dope, but I can't handle my own shit?" He gave Dee Dee a cold stare.

"Chill out, shorty. Damn, can't a bitch play with you? I swear, when y'all niggas start gettin' paper those heads of y'all just start blowin' up. I'm surprised those big mutha-fuckas don't just explode and pop." Dee Dee motioned for Lil' Man to close the door. She had business to talk over with him if she was gonna do this shit right.

Dee Dee was actually happy to see Lil' Man. As she drove she turned her head towards him and stared for as long as she could before her attention needed to be put back on the road in front of her. There was something about him that was different. She couldn't put her finger on just what it was, but there was definitely something different. She took another look at him then smiled when she noticed the little peach fuzz developing above his lips to one day form a mustache.

"So what you been havin' people search for me for?" he asked as he let the sun roof roll back up top.

"Look, I been thinkin' for a minute about this shit. I gotta hit the streets and hit 'em hard this time. I ain't got time to look for new people to put on my team, so if you want in, then just say so 'cuz I'ma just roll with the hood on this one."

Lil' Man reclined way back and went into thinking mode. Once upon a time he couldn't even beg her two brothers to front him some work, and now Dee Dee was asking him to be her number one man. It couldn't have happened at a better time. He looked her way. "So you gonna fuck with any of those other niggas that was on your team before you went down?"

"Those niggas took me for a joke before. I won't give them a second chance to think they can play me like a PlayStation or something. What I'm about to do is big, real big, Lil' Man, so either you in or out." Dee Dee looked at him once again.

"So, if I'm in, what you got planned for me to do?"

"Let me handle that when it's time, all right." Dee Dee patted him on his leg. "But what I need you to do right now is get on the streets and see what you can find out about who shot my brothers."

Lil' Man eyes got big when Dee Dee let those words come outta her mouth. He'd heard different stories about what went down, but through it all, he was hearing one thing consistently. Which was the cat that did the shooting wore a mask on his face.

In the past Lil' Man had been Dee Dee's ears on the street, and the information that he'd relayed to her always turned out to be helpful. That's why she took a chance and fronted him his first "key." Someone putting that kind of work in his young hands was just unheard of. Since his little mishap outta town a couple of months back, Lil' Man had been down and out, and now it was his time to shine once again.

"Look, Dee Dee, I'm sorry about what happen to your brothers. Those was two cool muthafuckas. They put me on when everybody kept passin' me by. What you just asked is on and poppin', and that's my word, home girl."

"Lil' Man, you don't know how good that makes me feel to hear that."

"So what you gonna do to the chump who did it when you find out?"

"Shit like that should never be talked about, Lil' Man, just dealt with when the time comes," she replied, her demeanor changing altogether.

Lil' Man already could tell that Dee Dee had something ruthless planned for the sucker muthafucka who'd pulled the funky on her brothers 'cuz it was written all over her face. The cold vicious act that her and the R.B.M Clique did to ol' boy with the dildo and pictures was enough for him to know that whoever killed her brothers was in for a fucked up situation if she ever got the word.

As Dee Dee kept driving Lil' Man leaned up from his slouched down position in his seat so he could see where they were. To his surprise he saw that they were rolling around in their hood. Lil' Man spotted TJ, the neighborhood weed man, shooting dice over by the bricks with some other cats from their hood. He told Dee Dee to pull over to the curb by the bricks so he could cop a sack from TJ. Dee Dee slowly pulled over and parked. TJ and the others put their game on pause for a moment, as they all knew who was driving the smooth-ass H2 sitting on phatties.

Both Dee Dee and Lil' Man emerged outta the ride. Dee Dee walked around her ride and went over and posted up on the stoop with all the fellas. The Jordan sweatsuit Dee Dee was sporting was looking more playa than what the fellas had on, not to mention she had on the matching throwback Jordan sneakers on her feet.

"Dee Dee, what's poppin', homegirl?" TJ stuck his clutched fist out to receive a pound.

"Same shit, TJ, just a different day poppin', that's all."
Dee Dee gave him a pound.

"Sorry about what that faggot nigga Junior did to you
and your brother's girl. She was cool. That bitch-ass nigga
got what he deserved for all I'm concerned."

"Thanks, TJ."

"The paper said you blew that nigga's dick off while the
police was right there. That's some ill shit, baby girl."

"Any rapist needs to have his shit cut or shot the fuck
off. And I mean ANY RAPIST." Dee Dee said it loud
enough for all the niggas around to hear, just in case they
ever got an idea.

The newspaper had made an error in their account
about what happened. Instead of saying that Dee Dee shot
Junior's dick off *after* the police shot and killed him, they
stated that Dee Dee had got a hold of a gun and fired first,
blowing Junior's dick off, *before* the police took care of the
rest when he tried to fired back. Dee Dee used that to her
advantage, 'cuz that was the way a real bitch came back—
hard—after what Junior did to her.

TJ turned his attention to Lil' Man and gave him a
pound. "Lil' Man, when they let you out?"

That caught Dee Dee's attention right away. Hearing
something like that, when a person didn't know anything
about it, was like hearing a nigga finally got a job after selling dope his whole life. Dee Dee just looked on as Lil'
Man answered the question.

"Muthafuckas let me roll last night. You know they can't
really give a juvenile that much time for dope possession.
Moms was tripping though. She wanted me to leave me up
there in the detention home, but I told her I was through
with the game and hanging out all night. She knows now

that I lied 'cuz I ain't even much seen the crib since I been out. As soon as we got back in town, I had her drop me off at Montreya's sister crib. Mom's cussed me out something serious, but what can a brother do when he gotta get paid?"

"I hear that, homie. And I see you rollin' with the best person to get paid with. Dee Dee, your hand better than some of the niggas that been hustlin' out here for years and think they got it poppin'." TJ smirked.

"Niggas just take the game for granted. It's like Master P said, 'Most niggas lookin' for bitches and blunt.' Now what is those two things gonna do for a nigga who's really trying to get paid, but hold them back from getting paid? Only those ashy-trashy bitches wanna smoke blunt after blunt. A real bitch wouldn't even wanna fuck with a nigga if he's only giving her a blunt, one after another, instead of a whole pound so she can get lifted whenever the fuck she chooses to, whether he's with her at the time she choose to smoke or not. Niggas just gotta step their game up or realize that all the hustlin' that they're doin' is for muthafuckin' nothin', and I do mean nothin'." Dee Dee told it like it was. One thing that she'd learned from all the years of watching her brothers hustle and hold it down was that in order to make it in the game one had to use the things that they had to get what they wanted outta life, even if the stakes was high on getting caught.

Dee Dee was still thrown for a loop on finding out that Lil' Man had been locked up and his little ass didn't bother to disclose that information to her after all the time they'd spent cruising. She watched him cop the sack of weed from TJ.

"Hey, Dee Dee, if you need someone to work with, I'm

game." Jesse threw his hands up in the air, just to let her know that he was serious.

Dee Dee smiled. "I'll think about it, Jesse, and get back with you, cool?"

"Yo! Dee Dee, you keep your head up, all right, girl. And by the way that new hairstyle fits you to a T, with your cute ass." TJ pointed his finger as if to say, 'You go, girl.'

"Thanks for the compliment, TJ. I got it did just for you."

"For real?" he asked, in a high-pitched tone.

Dee Dee teased her hair. "Psych!"

"It's good to see that you still got humor," he replied, "with your ugly ass—psych!"

Dee Dee hopped back in her ride and started it up. Lil' Man was already sitting in the ride when Dee Dee got in. She looked over at him rolling the blunt up. The smell of the weed was strong as the wind from the open sunroof breezed the scent her way.

"Lil' Man, why didn't you tell me that you got popped?"

" 'Cuz you didn't ask." He licked the rolled blunt to seal it.

"What the fuck you mean, 'cuz I didn't ask? Nigga, I'm in a business where that type of information should be voluntary, especially when it's my people."

"Dee Dee, all I'm saying is that if you would've asked then I would've told you."

"Well, check this shit out, Lil' Man. Now I'm asking, so tell me the deal on what's up with you."

"Well, since you put me on with that first shit, I been takin' trips down to Chattanooga, where I got family at. Business was good and all that, until the boys in blue got hipped to a juvenile called Lil' Man. Those hoes was trying everything to get at me, but I was duckin' and dodgin', stickin' and movin'." Lil' Man acted out the scene, bobbing in his seat, as he puffed away at the blunt. "Then those hoes finally caught up with a nigga at the hotel while I was with this little fine yellowbone. I know I should've kept pleasure separated from business, but the money made me slip. That same day I got a call from a nigga who wanted to get four of those OZ's. After the nigga left the room, me and baby girl got busy.

"Maybe about two hours later or so, when I got my shit back up and started crammin' that ass of hers like DMX was doing Kiesha in the movie *Belly*, I heard a boom outta nowhere. That was the boys in blue kickin' in the door and screamin' shit at my ass, like they was smokin' crack."

Dee Dee had to pull over to listen to Lil' Man's story. She still had her doubts, but the way Lil' Man told the story quick and all, and without any slip-ups, made her believe that he was telling the truth. And Dee Dee was waiting to hear a slip-up. She asked herself, as she looked at Lil' Man, whether she could trust him to where she could use him on her team. She needed him, but she didn't know what price she would have to pay down the line for having him on her side.

"Lil' Man, you don't think the nigga that came by to get the four "zones" before the police came set you up, do you?" Dee Dee took the blunt from him and started puffing.

"Shit! I never even thought about that. I mean, it was such a big time difference from the time I sold the shit to his ass to when they kicked in the door, you know." Lil' Man now realized that ol' boy could have set him up.

"You all right, Lil' Man?" Dee Dee asked, seeing his troubled look.

"Yeah, I'm cool. It's just that if that nigga did set me up then I gotta handle that shit. That's on my grandmamma, Dee Dee."

Dee Dee now believed in Lil' Man once again. See, when a nigga got busted by the law, it was no telling what they would do. In fact, Jay and Bee had a rule, which was to never fuck with a nigga that got busted ever again. Whether the cat turned or didn't turn didn't matter to them. As long as they never took the chance of doing business with the person again, then they would never find out if they were on the list to be set up. Maybe they would lose the friendship if the niggas wasn't hot and he got mad that they was playin' him close like a snitch, but if the person was hot then they was savin' their asses the chance of havin' to do time. Basically, they was like, "Fuck some friendship," when it came down to keeping their freedom.

Dee Dee rolled through traffic with Lil' Man still in the ride. It seemed as if all the problems that she had would disappear into midair as she puffed on the blunt. She now found the cure for her depression. With all the drama she had to deal with, she was finding comfort in getting lifted. But still nothing could make her forget the promise she'd made to her brothers while they lay in their caskets. Dee Dee was determined to find out who killed her brothers and kill them, no matter if she had to spend the rest of her life behind bars or get killed in the process.

Lil' Man told Dee Dee where she could drop him off, so she headed there.

Dee Dee parked in front of the apartment building

where Lil' Man's girl's sister lived. Just as he was about to get out of the ride, she grabbed his arm. "You got enough of that greenery?"

"And you know this." Lil' Man held up the plastic sandwich bag with the ounce of green weed. "Why?"

"You think a bitch can get some of that?"

"So you wanna get high all by your lonesome, huh. Well, do you, homegirl, 'cuz I don't know one muthafucka out here that ain't chiefin' and that includes my eighty-year-old great-grandmamma. She be talkin' 'bout she smokes it for her glaucoma." Lil' Man laughed as he put some of the weed in another bag for Dee Dee. "Here, this should hold you for a minute, but try buying you some with all that cheddar you got stashed somewhere."

Dee Dee took the bag from Lil' Man then gave him a pound. "I'ma call you tomorrow. Don't get lost on me now." Then she took off.

For the first time since coming out of jail, Alastair popped in her head. To her, there wasn't one relationship out there to match what they'd built. Alastair was the guy for Dee Dee and she knew it, but she chose to tell him about her horrible dream and that messed everything up for them. All that good loving got flushed down the toilet.

Even though Dee Dee cared more about Prat—At least, she thought she did, with how she was going out her way to get him back—she now knew that her heart was with Alastair. She wondered how and what he was doing right at that moment.

Chapter Five

Picasso walked smoothly through the Memphis airport lobby, carrying a black shiny leather briefcase in his right hand, and headed for the exit door. His square-toed Italian boots clashed against the waxed lobby floor as he made some long strides with his six-foot three-inch frame. Dressed in an Italian gray silk suit, he looked like someone important, and the black shades that covered his brown eyes and his short, thick, slicked-back hair only added to the intrigue.

Picasso exited the lobby door to the carport outside. The air was chilly on this day, mostly because of the hard rain that was pouring down. He raised his left hand up to his face and articulately removed his shades from his eyes and look around. Cabs and limos of all types lined the median, avoiding the doors in front of the lobby, and a sure ticket from one of the cops on patrol.

"Sir, you need a ride to take you to where you're trying to get to?"

Picasso turned his head and stared at the young brotha standing next to his cab, back door open and waiting. Picasso looked to his right then to his left, and still there was no sign of his limo. Patience wasn't Picasso's strong suit, except if it came down to him finding his target for his client. He was beyond irritated with the driver that was supposed to have already been there, parked and waiting for his arrival.

Outta nowhere a horn started blowing repeatedly. Picasso looked in the direction of the blowing horn and saw a gray Lincoln Imperial limo with tinted windows rolling up next to the cab.

The Mexican jumped out of the car and went straight to the black cabby. "Look, don't cut into my business as long as you live." He looked hard at the cabby. "Besides, can't you see you're out your league?"

The cabby nudged the driver in his shoulder. "Look here, money, I advise your cool ass to back the fuck up outta my face before you get your wig split."

The driver stumbled backward, only to be caught by Picasso. After gaining his balance, he attempted to go after the cabby, but Picasso grabbed the back of his black chauffeur jacket, making him jerk backward and almost having his feet slip from underneath him. As he held him around the neck from behind, Picasso whispered into his ear, "How can you get upset at someone for trying to give me a lift when you was the one that was late getting here? If I wasn't in such a hurry I would let him have a piece of your ass, but I'll let your boss take care of that."

"Señor, but I—"

"No need to explain to me. Save that for your boss when you tell him that you wasn't the one that drove me to where I had to go." Picasso broke his hold and headed for the cabby's open car door.

"My man, you made a wise choice, 'cuz this is the cab for a star to ride in. So where to?"

Picasso liked the cabby's humor and hustle.

Most people who laid eyes on Picasso instantly thought the worst, and their instincts were sound, 'cuz he was a killer for only the big people who could afford his price.

The driver looked on as Picasso got into the cabby's car. He knew he was in big trouble, and he only had his dick to thank for that, prolonging his conversation with the female he'd just met in the back seat of his Lincoln.

The cabby hit the highway cruising, blending in and outta traffic at the speed limit of sixty-five. As he drove he looked up at his rearview mirror and took a glance at his passenger.

Picasso looked out the window, his thoughts on his mission, and what he would do after completing it.

The cabby maintained his view on the road, wondering just who his passenger was. He felt that something wasn't right with this picture. It was like the way any black person who grew up in the slums could sense when something wasn't right 'cuz of all the shit that they had to endure growing up in the ghetto, where stuff was always going down illegally.

"Hey, boss. I can see that you're in thought, but I gotta ask you this 'cuz it's my job." The cabby looked through the mirror at Picasso. "But be assured that what don't involve me, I don't ask shit about. But I need to know where I'm going, so I don't be driving around in a circle."

Picasso took his stare away from out the window to the back of the cabby's head. He then noticed that the cabby was looking at him through the rearview mirror and let out a slight chuckle, caught off guard by the face in the mirror. "Do you know this city pretty good, my friend?"

"Do I know this city pretty good? Man, I know this city like you know your mommy vagina." The cabby looked through the mirror and saw the unpleasant expression on Picasso's face when he removed his shades.

Picasso leaned forward, making the cabby nervous.

"My man, look I didn't mean anything by that. It was like a joke, you know, 'cuz we all came from our mother's *you-know-what*. You get it, right?" He asked, hoping the big fella wasn't too upset.

Picasso cracked a slight smile, which really didn't look like a smile at all to the young cabby, but it was enough to let him feel relaxed again.

"So, big guy, why you asked, did I know the city good?"

"I need someone to drive me around full-time while I'm here on business because, as you already know, my driver isn't the most dependable person for me to keep around. So what you say?" Picasso drew a cigarette from his shirt pocket and lit it.

"My man, you know a cab ride is already costly, and you wanna keep me for how long?"

"Look, money is no object. Can you handle it or not?"

"My man, if you got the bread, then I got the wheels. And by the way, the name is Timmy." He looked through the rearview mirror. "And yours is?"

"Timmy, they call me Picasso."

"Picasso? Like the painter who created those crazy expensive pictures." Timmy had a slight grin.

"That's correct, Timmy."

"So what you do for a living? Paint like him?" Timmy laughed.

"Not exactly, but I do create a masterpiece of art when I go to work."

"I knew you was an artist. You just look like one of those serious spaced-out dudes. So what you workin' on now?"

"Let's just say that I'm working on my best work yet." Picasso took a drag on his cigarette then blew the smoke outta the slightly rolled down window.

Timmy took Picasso to his destination, which was to where Jay and Bee used to live. The whole time he kept taking a peek here and there in his rearview mirror at the strange Latin brotha in his back seat. Timmy still felt it was something about the guy that was strange, especially since he wanted Timmy to drive for him the whole time that he'd be in town. Picasso was just too smooth. And once he'd removed his shades, Timmy saw those small, brown, beady eyes, which gave off that scary feeling.

Timmy exited off the expressway then took the feeder road to enter the side of town that Jay and Bee lived on. Timmy took a right, a left, then another right and another left, bringing him one block from Langston Drive, the street that Picasso had asked him to drive to.

As he cruised down the street, Timmy looked at every house address. The flip-flop of numbers didn't confuse him, since he was so used to finding an address. As he went a little bit further down, he noticed that the address he was looking for was coming up, from the numbers on the houses he was going past.

"Picasso, I think this is the one coming up right here to your left." Timmy pointed briefly at the house.

Picasso turned his head to where Timmy pointed. His blood pressure started to rise as he felt his mission was just about to begin.

Timmy parked the car in front of the house on the street then looked back over his shoulder at Picasso. "This is it, my man, 2239." Timmy looked at Picasso holding the briefcase on his lap.

"Timmy, I need you to do me a favor."

"Just say it and it's done."

"I like that. You and me are going to get along just fine. But what I need you to do is go knock on that door and ask if Jay or Bee is at home. If they are, then tell them that Picasso is here to give them their check, but if they're not, then find out when they will be back home, okay." Picasso pulled out a lump sum of money and handed Timmy one thousand dollars in cold hard cash.

Timmy opened the car door and got out. "You got it, big guy."

Picasso watched Timmy walk toward the house. Then he punched in the combination to the security lock and popped open his briefcase up. His eyes rested on the high-powered long-barreled chrome .357 Magnum with the infrared beam. He placed his hand on the gun then let his fingers caress the steel that rested in the gray form-fitting case.

Picasso looked over at Timmy as he walked up on the porch before taking the gun out of its resting place. Then he took the speed clip that was equipped with deadly acid heads that would eat through the insides of a person on impact.

Timmy placed his hand out and knocked on the front door three times then waited.

"RODNEY, I told you I didn't wanna be bothered with you anymore, so just take your ass back on over to Teonna's crib where you came from." Janelle didn't even know who she was talking to.

Timmy took a look at himself. "Now I know I ain't this Rodney cat, so who she talking to?" he said to himself out loud. Timmy turned around and looked at Picasso, who was looking at him. Timmy shrugged, as if to say, "You got me boss," then motioned that he was about to knock again.

Janelle shouted again at the knock, this time swinging the door open with fierceness. "RODNEY, I—I'm so sorry. I thought you was somebody else." Janelle tried to straighten herself up from the housecleaning she was doing.

"It's all good. I take it that you and this Rodney cat just broke up, from the way you were shouting." Timmy immediately took a liking to what he was looking at.

"Me and him? Oh please. He was just somebody that's been buggin' a bitch, that's all. Niggas just don't know how to take no for an answer sometimes." Janelle puffed up her big titties in her bra.

Timmy couldn't help but looking at those big ol' thangs. He liked women with meat on their bones, and Janelle sure had plenty on hers. He looked her up and down, wondering what it would be like to be all up in between her legs, bumping and grinding all through the night. Then he suddenly recalled what he went there for in the first place.

"Look, ma! I'm here 'cuz I was looking for Jay or Bee."

Janelle couldn't believe her ears. Here it was, Jay and Bee had been dead and buried for some months, and this guy hadn't heard. Then for once, other than lust, Janelle really took a good look at him, but his face wasn't stirring any memories.

"You know Jay and Bee?"

"Not really. I'm just here to relay a message."

"I didn't think so 'cuz everybody that knows Jay and Bee know that they been dead for a minute. Plus, this isn't their house. Their house is across the street. Well, it was across the street. They gettin' it back together though."

"DEAD? What happen?" Timmy looked back to see where the house used to be, and where a brand-new one was being built.

"It was terrible. They were both gunned down on the corner and no one knows who did it."

"Oh, I remember reading about that in the paper. It happened about four or five months ago, right?"

"Yeah. It was sad. Then after that this nigga name Junior raped their sister, Dee Dee, and killed Bee's girl all in the same day. Dee Dee is so fucked up right now," Janelle said, giving just a little too much information.

Timmy turned around and saw Picasso looking at him. He knew that Picasso wasn't expecting to hear anything like what he had to relay. Timmy figured their sister Dee Dee could use the money, which he was sure was a lot, from the way Picasso acted.

Of course, Picasso had no way of knowing what was being said. All he wanted to see was the two that were called Jay and Bee so he could complete his mission, which also meant that he would have to drop two more bodies for free, Janelle and Timmy, 'cuz there could be no witness left.

"Hey, look, I'm sorry about all this bad stuff that happened, trust me when I say that, but I gotta ask. Do you mind if I get your number so maybe one day I can give you, you know, a call and we can go do something? My treat, of course." Timmy looked deep into her eyes.

"As long as you're not one of those niggas that play games," Janelle said, smiling excitedly.

"Trust me, games is for kids. I'm dead serious and I'm single, looking for love."

Janelle liked what she'd just heard and what she was looking at. Timmy seemed to be a nice brotha. She couldn't remember the last time she had a boyfriend. All her kids' daddies were just a fuck. As she wrote down her phone number, she felt cool about telling Timmy that Dee Dee could probably be reached through her other sister-in-law, Maya.

Janelle waved bye to Timmy, putting her hand up to her ear and mouth, signaling him to call her.

Timmy planned on doing that already, and he wasn't planning on doing it tomorrow either. Later on that day was gonna work just fine for him, 'cuz he figured a nigga never knew when they was gonna get lucky and get some pussy. He hopped in the car still excited, closed the door, then turned around to look at Picasso, who was still look-ing at him.

Picasso had placed the gun back in its case before Timmy got close to the car, knowing that he wouldn't be using it at that time.

Timmy explained everything to Picasso, word for word, about what he and Janelle had talked about, except the love connection.

No doubt, Picasso was upset about hearing that the two people he was seeking out had already been terminated by someone else. He now saw no reason to stick around in

Memphis, so he told Timmy to take him to his motel and come by in the morning to pick him up so he could drop him off at the airport. Picasso just sat back and smoked on yet another cigarette as Timmy drove smoothly through traffic on the expressway, playing Marvin Gaye's "Let's Get It On" on his car's CD player.

Chapter Six

Blawww! Blawww! Blawww! The sound of gunshots echoed through Dee Dee's old neighborhood. All the niggas that were hustling on the block, getting that cash, was now running for their lives, trying not to get plugged by the many bullets that were fired by passing cars.

The Robinson boys were making a statement, "We're back in town, so if you're trying to get that dough then you better do it on the low and not let us hear about it."

When the black beat-up 1985 Buick Park Avenue sped off, leaving burnt tire tracks and white smoke in the middle of the street, everybody came out of hiding, wondering if anyone got hit. It wasn't any secret about who did the shooting 'cuz the niggas didn't wear any masks. Plus, they screamed out, "Robinson boys for life!"

Everybody knew who gunned down D-Dawg except the police, and wasn't anybody gonna say anything if they knew what was good for them. If the Robinson boys got word about who was talking through the Motion of Discovery, which they would soon get access to through their lawyer, then they'd have the name and address of any witness.

"Those bitch-ass niggas wanna go to war?" TJ clinched his 9mm tight. "Then we can do that."

"Playboy, be cool. Ain't no need to add fuel to the fire. Those niggas just want some beef. If we give them beef, then we ain't gonna get none of this money out here 'cuz the law will sweat the block seriously, feel me?" Jesse tried to make sense out of the chaos.

TJ snapped, "Nigga, please . . . you sound like a bitch, talkin' the way you're talkin'. Those niggas just came into our hood and shot shit up and you talkin' logic. Get the fuck outta here with the bullshit."

"Hey, y'all! I feel y'all both. TJ, you got a major point."

TJ cracked a grin at somebody taking his side.

"You gotta a point too, Jesse, 'cuz the block will get hot."

"Lil' Man you was talkin' good until you let that weak-ass shit come outta your fuckin' mouth. I don't know what's up with you niggas these days. Niggas from the hood suppose to represent, not get disrespected. Am I right, Cheddar?"

Cheddar was slim but cut-up nigga who couldn't talk due to a motorcycle accident years earlier, but make no mistake about it, he chased that cash, hustling day and night, and he was a rider. You've heard the saying, Watch the quiet ones. Well, Cheddar was one of those niggas that people would be referring to. Cheddar just shook his head with the sinister look on his face.

TJ knew that other niggas, along with Cheddar, would

no doubt ride for the hood, especially the ones that wasn't around the block when the shit popped off. He knew Jesse was right, and he knew Jesse wasn't any type of ho.

In fact, Jesse had proved many times that he was 'bout it. It was just that the shooting shook him, and the last thing he needed was for someone to be talking payback to him right then. "Look, TJ, I'm down to ride. I wasn't sayin' that I wasn't, but to get off that subject, I'm ready when y'all are, all right."

"That's my muthafuckin' nigga. Much love, homie, and sorry for comin' sideways out the mouthpiece. A nigga just still trippin' from those ho-ass niggas," TJ replied.

Suddenly somebody yelled out for everybody to look down the street.

Laughs and chuckles erupted and fingers started pointing. What they was looking at was hood-funny. Toneya, a crackhead-slash-crazy bitch, was walking up the block with pants on and pissing.

"Oh shit!" Lil' Man said out loud. "The bitch is pissin' like a nigga standin' up. I didn't know a bitch could do that shit."

"Come on now, Lil' Man, don't make yourself look stupider than you already look. Hoes ain't no different from a nigga when it comes to pissin'. They got a pisshole just like us. We just got ours going through our long pipes." Then Jesse waved him off. "But, oh, I forgot you ain't old enough to have a long pipe yet."

Now everybody had two things to crack up laughing at after Jesse schooled Lil' Man's naïve ass.

"Yo, y'all ain't gonna be tryin' to ride me 'cuz I'm young. Hell, y'all niggas old as dirt and don't none of y'all know the shit I know now."

"Shit, little nigga, we don't need to know all the shit your little ass know, cause all that shit ain't worth shit, if you don't know shit about a bitch and her body," TJ said, cutting Lil' Man down.

"Fuck you niggas. All of y'all ain't nothin' but some old-school played-out niggas, anyways. I'll still be gettin' money out here on these streets in twenty years, while y'all wrinkle asses will be in some old folks' home, suckin' on straws, drinkin' Ensure like my great-grandmamma be doin'."

Lil' Man got them back good with his verse, and they knew it too. That's why everybody gave dap. "But, check, I gotta get goin', so whenever y'all get ready to ride on those bitch-ass niggas, if y'all old decrypted ass ain't fell out and died before, then let me know." Lil' Man walked off headed to check on some other business.

As he hit the Arab corner store, thirsty for something to drink, he went to the back, where the cooler were. He slid back one of the coolers and felt the cold rise up his way. The Arab store was known as the cold spot 'cuz they had the coldest beer, soda, water, and anything else you could drink. He reached down and grabbed a bottle of Schlitz Malt Liquor. He knew he wasn't old enough to cop it, but he had successfully purchased one or two in the past. He didn't know this particular Arab that was at the counter, so he cocked his Memphis Grizzlies Starter cap, which matched his Starter jacket, to the front to hide that he was a minor from "El Sheiky" at the counter.

As Lil' Man placed the beer on the counter, the Arab looked him over carefully. He knew the youngster wasn't old enough, but to him, the money was the only thing that mattered. "Is that all?" the man with the keffiyeh asked.

"Yeah, playa, that's all," Lil' Man replied, his voice full of bass.

The man was letting Lil' Man get by with something that he knew the boy wasn't even old enough to purchase but to get more cash outta the youth he played on him for a second. "Hey, don't you want some gum to take the smell of the beer away when you're done drinking it?" He put three big packs of Big Red on the counter.

Lil' Man wanted to raise his head, but he didn't want to blow his chance at copping the brew. *Three packs of gum? What the fuck I'ma do with this shit?* He peeled off a five-dollar bill from his bankroll to cover all the items and kept his hand out for change.

"You should buy these chips also. The chips will make you thirsty so you can finish the whole forty ounce."

Lil' Man now felt that he was being played on, or more like preyed on. He hurried up and left, leaving the man with the five and the two other funky-ass dollars. When Lil' Man turned around and looked back at the store, he saw the Arab waving bye, like he just had him a good ol' laugh. Lil' Man reminded himself to let that "bandaged-head" muthafucka know that it was truly on and poppin' the next time he saw him.

Lil' Man finally made it to the park. He saw the gray Crown Victoria parked in the same spot as always whenever he met the guy.

"It was nice of you to make it," the white guy greeted sarcastically when Lil' Man got in the car.

"Man, ain't nothin' nice about this ho shit." Lil' Man took a swig of the brew.

"Look, ain't nobody twisted your fuckin' arm to do this. I'm sure the judge wouldn't mind locking you back up, if you don't want to cooperate anymore. We white folks do know about the black street code. Tell on no one and see no evil, hear no evil. Hell, boy, that's the old saying. The new saying is either help yourself out and do your part or we send your little black ass up the river to be somebody's guppy. The choice is yours. And there's no two ways about that," Detective Gary stated.

Lil' Man soaked up what the five-O had just said. He cussed himself silently for going down to Chattanooga to slang. Nothing good came outta that move, except for all the females wanting to give the new ballin' cat some pussy. And the fame and glory of having pussy coming at him in every direction wasn't all of that because by being with pussy the night the laws rushed him in the motel he was now forced to go against the code of the street and get down with the boys in blue.

"Look, man, I'm meeting you like I'm supposed to do. I ain't tryin' to do no time for nobody, so don't be threatenin' me," Lil' Man said in a high-pitched tone. He took another swig of his beer.

"Man, I wish the guys from the DEA in Chattanooga would have told me that you was a little smart bastard before I agreed to be your liaison. I would have told them that I'll agree only if I could beat your ass like a runaway slave if you ever got outta hand—like now." Gary looked dead at Lil' Man.

"That's how you do shit, huh. I know y'all white folks really miss the slavery days."

Gary was tired of the youngster's high fallutin attitude. He'd worked as a DEA liaison before for the Feds with other people who got caught up and chose to help themselves out, but none of them had an attitude like Lil' Man.

Maybe it was just because they knew what they had to do to maintain their freedom and not get sent to the big house. He chalked the thoughts up in his head. Lil' Man wasn't mature enough to understand the severity of the charge when the DEA raided the motel room with him and his little Chattanooga female friend inside.

"Lawrence, why don't we get down to business and you tell me what I want to know, and we can move on from there, all right." Gary pulled his notepad and pen from his shirt pocket.

"Cool. 'Cuz the quicker we done here, the quicker I can leave."

Gary waited for Lil' Man to finish spilling his guts about Dee Dee, and all that she had been up to.

The reason that the Feds let Lil' Man go was because he gave up Dee Dee's name as his connect. The Feds wasn't dumb. When they'd busted Lil' Man and found all those ounces of crack in his backpack, they knew that a young kid like him had to be working for somebody. Lil' Man's ID stated that he was from Memphis, so they did a little investigating by calling the Memphis Police Department. All from a phone call, they found out everything they needed to know about Dee Dee, including her current courtroom battle. The Feds felt that the case with Lil' Man was one that would come in handy, so they gave him the chance to either work or be sentenced as an adult and do Fed time, like the rest of the wannabe big boys who thought the game was for them. Lawrence Devon Parker, aka Lil' Man, was now working for the law and not one hustling soul from his hood knew about his little charade.

"So you mean to tell me that all this time that you been out, you haven't got a supply of drugs from her yet?"

"Look, she knows I got busted, so she's just a little bit slow to put some work in my hands right now."

"So she don't trust you, is what you saying, right?"

"Fuck naw, man, that's not what I'm sayin'. What I'm sayin' is, she ain't no dumb bitch. Hell, she had two of the coldest brothers that was in the game who taught her right. It's just gonna take time that's all."

"I said a second ago, like she don't trust you. I guess I'll call the boys in Chattanooga and let them know that's it's a no-go."

He wasn't really planning on making the call. Besides he didn't have the power to pull the plug on a federal investigation. All he was just trying to do is lean on Lil' Man a little, so he could get some concrete evidence.

Gary wanted to surprise his partner Perkins more than ever. He didn't like for Perkins to go around working as hard as he did, and then think he wasn't doing the right thing. To Gary, everybody that was black driving around in fancy cars, wearing expensive clothes, and sporting all that bling-bling was guilty of something, and wasn't no innocent-until-proven-guilty shit going to fly with him, if he had any say-so in the matter.

"Man, don't do no stupid shit like that. I told you I got this. She'll come around. Besides, I roll with her every day, so it's gonna happen soon. Shit, she the one that told me that she got somethin' big goin' down soon."

"Okay, Lawrence, I'll take your word this time, but you better start producing real soon because every day that nothing turns up I jot it down in this here notepad. And you know who sees this here notepad, don't you?"

Lil' Man knew he had to play his cards right with the cracker or take the chance on letting Gary blackball him with the boys in Chattanooga by telling them he wasn't trying to help himself out, which was the deal they'd all agreed on. Lil' Man knew he had to produce something, and in a hurry, and that was the only way to maintain his freedom.

Gary told Lil' Man that he would see him the same time next week, and Lil' Man hopped outta the car, making sure that no one who knew him was around.

Chapter Seven

Dee Dee walked in the apartment building entrance. When she did, she understood why the big U-Haul truck was parked outside.

"Dee Dee, I'm glad I seen you before I left," Sondra said to her. Sondra was middle-aged, brown-skinned and had a slender track runner build. Her hair was just as short as Dee Dee's with her new haircut. She was dressed in an all-gray Fruit of the Loom sweatsuit. She had on that Sunday morning get-up that women wore when it was housecleaning time, except, she was moving furniture now.

"What's going on, Sondra?"

"I know this all of a sudden, but I got no choice but to move. My mom is in the hospital, and I gotta be there to take care of her when she gets out. Damn, strokes! Doctors need to hurry up and find a way to treat that shit. I don't know how much use of her body she has. Like I said,

I'm sorry for not giving you a notice, but this wasn't something I had to think about," Sondra said, tears in her eyes.

"Sondra, I am so sorry, but don't worry. Like you said, your mom needs you and you need to be there."

"Thanks, Dee Dee, and don't worry about the deposit either. You can keep that for my abrupt departure, girl." Sondra dried her eyes with her sleeve.

"Sondra, come now, is the apartment messed up or anything?"

"Oh God, no. Dee Dee, I take care of my things and even better care of other people's stuff I'm responsible for. Come check for yourself." Sondra motioned for Dee Dee to follow her.

"So why would I keep your deposit if the apartment is in good shape like how you moved in? Sondra, when you get to where you goin' just give me a call and I'll send you a check for your deposit, okay." Dee Dee leaned in and gave Sondra a girly hug.

Sondra embraced Dee Dee as if she was hugging her mother right then.

Sondra's situation made Dee Dee think of her own mother. She wondered how she was doing. Since the funeral she hadn't seen or heard from her. Their hug session was interrupted by the two men carrying Sondra's box spring mattress to her bed.

"Hey, Sondra, we'll meet you outside," one of the guys said, as they guided the mattress through the apartment building entrance and exit door.

"I'll be right there, Greg," Sondra replied.

"You need some help, Sondra?" Dee Dee asked.

"Oh, child, if you would have been here three hours ago, I would have said grab this, grab that, but that was the last of everything. So I guess this is goodbye, huh." A miserable look on her face, Sondra looked at Dee Dee.

"Never say goodbye. Just say, 'See you later on.'"

Dee Dee walked Sondra outside and then watched her get in her car.

Before rolling off, Sondra told Dee Dee thanks for everything and for her to keep her in prayer and she would do the same. As Sondra pulled off, the big U-Haul with her belongings in it pulled off right behind her. Sondra blew her horn one last time as she waved goodbye, and Craig did the same in the U-Haul.

Dee Dee walked back inside the building. She went straight for Sondra's old apartment. She opened the door and wasn't surprised in the least at how spotless the place was. The thing that tripped Dee Dee out was the fruity smell in the apartment. After walking to every room, she spotted the source of the wonderful aroma, the plug-in air freshener in every room.

Tired, Dee Dee headed up to the apartment where she not only did drop-offs, but had been staying in lately. As soon as she closed the door to the apartment, she kicked her royal blue and white Jordan's off. She plopped down on the couch then put her feet up on the armrest.

Dee Dee placed her hands on her head and started massaging her temple. The stress was working her over to the third power. Finding out who killed her brothers was all she could think about.

Dee Dee slid her right hand down to her purse on the floor. She picked it up and looked inside for the Phillie Blunt box. Dee Dee pulled two blunts outta the box. She reached her arm out and gently tossed one onto the coffee table. The other one met the flame of her lighter.

Weed had become her little stress reliever. She didn't understand, back in the days, why Jay and Bee was always firing up blunt after blunt, but now it was evident. Weed was the cheapest and quickest pain reliever to obtain. Dee Dee didn't bother with bullshit stress weed that was out there. No, she was paying twenty-five thousand-a-pound for that killer BC bud. British Columbia bud was one of the most expensive marijuana out there, and weedheads craved it. The price was so high that most people settled for that stress weed in their life, but not Dee Dee. Since the first day she smoked that blunt after killing Manny, the shit worked good to calm her down. TJ was her connect on the bud, and since he was already the neighborhood weedman, she didn't have to go looking for shit when it came time to re-up.

Dee Dee blew smoke ring after smoke ring in the air, trying to relax some. The smoke rings were doing the trick. Or was it the good weed? Whichever one it was, she was now tripping out, staring at the ceiling through the evaporating smoke.

Dee Dee took another puff then started choking like a muthafucka. "Jay and Bee, I bet y'all ain't never smoke no killa shit like this, huh." Even the weed couldn't keep her from feeling like she was alone without Jay and Bee around. "I promise, I'll get whoever did that to y'all. Mark my words, Jay and Bee. I promise that the muthafucka that killed y'all is gonna pay in the worst way." Dee Dee stared at a picture with all three of them posing in it.

Dee Dee got up off the couch high as fuck. She headed for the bathroom to ease her bladder. Just before she made it to the bathroom, her cell phone started ringing.

She quickly put her piss session on hold, figuring that the caller may just be Lil' Man with word about who killed her brothers. Dee Dee plucked her cell out of her purse and noticed that the caller information wasn't available. She flipped the phone open. "Yeah, who this?"

"*This is a prepaid call from a federal inmate. You will not be charged for this call. This call is from*"—The voice of the automated speaker paused to allow the person trying to get in touch with Dee Dee to announce their pre-recorded name—"Chills! *If you do not wish to speak to this person at this time, just hang up. If you do wish to speak to this person press five, if you do not want this person calling you anymore at anytime just press seventy-seven.*"

Dee Dee quickly pressed the number five. "Chills!" Dee Dee shouted with excitement in her voice.

"What's up baby girl? How you holdin' up?"

"I'm good. A little twisted right now, but still I'm good, especially after hearing your voice."

"Aww, heiffer, now you wanna talk like you wanna give me some now that I'm in here," Chills said, making fun of the way they'd first met.

"If you don't cut the games, 'cuz it's still the same. I'm strictly-dickly. Besides, I'm sure you got hoes in that bitch that's just fighting over your pussy-eatin' ass."

They both laughed. Dee Dee really missed Chills, and Chills really missed Dee Dee.

Dee Dee didn't think that Chills would call her back anymore after the first time that she called to let Dee Dee know that they was in jail for robbing another bank. Dee Dee lost her girls to something that was just in their blood, and when something is in someone's blood ain't no gettin' it out, like HIV, the crippler.

"So the cops found out who did that to my homeboys yet?"

"Nawh, not at all, but you know I'm on it."

"That's cool. Just be careful, so you don't see a place like this in the future, feel me?" Chills gamed Dee Dee, basically telling her to do it the right way, 'cuz the wrong way could lead her to a cage, like it did her, Diamond, and Tricksy.

"Fuck all the talk about that. You been gettin' the magazines, money, and books I been sendin'?"

"Yeah, Mom's been sendin' everything. Speakin' of sendin' shit, I want you to go back to whatever bookstore you been gettin' those books you been sendin' me and get all the books by that nigga, Uncle Al. I just got through readin' one of his books called *Super Starr Jack'n*. Dee Dee, a bitch ain't really read before, but this nigga took me there. His shit is fire."

"I didn't send you no *Super Starr Jack'n* by some Uncle Al dude."

"I know. Some other bitch in here that's my little side-piece had it. That shit was like it was written after my life story. I'm telling you, Dee Dee, the shit is good. The nigga can write and tell a story. I finished that book in one night. Just look out for me and send all the ones he got in the stores and get yourself copies too. You for sure gonna like them, just mark my word, and that's real."

"Hey, Dee Dee. Miss you, girl."

"RBM for life, Dee Dee! I miss you too. Keep my ride tucked away in a safe place 'cuz I'm comin' home one day. It will be in nine years, but I'm comin' home one day."

Dee Dee knew the voices just as well as she knew Chills's. "That was Diamond and Tricksy?" she asked.

"Yeah, that was those hoes. They buggin'. Diamond stay fightin' over these bitches in here. On the outs, she loves dick, in here the bitch loves pussy. I don't get her ass sometimes."

Dee Dee did, especially after seeing Diamond fuck the shit outta Trey's ass before Chills really fucked him in the ass with the dildo they had on hand that time when they checked his punk ass.

Their conversation was interrupted by the automated beep, which signaled that the call was about to end. Well, at least Chills knew what the beep was for. Dee Dee, on the other hand, hadn't heard it enough to know what it meant.

"Did you hear that noise, Chills?" Dee Dee asked.

"Yeah, that means that we only got maybe about a minute left to talk. It's crazy how the Feds got all this money and they only allow us three hundred minutes each month, and fifteen minutes to talk every time we call. Hell, for seventy-two dollars to buy the three hundred funky-ass minutes these hoes should let us talk however funkin' long we wanna talk."

CLICK.

"Hello! Chills! CHILLS!" Dee Dee didn't know what happened to Chills, but then she remembered what Chills said about the beep. Chills was right. Fifteen minutes was too short to be talking to your loved ones in prison. Their conversation didn't even get a chance to warm up, and she had so much to say to her. She was also happy to hear Tricksy's and Diamond's voice again.

Thinking about her homegirls, Dee Dee went into the restroom and stood in front of the mirror. She pulled her Baby Phat white with royal blue letters shirt off. She looked at the tattoo just above her nipple on her breast. She traced her finger around each letter. "RBM Clique 4 Life," Dee Dee said out loud.

Dee Dee then placed her shirt back on so she could go to the bookstore and grab the books that Chills wanted. She couldn't remember the name of the book, but the name *Uncle Al* stuck with her.

Chapter Eight

Dee Dee drove swiftly through traffic as she headed to Janelle's crib to get her hair done as they'd agreed. She was looking good in Jay's big gray Ford Excursion. It was a nice ride to Dee Dee, but she felt like it was just too big for her to sport around for personal use.

Jay had bought it because it fit his style. Plus, it handled like Cadi, riding all smooth and shit. The stereo system was a monster in the banging department. He only believed in having the best, so he had the shop install the reliable Pioneer system throughout the whole ride. Four twelve-inch speakers in a custom-made Plexiglas box that blended in with the ride like it wasn't even there, and six ten-inch speakers mounted in place of the six by nines made his shit one of the most pounding, bass-thumping vehicles rolling on the Memphis streets.

Dee Dee turned the music down when she turned onto the street. She slowed the ride down as she pulled over to the curb and parked. The CD player automatically flipped over and folded into the console, so a thief couldn't notice it just by looking inside, trying to hit a lick.

She sat in the ride for a minute and stared at her and her brother's house. The construction workers were moving quickly, putting up the new prefab two-story crib. Dee Dee knew that she'd done the right thing by giving Janelle and her kids a place to call their very own. It made her feel good to help Janelle out like that. Besides Dee Dee didn't figure that she could handle all the old memories if she stayed there.

The loud yell from Janelle's mouth brought Dee Dee outta her trance just as she was about to go into the land of the lost, reminiscing on all the good and bad times that she'd shared with her brothers.

"Girl, if you don't get your butt in here right now . . ." Janelle said to break the ice.

Dee Dee stepped outta the ride. "What up."

"Ooooh, girl, let me get started on that crop of yours right now." Janelle rubbed her hand through Dee Dee's short, overdue-for-her-appointment hair. "I told you, Dee Dee, that I would do your hair two times a week and you ain't came in two weeks. Now am I gonna have to call and remind you when you're suppose to be tended to?"

Dee Dee just smiled. She wasn't really tripping on whether Janelle did her hair or not. She had given Janelle the money for GP 'cuz she had so much, and she knew all the money that she had was no good if she couldn't show a little love to somebody that needed help.

For the past two weeks Dee Dee had missed her appointments. Usually she would miss the one at the beginning of the week. At the end of the week she would just lay her hair down smooth-like with the black gel that made her hair hard and stiff to where it still looked good. But on Friday, like clockwork, she'd be at Janelle's crib to get her 'do done up.

"Come on in here," Janelle said, ushering Dee Dee up the porch steps.

As they walked up the steps, Dee Dee heard a noise coming from down the street. She turned her head and spotted someone riding a bicycle. The noise coming from the bike was caused by a playing card flipping back and forth against the spokes on the back wheel. She wished it was Mikey. She then got sad just thinking about him. She threw that notion outta her head, knowing he was gone and never coming back.

Once inside, Janelle checked all her little "bebe kids" right then and there. They called it playing around in the house. Janelle told all of then to take their little bad asses outside before she wound up putting the switch to their backside.

Dee Dee chuckled.

"Hi, Dee Dee" came outta each one of the kids' mouths as they walked by.

The one thing that Dee Dee peeped out was that Janelle had her kids trained to a *T*. The cute little jokers were so mannerly.

After washing and conditioning Dee Dee's hair, Janelle had her sit under the blow dryer. Janelle had time to kill, so she went in the kitchen and grabbed two Jack Daniels Wild Berry Wine Coolers outta the fridge.

They both sat drinking and talking about the new nigga in Janelle's life, Timmy, who was taking care of business and making her happy.

Dee Dee was glad for her girl's newfound happiness, which brought back memories of the nigga that had made her beyond happy. Thinking about Alastair, an ugly but realistic thought popped in her head. "Now you're thinking stupidly, Dee Dee," she said out loud, battling her thoughts.

"You talking to yourself, girl. You better quit that shit before I get to thinking that you goin' crazy or something." Janelle raised the hair dryer off Dee Dee's head and bent over to look at Dee Dee.

"You lost something?" Dee Dee asked Janelle, who was all up in her grill.

"Not at all. I was just checking to see if you was cool, 'cuz it ain't like you ain't been through enough drama lately."

"I'm cool. I was just thinking about something."

"Wanna talk about it? You do know that's what women do in salon shops."

"I don't know if you know this or not, but Janelle—this ain't no salon shop. Now by you sayin' some shit like that, maybe I should be the one wondering if you're okay." Dee Dee cracked a smile.

"Okay, you got that off, but how would you like it if I left this ol' raggedy hairdo fucked up?" Janelle rubbed her hand through Dee Dee's hair to see if it was all dry. "Oh yeah, Dee Dee, I forgot to tell you about how I met Timmy."

"Well, you gonna spill the beans or what? This should be interesting to hear." Dee Dee put her hands out as if to say, "Let it rip."

Dee Dee sat listening to what Janelle had to say as she worked on her hair at the same time. The news was baffling. Timmy had brought some guy who looked like a guy that plays in Mafia movies to Janelle's house. Dee Dee knew her brothers knew a lot of high-powered people, so she chalked it up as someone from outta town who knew Jay and Bee, but didn't know that they were now dead.

"You didn't tell him nothin' about me, did you?" Dee Dee asked quickly, thinking that maybe the guy could have been the police.

"Hell no!" Janelle lied. She did tell Timmy that Dee Dee's sister-in-law, Miya, could probably help the guy out. Janelle wanted to now kick herself in the ass for ever opening her big-ass mouth. She'd thought that the guy was a friend of the two brothers.

"Good! Keep it like that, 'cuz the police is really trying to sink my ass, and it ain't no tellin' what they would try or who they would try and send my way, you know what I mean?" Dee Dee turned around in her seat to look at Janelle to make sure that she got the hint.

Janelle continued to fix Dee Dee's hair until she was once again looking like a star. Dee Dee didn't need to look in no mirror, but Janelle held one up to her face anyway. And just like always, her 'do was looking tight.

Janelle walked Dee Dee outside and to her ride. The Excursion was gonna go to Janelle, so she would have decent transportation for her and all her kids. But something was telling Dee Dee to hold out for a while.

Just as Dee Dee got inside of her ride, Timmy's cab pulled up behind her and parked.

Janelle looked in the back and saw Timmy smiling and waving, and the biggest smile leaped onto her face.

Dee Dee noticed and was really happy for Janelle. "Janelle, remember what I said. Don't mention me or that you seen me to another person who we don't know. Hell, that goes for anybody. I don't care if I do know them or not. You ain't seen me, okay."

"I got it, Dee Dee, I got it. Now get outta here, so me and my baby can have some freaky-freaky time to ourselves." Janelle patted the door as if to say, "See you later, girl."

Dee Dee pointed her finger at Janelle. "Nasty, nasty."

Janelle just laughed and showed Dee Dee with her hand to get the tires turning, and Dee Dee blew her horn and rolled off.

As she rolled on Fulton, she fired up yet another one of those fire-ass blunts that was filled with the BC bud. She pumped the music as she smoked and cruised. All kind of thoughts went through her head. She knew the time was now at hand for her to take matters into her own hands since Lil' Man wasn't coming up with any leads about who killed her brothers. After thinking about it for a second, she knew it wasn't his fault. She understood that nobody out was just gonna up and talk about a murder, let alone two murders.

To find something out she told herself, that she would have to be in the streets where the action was. It was time for her to get to pushing some of those many kilos that she was in possession of. If the hustlers wanted to get some work, she would be right there on the block with them, ready to sell to them, morning, noon, and night. The candy shop was officially about to be open, and somebody was gonna tell her something. If she had to give a nigga some pussy so he would talk, then that's just what she was gonna have to do 'cuz somebody was gonna pay with their life.

"Did you kill my brother's cuz I told you about my

dream? Did you take revenge out on my brothers 'cuz I killed your cousin?" Dee Dee asked out loud. Alastair was the only person that popped in her head who she knew would probably want to do something like that. It was adding up. Jay and Bee did have a lot of enemies floating around the city, but Alastair was the best suspect she could come up with 'cuz he flipped when she told him about her dream and he found out she was the one who killed Manny.

Then shortly after Jay and Bee got out of jail they got killed. That was all too close for comfort to rule Alastair out as the one she needed to see in a dark alley somewhere in town.

Chapter Nine

Picasso stepped outta the limo, then took the time to straighten out his cream, tailored Hart Schaffner Marx suit. Picasso didn't need Don Ruiz's driver to escort him through the house, nor did he need the bodyguards at the front door to guide him in.

Even though Don Ruiz's men were heavily armed and straight killers, they were no match for Picasso. Before Picasso became a hired killer, he acquired his skills from the Costa Rican army. Excelling in hand-to-hand combat and winning numerous honors in target practice earned him a spot on the sniper unit. He was a dead shot for any target in his scope. And martial arts became a passion for him, as did meditation, which came in handy. After killing a person, he needed a way to get at peace with himself again, and meditation was the way.

The front door bodyguard opened the door and allowed the sharply dressed assassin to walk in. The maid was waiting right there for him so she could take anything that he may not have wanted to lug around. After she took his trench coat she escorted him into the lavish dining room of the ranch-style estate, where Don Ruiz was awaiting his entrance.

"Picasso, my friend. *¿Cómo estás, compadre?* Please have a seat." Don Ruiz motioned to where he should sit.

"*Muy bien, Señor Ruiz.*" Picasso took the suggested seat in the expensive white chair that was big enough to fit two people.

"So, *mi amigo,* tell me, have my little friends been taken care of and my property recovered?" Don Ruiz asked, referring to Jay and Bee.

Picasso removed his Prada shades from his face, revealing his straight, stern expression, and meticulously folded it and placed it in the outer pocket of his suit coat.

"*Señor,* your problem has been taken care of—"

"*Fantástico!*" Don Ruiz leaned over and slapped Picasso on his thigh. Don Ruiz was booming with so much joy that he forgot to even ask about his five thousand kilos of coca.

"Contresa, bring me and *Señor* Picasso some of my finest brandy and a couple of my Cuban cigars."

Contresa whisked away in her black and white maid's outfit and returned with the order on a silver tray. She placed it on the rest stand then poured both men a drink in cognac glasses. She handed one to each man then grabbed the snipper cutter so she could clip the tip of the cigars. Once done, she gave each man a cigar and lit them with the hand-size marble block lighter.

"Drink up, *compadre.*" Don Ruiz took a sip of his brandy.

"Don Ruiz, please forgive me for interrupting your joyous moment, but I didn't get to finish speaking on the extent of my trip." Picasso never even blinked.

A puzzled expression leaped onto Don Ruiz's face. He didn't understand where Picasso was going and he couldn't read his expression. Picasso had one of those faces that never changed. It always stayed blank, giving him a mysterious look.

"It's true that the targets, Jay and Bee, were taken care of, but it wasn't by my hands."

Don Ruiz quickly put his glass on the coffee table then sat all the way back in his seat to hear Picasso's story.

"On my arrival in Memphis, I was able to track down the two, but I found out that they were already dead, shot in the head at the same time. Who killed them, *señor*, I have no idea."

Don Ruiz leaned forward and grabbed his glass of brandy. He needed a drink after hearing that type of information. "So they was robbed for all my drugs then killed I suppose. That fuckin' *maricón*, Ricardo. Because of him I'm now outta five thousand kilos and no leads as to who has my shit. "*CHINGA SU MADRE*!!!"

"*Señor*, I was able to get some other information though."

Don Ruiz's whole expression changed.

"The two have a sister. I haven't attempted to track her down because I felt it was best to check in with you to see if you wanted to further this venture, even though the two are already dead and there's a possibility that your property is lost."

Don Ruiz sat up once again and took another sip of his brandy. The new information was promising. He knew that he just might not see his property again, but before coming to that conclusion, he wanted Picasso to move his ass. He gave Picasso a hateful look. He felt like Picasso could have called that information in, and because he didn't just take it upon himself to follow up with leads he had acquired to track the sister down, his drugs was now getting farther away by the second, especially with Picasso now being all the way across the country back in California.

Don Ruiz stood up with his drink in hand and asked Picasso to take a walk with him. Don Ruiz showed off his estate as they talked and walked along the dirt trail that led to a beautiful forest with autumn leaves all over the ground. Don Ruiz was telling Picasso how much he would appreciate it if his drugs could be retrieved. He didn't care how it got done, as long as it was taken care of without him coming back to California to deliver a message of no importance.

After their talk, Picasso left the estate set to head back to Memphis the next morning with the intent of following up on Timmy's lead. Now Timmy would come in handy once again, as his first stop would be to seek out Miya.

Don Ruiz walked into the pool area where all his personal playthings waited in the big Jacuzzi to tend to his every need. Contresa was right there when Don Ruiz motioned that it was time for his robe to come off.

Once off, he carefully stepped in the water with the gorgeous butt-naked bodies. Immediately, one of them went to massaging his neck, another, his temple and head, and a third, his dick with her mouth.

Don Ruiz looked over and saw a couple of his girls smoking opium from the multi-stem Asian bong. Don Ruiz allowed it since, after all, they weren't allowed to go anywhere other than around the compound. He signaled the girl to hand him one of the many stems. Matter of fact, he gestured for all the girls to join in.

With laughter and giggles they got high. The first hit had him feeling woozy. He leaned his head back, his arms spread out on the edge of the Jacuzzi, and one of the females took his little soldier into her mouth.

Don Ruiz got to thinking about how ignorant Picasso was to not handle the business like he was supposed to. And that look on his face, like he was a Don himself, made Don Ruiz sick. Don Ruiz made up his mind that Picasso would no longer work for him, nor anyone else for that matter. He felt that once Picasso made his way back to Cali, he wouldn't be leaving, nor would that look be on his face anymore. Especially after his bodyguards cut it all off while he was still alive. His service was going to be terminated indefinitely.

Picasso was back in Memphis, and his incomparable chauffeur was waiting this time, but not to drive him around. He was only there to give Picasso the leather briefcase with the powerful gun inside it and the other suitcase with undisclosed contents. Timmy was also there, his cab ready and running. As he opened the door, Picasso walked his way with both suitcases in hand.

Timmy looked back at the Mexican chauffeur and blew him a kiss. Then he closed the back passenger door and rushed around to the driver's side and got in. He looked through the rearview mirror. "Where to, boss?"

"The Hilton this time, *amigo*."

Timmy fastened his seat belt then put the pedal to the

floor. He moved through the crowded airport traffic like he was on the highway during traffic jam hours.

Picasso watched Timmy handle the car with precision as he drove. Timmy was a likable guy, and Picasso liked him. It was just too bad that he had to be erased from the earth. See, Timmy knew what Picasso looked like, and Picasso didn't become the best in his field by being careless and leaving loose ends behind, like someone who could give any type of information to the police that could harm him in the long run. No two ways about it, Timmy was going to be put six feet deep.

Timmy pulled into the Hilton cul-de-sac parking entrance then parked. He then threw his right elbow onto the back headrest and turned around to look at Picasso. "We're here, boss. You want me to wait for you while you get settled?"

"That won't be necessary today, *amigo*, but tomorrow is a new day. I need you to be here early in the morning to pick me up. Very busy day tomorrow, so let's not be late. And just like last time, this should take care of you for your time." Picasso pulled ten crisp hundred-dollar bills from his inside suit coat pocket.

"You got that, boss." Timmy took the big-face bills. "Early tomorrow morning I'll be here just like you want me to." He hopped outta his seat and ran to the other side of the car to open the door.

Picasso got out and didn't look back as he walked with his cool stride, leaving Timmy with an eerie feeling.

Picasso opened the door to his room with the electric card key. Once in, he headed to the bedroom, where he placed both of the black shiny suitcases down side by side on the nice, soft queen-size bed.

Picasso opened the bigger suitcase, and lo and behold there was the makeup kit with designer wig and all inside. After seeing that part of the suitcase was right, he opened the bottom half to check out the all-black high-powered rifle and feasted his eyes on the marvelous piece of weaponry. Without doing anything else, Picasso walked over to the other side of the bed and lay down, his hand clasped behind his propped up head, and thought about his visit to Miya.

Chapter Ten

Dee Dee pulled onto the street where everybody was hustling. She'd kept her word about getting down and dirty, just like everybody else. She figured if she was in the gutter like everybody else, then they would look at her like one of the guys. But the thing about it was, Dee Dee wasn't one of the guys. She was a fine female with the product they needed. Even though some of the niggas that had been hustling for years hated 'cuz their pockets wasn't even close to hers, they kept quiet about it, afraid that what had happened to Trey could happen to them.

As she spotted the fellas on different blocks of the street getting money, she chose to pull over and park where TJ was. TJ was hitting a lick with one of the many dudes that was hanging out. The weed that he had for sale damn near went quicker than the crack other guys was selling.

TJ gave the dude that he'd just sold the ounce of weed to some dap and tucked the cash in his right pocket. As he did, he turned around and spotted Dee Dee waving him to come on over. TJ placed both his hands on his black and white Avirex jacket then flipped it out like if he was popping his collar. Then he removed his heater from the waistband of his sagging baggy pants, so it wouldn't fall out while he stepped to chill with Dee Dee for a sec.

TJ opened the passenger door to get in. "What's poppin', Dee Dee?"

"Same shit, gettin' money like you. You wanna hit this?" She passed the blunt in his direction.

TJ was happy to get out of the chilly weather for a moment. As he took the blunt from Dee Dee, he took his heater and placed it on the seat, between his legs.

"I respect your hustle, Dee Dee. I mean you got so much of your brothers in you. I know they would be damn proud of you."

Dee Dee leaned her head back and soaked it all up.

"Yo, I didn't mean to bring up no ill feelings. All I was just saying is that you been out here on the grind with the rest of us handlin' your business. Actually, it's a smart move 'cuz you get to keep watch on your cash. Niggas can't come with no lame-ass excuse about they ain't got your cheddar, if you're watching them, feel me?"

"TJ, peep. By me being out here with these cats watching my money is probably the only reason why I haven't had anybody trying to play me, but the real reason I'm out here"—Dee Dee looked at TJ and searched for a reason why she shouldn't let him in on why she was on the block morning, noon, and night. His giving her brothers and her props just a second ago gave her the green light to go ahead—"Look, TJ, I'm really trying to find out who put my brothers to rest, and the only way it seems like I can do that is if I'm out here on the front line 'cuz you know the streets are always talkin'. That I do know, feel me?" Dee Dee reached out to retrieve the blunt.

"DAMN, BABY! That's deep, but I feel you. I ain't heard nothin' about that, but I'm on your team. If I hear something, guaranteed your cell will be ringing off the hook. I can't believe we ain't heard shit about it yet."

"Me either. Somebody gotta know something. Shit like that just don't stay hush-hush. Hell, Sammy the Bull even told somebody about the bodies he had. It may have been the Feds, but he told somebody. Feel me?" Dee Dee couldn't help laughing.

TJ chuckled. "Gimme that, girl." He took the blunt back. "Here I am thinking you're serious and you crackin' jokes."

Dee Dee's expression changed up quickly. "Nigga, best believe this bitch right here is dead serious. I ain't playin' no games, TJ. I want the nigga's head who did that to my brothers. Either by my own hands, or by somebody else. Matter of fact, shit is moving too slow by me trying to find information out."

Dee Dee started blowing her horn, crazy as fuck, repeatedly. She wanted to get the attention of all the niggas on the block. To make her message understood, she opened up the driver's door then stood up on the running board and waved the fellas over. They would soon understand what all the honking was for.

Once they was all huddled around the big Excursion, she hopped onto the hood then got on top of the roof. She stood up there and looked down at all of them.

TJ opened the passenger door and braced himself between the door and roof as he too stood on the running board.

"Look, all y'all know how my brothers got killed."

Everybody started looking at each other like, *What the fuck's going on?*

"What we don't know is who the fuck shot them. I know it wasn't one of y'all. That I'm sure of 'cuz shit would have got out way before now. The bottom line is, I wanna know who did it, so whoever can find that shit out, I got ten bricks for your ass as a reward. I don't want nothin' to happen to the person. Just let me know, and I'll take care of that."

Ten bricks sunk into everybody's head quickly. Niggas got to calculating all the shit they could buy with that much shit. Hearing big dollar amounts brought the motivation out in the best of people. Plus, it also brought out the plotting in a muthafucka, which Dee Dee would soon encounter.

"Ten bricks to find out who did them? Hell, I'll mark the nigga for you, Dee Dee, for ten bricks." Roy, wearing sagging Rocawear jeans, gripped his nuts.

"Fuck what he said, Dee Dee." Jon Jon pushed Roy in the back. "Jay and Bee was from our hood. We lookin' for the busters just like you. It don't take for you to offer us no reward. We ain't the white folks on TV. If you wanna give the nigga who hip you to what you wanna know the ten birds, then that's on you, but we're a hood and a hood stick together."

Some nigga agreed with what Jon Jon said, while others cringed. Ten bricks was a come-up and that was the main reason that they was hustlin' the block, taking penitentiary chances, trying to come up in the first place day in and day out.

After Dee Dee was done talking, niggas broke off back into their own little groups, and Jon Jon stayed around to lend Roy a hand in getting her down off the roof of the ride safely. Dee Dee found a new respect for Jon Jon. The stuff he'd said made her feel like her brothers wasn't forgotten.

She made it a point to take care of Jon Jon from then on out. To her, he was "work-worthy" of her help, seeing that he was one of the older *G*'s on the block getting money. He was also a good friend to Jay and Bee. If anybody had close ties to Jay and Bee, it was Jon Jon and Terry Tee. Even though Terry's brother was dead, he understood that it wasn't Dee Dee's fault. He missed his brother, but his brother was sick and the bullet that laid him to rest was probably the best thing to take him out of his misery.

Dee Dee knew she had to get back to the apartment building to meet the furniture man, who was supposed to meet her there to finish the place where she would be laying her head. Sondra's old apartment was now Dee Dee's. The whole arrangement was a good fit. She could lay her head, collect her cash, and get easy access to the dope. Since they all had something to do with the building, it surely was gonna work to her advantage. Dee Dee smoked and cruised, trying to make it to the building on time.

No sooner than she broke from the hood, she was pulling up to the two-story brick building. The delivery people were already there waiting, standing outside the truck on the sidewalk, puffing on their cigarettes. Dee Dee blew the horn as she pulled up behind the furniture truck and parked. The two big guys, one white, one black, hurried up and tossed their smokes when they heard the horn, figuring Dee Dee was the person they'd be delivering the furniture to.

"I'm sorry, fellas, for being late. Y'all ready?" Dee Dee asked as she was getting outta her ride.

The movers couldn't believe that the female that they was looking at was that fuckin' fine. Only when she spoke again did they break out of the hypnotic gaze.

"Y'all ready?" she asked again, knowing that they were looking just a little hard.

The guys jumped to attention, pushing one another like they were telling the other to come on for the longest.

Dee Dee walked up to the entrance to hold the door open, but to her surprise the white guy with the long hair like a rock 'n' roller walked up with the door jammer in his hand.

"You ain't gotta stand there and keep the door open for us. That's what this thing is for. I think you chose some of the store's best pieces. I believe you gonna like all of it."

"Thanks. This the apartment that everything's gonna go in. Just use your logic on where you think something should go. I'll be upstairs in apartment seven," Dee Dee said, referring to the pick-up spot.

Dee Dee had decided to move into the vacant apartment when she found out Sondra was moving. This would be her very first apartment. She wanted everything in the crib to be laid out, so she went and purchased nothing but the best from Lawinski Furniture Store.

Dee Dee walked up the stairs, leaving the movers to do their job. When she got upstairs she figured that she might as well get the work ready for everybody outta the stash apartment, so she wouldn't have to do it later.

As soon as she got to the apartment, she headed straight for the security monitors and peeped the movers handling their business. She couldn't wait to chill in her own crib. With thirty-three million in cold hard cash and enough dope to remake three times over the money that she would spend, yeah, she could have bought any crib she wanted, even a mansion, but the apartment was perfectly suited to her needs.

She then walked over to the thermostat and turned it, and the wall cracked open. She grabbed the black duffel bag off the desk then started filling it up with kilos from off the shelves. Once done, she zipped the bag then looked at all the bricks on the shelves. It was like looking at "white heaven."

Dee Dee closed the wall back and walked over to the security camera. It was always wise to look at the monitors when she was exiting 'cuz she didn't want to meet a stickup kid looking for a come-up.

Dee Dee walked out the front door of the stash house then headed for the collection pad, where she placed the big duffel bag in the bedroom. She picked up her cell and called TJ.

TJ answered right away, figuring Dee Dee needed a new supply of that BC bud.

Dee Dee explained that she wanted everybody to come through about six o'clock, which would give the movers enough time to be long gone. After TJ told her that it was on and poppin' and not another word needed to be said, Dee Dee then placed a call to Lil' Man's house.

After three rings Lil' Man's mom answered the phone.

"Is Lil'—I mean, is Lawrence in?"

"Who's calling?"

"This Deondra."

"No, he's not, but I'll tell him that you called, baby, okay."

"Thank you, ma'am."

Dee Dee had never met Lil' Man's mom, but the feeling that she got from talking to her was that she wasn't young, considering Lil' Man was only sixteen.

Usually, if a person had a kid about sixteen, then they'd usually be in their early or late thirties. Ellen wasn't even close. She had Lil' Man when she was thirty, which now made her forty-six.

Ellen had been coughing real bad lately, and the cigarettes weren't helping her none. She wanted the best for her only child. That's why she wanted to find out just who this Deondra girl was, 'cuz she sounded too old to be calling her house for Lawrence.

The knock at the door interrupted Dee Dee as she watched *Sanford and Son*. She rose up off the couch and walked over to look through the peephole.

"Ma'am, we all done," the burly brotha said.

Dee Dee didn't say a word. All she did was walk outside the door, closing it behind her, and then followed him downstairs.

The white mover stood to the side as Dee Dee walked inside her newly furnished crib. At the sight of her furniture all arranged in pretty good order, Dee Dee covered her mouth with her hands. Then she said, "All right now, y'all did y'all thang." She looked back at the two movers in time to see them grinning from cheek to cheek.

"Okay, fellas, time to go. I gotta see what I'm working

with." Dee Dee scooted them out the door and gave them a generous tip.

On each end of the Italian leather green couch, Dee Dee placed white, redwood pillars with African male figures. The love seat was positioned opposite the couch, while the chair was backed off towards the balcony glass door.

There had to be about ten artificial silk trees throughout the living room. Dee Dee walked over to the large picture of the waterfall mounted on the wall, plugged the cord into the socket, and watched the water start running down, as if it was a real waterfall.

The rug in the center of the floor helped set the three-piece living room set off, the redwood end tables adding to the atmosphere. The two curio cabinets and the big china cabinet reminded her of her mom's living room. Up against the wall was the big-screen TV, which sat in the front of the couch, and next to the couch stood two massive chest-high all-black speakers. The stereo was mounted on the bookshelf in its pre-designed slot.

Dee Dee ran to the bedroom. She was feeling the wooden king-size canopy bed, a nightstand on each side of the bed, while the dresser with mirror was to the side and the two other dressers spread out in the bedroom. Dee Dee leaped onto her bed, feeling the perfectly soft pillows and soft mattress. Her money had been well spent, and the bed was the best indicator of that. She just lay there and rubbed her stomach.

Now, all that was left to do before she could move her clothes and bedding into the crib from the collection apartment was handle the business with the fellas with their pickup, and her collection.

Chapter Eleven

As she waited in the "collection apartment" for everybody else to stop and pick up their orders, she paged Lil' Man. Dee Dee couldn't wait to talk to him. In fact, she wanted to know more about his mother, who seemed to be a nice lady.

The knock on the front door brought Dee Dee to her feet. She walked over to the security monitor and saw Franky J. and Cannon, two of the hustling cats that roamed the hood. The only way they was able to stay up all night and hustle was by snorting about a half-ounce of coke every night. That, for them, was better than taking NoDoz pills or drinking coffee.

After they got their issue, she walked back over to the monitor to make sure that everything was cool. Once she'd seen it was cool, she gave the sign, and they left out the door quickly. Dee Dee cracked a smile as she walked to the chute to drop the money in. For two guys who weren't related,

Dee Dee thought Franky J. and Cannon had a strong resemblance. Plus, they were neat freaks who always kept her money straight.

A couple more of the fellas came through, and Dee Dee went through the same process, counting the money, giving them their issue, looking at the monitor to make sure it was clear, then dropping the money-bag in the chute. The system that she'd inherited from her brothers was proving to be valuable.

Time flew as everybody came by and got their work. The rest of the night was left to her to spend in her new lavish apartment. Dee Dee walked outta the apartment and headed back to the stash apartment to put the newly collected money behind the wall.

The time that Dee Dee had spent in retirement from the game, from being in jail to getting her mind right because of what had happened to her brothers, had made her forget what the feeling of being in control was like. Now she was feeling it again and loving every bit of it. But make no mistake about it, she was still focused on finding the person who snuffed her brothers, and that's all that really mattered to her.

As Dee Dee got downstairs, she realized she didn't have any food in her fridge to eat. In no time, she was out the door, bound for Wal-Mart, which had everything she was gonna need, including little knick-knacks for the crib.

Dee Dee pulled into the packed parking lot, filled with people coming and going from the store. As she cruised around looking for an empty parking spot that wasn't too far from the door, her cell phone started ringing. She reached down on the seat and plucked it from the portable charger.

"This Dee Dee," she said into the receiver.

"Yo, what's up, girl? Moms told me that you called."

"Nigga, where the fuck you been?" Dee Dee fired back. "This disappearing shit ain't gonna get shit poppin', and you talkin' 'bout you wanna do this. I can't tell." She peeped a soon-to-be-available spot to park. The white lady had her yellow Dodge Stratus reverse lights on in the back, but Dee Dee didn't see her making no attempts to back the car up. She had time to kill, 'cuz Lil' Man had shit to say, so she waited patiently in the still-running Excursion.

"I been handlin' up, playin' detective and shit. Plus, I got your cash and now I need to get the re-up."

The white lady in the yellow two-door Stratus finally made the move to vacate the parking spot.

" 'Bout time, heifer. Acting like people got all fuckin' day." Dee Dee blew her horn just to let the lady know it was about time, seeing as she knew Dee Dee was waiting for the spot. Dee Dee cracked a smile when the lady tossed her hand up and waved like it was all good. She wanted to put her middle finger up at the lady, so she wouldn't get the horn-honking confused with thinking Dee Dee was saying thank you or some bullshit like that.

"Look, I'm about to go into Wal-Mart," Dee Dee stated as she emerged outta the big cruiser. "So answer my fuckin' page immediately when I hit you back up, feel me?"

"It's on and poppin'. Just don't forget, I need to see you when you're done treating yourself, all right."

Dee Dee couldn't believe Lil' Man. It was all good when *he* wanted something, but when she had to look for his ass, it ain't all good. She was gonna make sure that they had a long talk when she got him face to face.

The automatic doors opened as Dee Dee walked up to them. She was greeted by one of the friendliest ladies ever. She thought Wal-Mart was bogus for having what seemed to be a sixty- or seventy-year-old white lady working this late as a door greeter. *They couldn't give this old lady a morning shift?* Dee Dee grabbed one of the shopping baskets then headed on her venture to buy up shit.

Guys was looking at Dee Dee as she strolled by, looking sexy. One tried his luck. "Hey, little momma, want me to pay for your stuff when you're done?"

Others just admired the tight JLo jeans that made her ass stick out.

Dee Dee kept it all cool and kept stepping. The comments was cool to her. Actually they made her feel like she was missing something in her life.

As Dee Dee turned onto the aisle with canned goods, she noticed a brother bent over, checking out some waist-high items. His ass was facing in Dee Dee's direction, so she couldn't see his face. She thought he had a cute butt. Dee Dee cracked a smile when he knocked a can of beans off the shelf. Then she let the laughter be known when three more cans fell.

The guy heard the laughter, so he stood up and turned around.

Dee Dee stood there biting her clenched bottom lip, her hands gripped tight to the basket's handle. Her feet felt like they couldn't move an inch. Nor could her body. She couldn't believe the guy was Prat. Dee Dee hadn't seen him in so long, and now that she did, all the feeling that she felt for him in the past stormed right into her heart.

Prat himself couldn't believe that it was Dee Dee. He

was nervous for all different reasons, as he stood there looking at the female whose brothers had put a helluva ass-whuppin' on him because of her. He walked towards her with his almost-full portable blue basket. "Hi." He looked into her eyes. There was no denying that she was attractive and beautiful. The last time he'd seen Dee Dee, she had long black thick hair. Now she no longer had it slicked back in the ponytail that she used to sport, but in a Halle Berry style that surely appealed to him.

"Hi," Dee Dee answered back, her stomach full of butterflies.

"So how you been doin'?"

"I guess, okay. You?"

"Good. Just living, that's all." The word *damn* leaped into his mouth, but he quickly caught it. He didn't mean to say the words *Just living* to her and have her thinking of her brothers, but to his surprise it didn't faze her.

Dee Dee was thinking about the day her and Prat did their thang, and the way he worked her thang. Nothing else was ever coming close. She was just happy that he wasn't trying to avoid her. She reached in his basket and picked up the bag of candy that rested on top of the other stuff. "Got a sweet tooth, huh?" Dee Dee looked up at him. "Well, you better watch it, 'cuz these things really aren't that healthy for you."

"So what you doin' here?"

"Trying to fill my fridge up in my new apartment, and buy some little knick-knacks too."

"Damn, Dee Dee!" Prat blurted out. *Why did you ever have me come inside that day?*

"Why you just said, 'Damn, Dee Dee'?" she asked, not knowing if seeing her was a good thing or bad thang.

Prat had to think quick. Dee was demanding when she wanted something. It was still evident to him that, except for the new cute hairdo she was now sporting, she hadn't changed any. "I just can't believe that I'm looking at you right now, that's all." Prat cracked a simple smile, revealing his all whites.

"Well, believe it, but actually you could have been looking at me a lot sooner if you wouldn't have been avoiding me like you been doin'. Prat, you gotta know that I was truly sorry for what happened to you. My brothers was really wrong for that."

Prat changed his facial expression, the memory of that beat-down blasting back into his head. Shit, Jay and Bee damn near killed him. Hell, to try and escape he had to jump outta a two-story window at their house.

He wanted to just take off right then and there and put Dee Dee back outta his mind, but she was looking finer than a muthafucka. He wanted to pick up from where they had left off. Just getting the ass only once wasn't enough for him, knowing just how good it was to be in-between her legs, in her love box.

"You all right, Prat?" Dee Dee asked, her hand on his arm.

"Oh yeah, I'm cool. But how you been doin', I mean, with losing your brothers and all?"

"You know, what can I say but living, that's all." Dee Dee put her hands up, shrugged her shoulders, and tilted her head slightly all at once.

Prat, seeing the despair in her eyes, took her in his arms and gave her a nice snug hug. To his surprise Dee Dee clasped her hands around his waist and caressed him like he was doing hers. As he had his hug firm on her body, rocking slightly side to side, his nose took in the scent of her perfume. He leaned his head to the side and kissed the top of her head. To him, this wasn't the same Dee Dee. Even though she looked the same to him there was a total difference in her. The hair was changed. Her clothes game did a three sixty.

Back in the days, Dee Dee only got geared when she wanted to. She felt like she didn't have to impress no one, but now she was a true "raw dawg" diva, handling major business.

The only thing that he felt that was the same was the attitude and sass, but it seemed to him that she had toned it down some, which was good.

"So where that girl at that I seen you with a while ago?" Dee Dee leaned back, so she could see his face.

Prat was like, *What?* This was his first time seeing Dee Dee since the incident at the house.

"Come on now, Prat. I seen you one day at this one house with some cute girl. I ain't gonna hate 'cuz she was cute and you had your lips all on hers like it was the first kiss you ever got." Dee Dee still had her hands clasped around his.

"Oh her? She ain't nobody important." Prat was wondering how the fuck did Dee Dee know where Tiffany stayed at, and was she following him or something.

"So you not with her like that?" Dee Dee wanted a serious answer before she said what she wanted to.

"That's old news, and there's no new news," Prat said, a straight look on his face.

"Well, it looks like I'm gonna need some help taking these groceries to my car. Then I'ma need some additional help taking them inside my apartment."

There it was, the new and improved invitation. With no

fear of someone coming home and breaking him off with a beat-down, Prat took her up on the offer.

They finished up Dee Dee's and his own shopping then bounced outta the store, feeling good and having good conversation at that. As he pushed the basket in the direction where Dee Dee had parked, he was surp. ised to see her pushing the big-boy Excursion.

Dee Dee turned around and looked at him, telling him that the back door was open.

Prat placed all the bags in the back then closed the door back up. He wanted to ride with her, but he wasn't gonna leave his brand-new all-white four-door 2007 Cadillac Seville in no fuckin' Wal-Mart parking lot. There was just too much that could happen to it, so they agreed that he would trail her to her apartment.

Once there, Prat walked up to the back of the Excursion. When he grabbed a bag outta of it and turned around, Dee Dee was right there to plant a kiss on his lips. Their lips locked as the chill breeze whisked across their faces. Dee Dee kept her eyes closed, while Prat looked on, liking every second of their kissing session.

Dee Dee finally opened her eyes then broke the kiss off.

"What was that for?" Prat didn't mind that she took the initiative, he just wished that he had his hands free, even though he enjoyed the kiss without wrapping his hands around her fine sexy self.

"I don't know. I think it was just, well, overdue; don't you?"

When they walked into the apartment building, Prat was amazed to see that the building was so nice inside.

Dee Dee placed the grocery bags down on the floor by the door, then took her key and unlocked the door.

Once it opened, Prat was instantly feeling Dee Dee's new pad. *Plush* was the ghetto fabulous word that ballers would use to describe a nice decked-out crib like Dee Dee's.

She took two of the bags that contained the long pillows and the matching four-piece bedding into the bedroom. After fixing the bed up, she pulled the house slippers out, then took off the shoes that she had on. She loved house shoes. That was one thing that would never change about her. Nor would her sassy attitude. If she would just so happen to change the attitude the niggas who she dealt with on a regular would no doubt take her for a sucker again like when she first took over her brothers' business.

Dee Dee walked back out into the living room in time to see Prat putting the groceries away. She smiled as she looked on. Prat was definitely winning some brownie points to get some booty tonight.

With sweat all on their bodies and lips locked, both felt that fucking never felt better. The sex was off the hook to Dee Dee. All the tension and stress that she had built up inside of her was just about to be released. With her legs up in the air, nails sinking deeper and deeper into Prat's back, and her teeth clenched, she was gone beyond belief. Getting her some dick was the best medicine that she could have ever got prescribed.

Prat stroked and jabbed, working what he had in Dee Dee, whose words were replaced with moans and heavy breathing.

Dee Dee couldn't hold it any longer. It was about to come. She was about to cum. Her mouth clamped onto

Prat's right shoulder. She couldn't believe the orgasm she was having.

After it was all over, and Dee Dee was able to get her body to quit trembling from pleasure, she managed to rise up out of the bed and head to the bathroom. She grabbed a warm wet soapy towel and some toilet paper. The towel was to clean the juices off Prat, and the toilet paper, to take off the condom that was still on his dick.

As Dee Dee tossed the rubber in the bathroom's wastebasket she suddenly became queasy. A dizzy spell hit her hard, forcing her to brace herself against the wall to avoid stumbling and falling. She flipped the toilet seat down then took a seat. She didn't know where that spell came from, but it had her tripping. Maybe it was just from all the good loving that she'd just had.

Once she felt better, she walked back into the bedroom, feeling like nothing had even happened just a little bit ago. She hopped in the bed underneath the comforter and snuggled up against Prat, where they both enjoyed each other's body heat and fell asleep exhausted.

Chapter Twelve

Dee Dee's ill feelings had been recurring to the point where she was about to visit a doctor. Her appointment was at nine-thirty. Before she would make it there, she felt like eating something from McDonald's. As she drove along the way, she jammed to sultry neo-soul singer Vivian Green's CD. "Emotional Roller Coaster" was just one of the many songs she liked on the album.

Dee Dee pulled into the McDonald's parking lot and parked. She wasn't the only person that wanted a taste of the fast food. She grabbed her purse then headed for the door.

As she walked across the parking lot, a beige Lincoln Imperial started driving off very slowly from the drive-through window. Dee Dee was now at the door, with it partly open, when she noticed who was driving. All she could do was stand there and look as if she'd seen a ghost.

She hadn't seen Alastair since revealing her ugly dream to him.

His car moving slowly, he didn't even notice her. He was too busy checking his food order in the bag. But then he suddenly looked up. When he did, he saw Dee Dee staring at him. He quickly turned his head, but before he did, he gave Dee Dee a look that said, "Fuck you," or at least, that was her interpretation.

Dee Dee found herself standing in awe at the entrance, holding the door open. She was in deep thought. Mixed feelings jumped into her body. It was good seeing him, but she believed that he was the one who'd killed her brothers.

"Excuse me," a short thin white man with his family standing behind him said.

Dee Dee snapped outta her trance and moved out the way to let them by, letting the door close after the white family exited the restaurant.

Not having the same urge to eat, she went back to her H2. She couldn't believe that within a two-week period she had run into Prat and Alastair, two of the only three men that ever meant anything to her. One of them, she was happy to see, the other, she was having mixed emotions about.

She didn't expect him to say anything about what happened. She didn't think about him killing her brothers nor did she think about him leaving her 'cuz of what she did. The only thing that crossed her mind was that she was happier than a fat person losing weight when she was in his presence.

Dee Dee finally made it to Doctor Regan's office, which was located in a new medical plaza with a lot of other doctors with different practices. She parked her SUV then got out. Thick dark grey clouds covered the sky above.

As Dee Dee opened the door to the office, the older black receptionist pulled back the sliding window. "Good morning," the lady greeted her. "You must be Deondra Davis."

Dee Dee nodded her head in acknowledgment.

"Just fill these papers out, and Doctor Regan will be seeing you as soon as he's done with his present patient."

Dee Dee took the clipboard with the papers on it and took a seat in one of the six colorful cushion chairs.

The receptionist kept looking over at Dee Dee in amazement. The thought that Dee Dee had all the men chasing her leaped into the receptionist's mind. She could see a special glow in Dee Dee. There was just something about her skin that was giving it all away.

Dee Dee walked back up to the window and handed the lady the questionnaire.

"Deondra, don't think I'm poking, but are you here to have a pregnancy test?" the receptionist asked, her glasses tilted on her nose.

Dee Dee had left that part out that asked, *Reason For Visit*, intentionally, figuring she could tell the doctor in private.

The receptionist didn't need an answer. She was a woman, a mother, and had seen it all too many times. Now she was getting good at telling who was pregnant and who wasn't. She saw that Dee Dee didn't really want to answer the question. "Baby, I could be wrong by saying this, but only the doctor will prove me wrong when he gives you the test, if that's what you're here for. But that's what I think."

Dee Dee was thrown for a loop. She was used to missing

periods by months, so she never had any reason to ever think that she was pregnant. Besides, it had been months since she'd had unprotected sex with Alastair, and she sure didn't have unprotected sex with Prat the other night. Dee Dee sat there in deep thought.

Doctor Regan came out from the back and walked into the receptionist's office. He glanced across the room and spotted Dee Dee sitting in the chair. He then looked back down at Miss Johnson and talked to her about his last patient.

"Doctor Regan, thank you so very much for all you done," the elderly black lady said, a wide smile on her face.

"Miss Mattie, you just remember to get this prescription filled and take your medication on time and everything should be fine." Doctor Regan gave her the prescription.

"Now I wanna see you back here in two weeks, okay?"

"I'll see you then, and if you want, I can bring my single daughter with me that I been telling you about. She'll make you a good wife," Miss Mattie teased.

That was a little inside joke that the two shared, so he didn't bother responding. He just smiled and called out Dee Dee's name.

Dee Dee raised up from her seat, grabbed her purse, and tossed it over her shoulder.

Doctor Regan held the door open that led to the back of the office. When they got to the examining room, he let Dee Dee go in first, as he looked over her chart. Then he walked over to one of the cabinets and grabbed a clear plastic cup from it.

"Just put this on. I'm sure you know what this is for." He handed her a gown and the cup and left the room.

Dee Dee got undressed. When she had everything off except her panties and bra, she rubbed on her little puffy stomach. She pulled the little excess skin out, just to see how her stomach would start to look if she was pregnant. Dee Dee had missed plenty of periods in the past, so being pregnant was the last thing on her mind.

She stopped playing around with her stomach and grabbed the cup. As she held it in her hand and looked at it she became disgusted. The thought of having a baby wasn't a good one. She figured if her and her mother's relationship wasn't all that tight, then how could she have a strong bond with her own.

Dee Dee went to the bathroom, filled the cup up, and capped it.

There was a light knock at the door. "Are you decent?" Doctor Regan asked. As he came in, he saw the cup in Dee Dee's hand and the distraught look on her face. He took the cup from her then told her to give him a second to go drop it off up front.

Dee Dee stared at the plain walls in the room as she waited. The thought of raising a child without the father or her brothers wasn't settling well with her.

The doctor came back in and told Dee Dee to lay back and get comfortable. Dee Dee felt comfortable with Doctor Regan performing her Pap smear. She didn't go to her own doctor that she went to for everything else since she and her brothers were kids. She thought there was just something gross about a man who'd watched her grow up looking at her precious spot. And so she chose Doctor Regan for this particular examination, a nice white man who everybody knew was gay, including the Miss Mattie, who always teased him that her daughter would make him a good wife.

After the examination was over, the doctor told Dee Dee that she could call in three days to get all her test results. She didn't really care about the Pap smear test results because she knew she didn't have any STD's. All she wanted to know was if she was pregnant, and if so, could he set her up for an abortion appointment. Dee Dee's mind was really made up about what she had to do, and what she was gonna do, and nothing in the world was gonna stop her either, if she could help it.

Dee Dee cruised back on over to the block, where the fellas were. She pulled up to the curb and signaled for Jesse to come over. He fixed his baggy pants, so that he could walk right before he got to stepping. With a forty in one hand and his cell in the other, Jesse headed toward Dee Dee.

Dee Dee remembered what Jesse had asked her the day she'd first met back up with Lil' Man when they were riding together. Jesse wanted to get on, and Dee Dee was now about to keep her word when she told him that she would get back at him on her decision.

The door opened, and Jesse looked at Dee Dee, waiting for the signal from her to get in.

"Nigga, get in and close the fuckin' door." Dee Dee held her body with one hand and turned the heat up with the other. The fall weather was dropping fast on Memphis.

Jesse put the forty-ounce that was in the brown paper bag between his legs. Then he placed his own hands in front of the high-blowing vent that was providing heat to Dee Dee's hands.

"So what's poppin', sexy?"

"You tell me, 'cause I can remember you putting a bug in my ear a while back." Dee Dee looked at him, one hand on the steering wheel. She sat at an angle, part of her back on the door, part on the seat, the manicured fingers of her left hand playing follow the leader as she kept them tapping, going up and down over and over again on the steering wheel. Her right leg propped up on her seat, she was waiting to hear Jesse state his claim.

"I'm trying to move some things, if you know what I mean, Dee Dee." He put his bottle up to his mouth and downed some.

"Just what is 'some things'?" Dee Dee hated when a muthafucka thought she could read their minds or some bullshit like that.

"I can handle ten. My money is right for half of that, if you front me the other half, feel me?" He gripped his pockets for emphasis.

"Listen, Jesse, if you got the cash for five, I'll go ahead and front the other five. You keep business cool with me and bring back my money and enough to buy ten of those thangs next time, I'll front you ten. So it's like this, whatever you buy after that, I'll match. But get this straight—Don't fuck me. Please don't fuck yourself."

Dee Dee was dead serious about what she was saying, and it was best that Jesse heed that shit.

"Girl, now that's what I'm talking about. Shit! We could've been doin' business like this a long time ago. So when can we do this—?"

Suddenly, TJ banged on the hood of the car then ducked out of sight. It was a warning sign, but Jesse and Dee Dee was already caught in crossfire.

Pop! Pop! Pop! BOOOOMMMM! ZZZZZZZZ!

Mad shit was being ejected their way from the niggas up the street. The Robinson boys had crept up on the fellas and caught them off guard. Only TJ had spotted them, but by the time he'd seen them, the riot pumps, 9mm and Uzi were already firing.

The Robinson boys meant what they'd said when they'd first run up on them. They wasn't just hitting Dee Dee's hood up, but other hoods where they used to roam also. Those boys were making enemies everywhere. There were so many of them, not to mention all the niggas that chose to roll with them 'cuz of who they was. They didn't get too much static back from niggas from other hoods.

TJ pulled his heater out and started busting back.

Jesse told Dee Dee to get down, as three bullets crashed through the back window and shattered it to pieces. Jesse opened the door and slid out, his piece in hand. He raised up, letting that .45 canon boom away.

No place to run, Dee Dee was down on the floor of the ride. She was scared like a muthafucka. Dee Dee was squirming all around, her body curled up and her hands covering her head, as she heard each new shot being fired. It seemed like the sound of each shot was ripping her eardrum apart. The little fragments of glass that she was laying on from the shattered back window seemed to be everywhere.

For the first time since she'd made the decision not to have the baby growing inside of her, she found herself now praying for the fetus to be kept safe.

It seemed like the gunfight lasted forever. Then Dee Dee's ears ceased to hear any more shots being fired. Still, she was skeptical about raising from her somewhat secure hiding spot.

Jesse stood up and opened the door. He saw Dee Dee curled up on the floor. "You hurt, Dee Dee?" He reached inside to help her get out.

"What the fuck was that all about?" Dee Dee asked, as she shook broken glass out of her hair.

"That, baby girl, was those faggot-ass Robinson boys. And let me tell you, this shit is getting outta hand. We gonna have to find those bitches and take care of them before one of us gets killed or something." Jesse kept pacing around. He knew something had to be done. Shit was getting too hectic, and this little stunt by them, sneaking up, was the last straw.

Jesse may not have been seeing eye to eye with TJ at first when they had the first encounter with the Robinson boys, but now all he could see was hitting them before they took one of them out.

"Look, Dee Dee, you sure you're all right?" He looked her over carefully.

"Yeah, I'm cool," Dee Dee said, looking around.

"Cool then. Now maybe you should ride out before the laws get here. They for sure coming." Jesse could see that she was still shaken from all the shooting. He leaned in and gave her a hug.

Before leaving, Dee Dee tried to gather her thoughts. "Get with me later about what we was choppin' up, Jesse."

As Dee Dee drove off, she began to recall the rumors she'd heard about who'd killed D-Dawg and the girl he was with. The story involved the Robinson boys. She thought for a second about whether they could have been the ones who killed her brother. As far as she knew, there was no static between them and her brothers. She could even recall her brother talking to Bow Wow, aka Drew Robinson, on the phone before they got busted in Ohio. The phone call didn't indicate any tension between the two, so it was hard to see how they could have killed her brothers. Then again, Dee Dee couldn't rule anything out, because there could be no telling if one of the ten brothers had something against Jay and Bee.

As Dee Dee cruised on the expressway, she listened to one of Bee's tapes. Bee had a thing for the old-school rap artists, and the song she was now listening to was from one of Ice Cube's solo albums, "Today Was a Good Day." Dee Dee couldn't see how shit had turned out to be a good day, with her being in the middle of a gunfight and having to drive around with her window shot the fuck out.

She pulled up and parked in front of the apartment building. She didn't waste any time in rushing inside and calling her insurance company. After that, she called the guy she'd bought the ride from. She didn't see why she should take it somewhere else when she had a good relationship with the owner. Besides, Dee Dee had been planning on getting a newer model big-body Benz.

While on the phone, she clicked over to answer an incoming call.

The phone call was from Alastair, but he didn't say anything. All he did was just enjoy Dee Dee's precious voice. He missed the shit out of her, but he couldn't fix his mouth to say one goddamn word. Finally, he just hung up.

Dee Dee was still saying, "Hello," when she suddenly heard the dial tone buzzing in her ear. She hung up the phone and sat down on the couch thinking about all the shit that took place earlier. She had to get her thoughts together if she was to become the baddest bitch. Recalling how she acted when the shooting went down made her tell herself to get it together. There was a lot of shit she had to do.

Chapter Thirteen

Picasso had Timmy drive him back over to Dee Dee's old street, not to see the house, but just to get a layout of the neighborhood for when the time came to erase all the loose ends, including Timmy. He wasn't going to leave anyone behind.

As Timmy turned onto the street, Picasso made sure to pay close attention to his surroundings and sat back calmly just scoping out the scenery.

Since they were on Janelle's street, Timmy was wondering what she was doing, even though he'd left there at six o'clock that morning. As he got closer to Janelle's house, he saw her sweeping the porch. His feelings for her had become strong. He was now in love, and so was she. They had managed to build a good and loving relationship. A perfect match.

Janelle took a break from sweeping and looked up. She placed her free hand on her hip and stretched, bending backward to get the cramping ache out of her back. As she did, she looked the other way down the street and saw Timmy's cab. They were both smiling as he got closer. He couldn't help stopping when he saw her waving with that big-ass smile on her face.

For a second, Timmy forgot all about his passenger because he chose not to keep business separated from pleasure.

Picasso, seeing what was going on, now knew just how he would kill two birds with one stone, and all thanks had to go to the fool who was now in love, Timmy.

"Oh shit! Sorry about this, Picasso," Timmy said to him when Janelle jogged his memory by asking who he got in the back seat. "Look, baby, I'll see you when I get off." They waved bye to each other before Timmy pulled off.

Picasso thought Timmy had played himself, so what he had coming was on him. But since he liked the kid, he made a mental note to himself to make their deaths as quick and painless as possible.

Picasso had Timmy take him back to his hotel, where he placed a call to the chauffeur he'd taken a disliking to for making him wait at the airport instead of being there, ready to pick him up. After telling the chauffeur what he wanted him to do, and giving him the exact time to pick him up at the hotel, he hung up. Picasso then went into the restroom and began to wash his face, getting it free and clean of dirt and oil, so that his disguise would hold up under any circumstance.

After that was done, Picasso grabbed the bath towel from the rack and began to wipe his face dry. Before going back into the bedroom, he grabbed the hotel's hair dryer. He unplugged the blow dryer then walked back into the bedroom. Then he went to the closet and pulled his two black briefcases out. It would be here in the room that he would make his face look like somebody else's.

Picasso sat in front of the dresser mirror placing the adhesive to his eyebrows and upper lip. The process of putting on a disguise required the technique of an expert, which Picasso certainly was.

When he would go on special ops missions for the military in his country, he had to be creative to get past security, which required him to change his appearance drastically so no one would know who he was. Every time he went on a mission, he had to acquire a fake ID to match his new look. And all the contacts that he'd made to get certain tangible items, such as high-powered guns, money on quick notice, including counterfeit money, explosives, automobiles, helicopters, planes, houses, including mansions, or whatever he needed, had all been maintained over the years.

Picasso wasn't the ordinary Latin-looking person. His complexion was lighter, like the Spaniards from Spain, and now with the new face, all he needed to complete his disguise was the wig. He pulled the wig out of a clear plastic bag and teased the short curly hair on it, to give it that fresh look. The wig was made with real brunette human hair, so styling it was an easy task.

Picasso carefully placed the wig on his head. If it wasn't put on right, someone would be able to tell that the headpiece was a wig, but with it put on correctly, no one could pick him out of a lineup filled with a bunch of people with real hair. Then to make the wig secure, he glued the outer edge, on the inside of the wig, to his forehead. Once that was done, Picasso stared in the mirror to make sure that the wig was looking straight.

He took the special makeup that was made by one of his secret contacts and the small makeup brush out of the suitcase. This was no ordinary makeup. Revlon didn't have anything on the shit Picasso had. That stuff not only matched his own skin to a *T*, but it wouldn't come off unless he used the special liquid in the suitcase to remove it. He took the white handle of the soft-bristle brush and began adding the makeup all around the hairline of the wig. The wig had excess skin so it could be blend in with his real skin. That was just one of the other things that made this wig a very special and expensive knockoff.

As Picasso looked into the mirror, his eyesight moved slightly to the left to look at the ringing phone that sat on the nightstand. He knew who was calling him, so he started placing everything back in the suitcase, not wanting to leave anything out for a snooping housekeeper.

Picasso placed the bigger suitcase back in the closet and took the other one out. He walked out of the door and headed down the hallway towards the elevator. He pushed the red button with the black arrow on it and cast his eyes up to the numbers that indicated which floor the elevator was on. The numbers kept changing, right and left, as it was coming to his floor. When the elevator finally arrived, the door chimed and opened slowly. Picasso stepped in then pushed the button for the lobby floor. His mission was on his mind, his fingers tapping impatiently on the suitcase.

The elevator stopped and chimed again as the doors opened up. He walked smoothly through the hotel lobby and right out of the side doors into the chilly Memphis wind.

The chauffeur that Picasso had taken a disliking to was ready and waiting with the back passenger car door open. Picasso laughed inside as he thought to himself that the chauffeur must have taken a lesson or two from Timmy on the low.

"*¿Cómo estás, señor?*" the chauffeur said hesitantly, knowing he was on probation from the incident that happened at the airport.

"*¿Seguiste las instrucciones como yo pedí?*" Picasso walked toward the grey Lincoln as he removed his suit coat.

"*Sí, señor.* It's all inside awaiting you," the chauffeur replied humbly and with fear.

Picasso didn't report the driver to his boss for his incompetence at the airport, like he told him he would. He felt that Timmy had added more insult to his honor and status than what his boss could've ever done with a bullet. Sometimes Picasso felt that a bullet wasn't the only way to solve a problem. He felt humiliating a soul had just as great an effect as taking a soul.

Killing wasn't in Picasso's future plans after this job. He'd seen enough and killed enough to last him a lifetime. This job was going to be his last, but he didn't know how much this job would really entail, namely, his no longer breathing when he returned to California to see Don Ruiz. Picasso slid into the back seat and began to take off his square-toed Italian boots.

The chauffeur closed the door and quickly rushed over to the other side of the car. He knew what his passenger was doing, so he fastened his seat belt and pulled off from the hotel. He didn't bother to speak. He knew that Picasso would let him know where he wanted to go.

Picasso was fully undressed except for his white boxers and T-shirt. He unzipped the clothes bag that rested on the clothes hook by the car door. The gas man's uniform was looking him in the face, the name *Ben* printed just above the right chest pocket.

Once he had the uniform on, he placed the black work boots on his feet. The hat and the clipboard were the last items to complete his look.

The chauffeur drove though the thick traffic, trying desperately to get Picasso to his destination. He cussed out loud as the car in front of him slammed on the brakes suddenly. Luckily he was able to do the same, which didn't sit well with Picasso, as his whole body jerked forward. The chauffeur quickly looked in his rearview mirror to see if Picasso was okay. What he saw was what he was hoping he wouldn't see.

"Sorry, señor. *Pinche pendejo* slammed on his brakes," the chauffeur explained, trying to take the heat off of himself.

Picasso held his words. The look on his face told it all. He wished that he could put one or maybe two bullets in the chauffeur's head when the mission was accomplished, 'cuz he felt the driver was the true definition of incompetent and ignorant.

When he noticed the facial expression on Picasso's face had once again changed up, the sweat seemed to be drying up on his forehead. All the driver wanted to do was hurry up and get his passenger to where he needed to go.

After getting free of the congested traffic on the expressway, he turned off onto one of the feeder roads. He drove down the road toward the waterfront, where the warehouses were located. Once fully at the location, he pulled over to one of the many warehouses located on the wharf.

Picasso placed his hand on the suitcase that he'd brought with him then stepped out of the ride. Without saying a word, he walked into the front door of the warehouse. There was no other person in the warehouse but Picasso, and that's how it was supposed to be. He walked quickly up to the stolen white van, which was painted to look just like one of the city's utility gas vehicles, opened the door, and hopped in. He took in the smell of the van, looking around to make sure he had a sense of the automobile's interior. He then reached his hand out and turned the ignition key. He pressed on the gas slightly, just to hear the purr of the engine.

Everything seemed to be okay with Picasso, so he drove the van up to the big steel door and blew the horn. The chauffeur acted with promptness and slid the door open. Picasso placed the van back into drive then rolled out and headed for his destination.

It didn't take long for him to arrive at the house that Dee Dee had purchased for Miya. The house and some added money was the least she could do for the person that she considered family. Actually, since Jay, Bee, and Ronshay were deceased, and Dee Dee and her mother didn't really talk or visit each other, Miya was her only family.

Picasso parked the van right in front of Miya's two-hundred-and-fifty-thousand-dollar home. The whole idea was for the van to be visible, to win Miya over and not bring suspicion to himself. He got out of the front seat and went to the back of the van. There, he opened the briefcase and placed the two things in the workbag that he had the chauffeur place inside.

Everything was set. Now all he wondered about was whether Miya was at home. Sure, he saw a Benz in the driveway, but he knew that one car in a neighborhood like this was rare. He then settled the items in the yellow bag that had *Gas Sensor* written on it.

He emerged from the back doors of the van then closed them gently. He scanned all around the lovely upscale neighborhood before moving on to the sidewalk and toward the house. Once at the top of the stairs, he reached his hand out and pressed the doorbell. The chime of the doorbell was loud. Loud enough that somebody in the backyard could hear it if they were outside.

Miya was washing her hair when she heard the doorbell. She wrapped the pink bath towel around her dripping wet hair and went to the door. When she got downstairs, she could see a man in a gas company uniform standing at the front door. The first thing that Miya could think of was that she hadn't paid her gas bill. She wasn't wrong in thinking like that, 'cuz she was from the bottom, where people had to worry about seeing a person like him when they didn't pay a bill that was due.

Miya opened the door. "How may I help you?" For some reason, she had a bad feeling.

"Good evening, ma'am. We had reports that there may be a gas leak in the area, and I was sent out to check everyone's gas meter in the vicinity."

"Oh my God! Please, come in and check it. The last thing I want is for me or my kids to inhale that stuff and die." Miya was now happy that her kids' father had come and picked them up.

"That's why I'm here, ma'am," Picasso said, "to stop anything like that from happening."

"I think the meter is in the back. Well, I think that's what it is. Follow me and I'll show you what I'm talking about." Miya headed for the back door.

Picasso reached in the bag and grabbed the stun gun, one of the items he had the chauffeur place in the van.

Miya began to speak, but only part of the word escaped her mouth, as the volts from the stun gun made her do the "body rock" dance. Poor Miya didn't know what hit her.

Picasso grabbed her limp body before it could hit the floor. Then he picked her up and carried her to the kitchen and placed her in one of the brown wooden chairs at the table. There he pulled out the duct tape, which was the other item he'd requested. Picasso taped her arms tight as hell behind her back, then began to do the same thing to her ankles. Once this was done, he connected the tape from her hands to her feet, so there was no chance of her escaping. After that, he stood up and just looked at Miya slouched over in the chair, the towel dangling from her head.

Picasso felt it was now time to get the information that he needed. He raised her head up then laid a vicious open-handed slap across her right cheek, which was enough to bring the dead back to life.

Miya's eyes weren't able to focus at first. She couldn't even tell where she was after being hit with one of the more powerful stun guns on the market. Slowly, her eyes started to focus on the man standing in front of her. She was startled and reacted by trying to jump up, but that's when she realized that her hands and feet were duct taped.

"Listen, and listen good. I'm going to ask you a couple of questions, and if you tell me what I want to know, we will both be on our way." Picasso circled Miya like a vulture looking for scraps.

"Why are you doing this? I haven't done anything to no one," she pleaded, tears in her eyes.

Picasso waited for her to finish what she had to say, but he had to get some things straight right then and there before he went any further. He came around to where she could see him and released a thunderous right hook to her forehead. The blow snapped her head backward then forward. A head was hard, but Miya's head was no match for Picasso's football tight end's big-ass hand. He chose to hit her there because he didn't want her to think that she'd be killed. He wanted the information, and he needed it to be spoken as clearly as she understood what that blow to her head was for.

"Now, like I was saying, I ask the questions, you just open your mouth when I need an answer, is that understood?" He snatched the towel off her head.

She was dazed but soon came back to consciousness. Still a little groggy from the dome shot, Miya didn't answer right off the bat.

Picasso shouted, "I said, is we clear on everything?" He gripped a handful of hair and yanked her head back.

"Yes, I hear you. Whatever you wanna know, I'll tell you," she blurted out quickly.

"Now, I'm glad we came to a mutual agreement." Picasso sat down in one of the chairs around the table. "So, tell me, where is Jay and Bee at again?"

Miya looked Picasso over as he crossed his legs and sat there like he didn't have a care in the world. She, on the other hand, had tears flowing down her cheeks, a splitting headache, and muscle spasms from the many volts shot through her body.

Picasso saw that she wasn't as responsive as he made her out to be after the serious talk they'd just had, so he picked up the stun gun from the table and pulled the trigger. The little bright light between the two chrome prongs on the stun gun looked like a miniature lightning bolt.

The loud crackling and clicking noise from the stun gun made Miya jerk back in her seat. She didn't know what was going on, but she knew it wasn't anything good.

"Now I must tell you that patience is not one of my character traits, so don't take too long to answer me. Now, do we understand each other? Because, if not, this little thing will send so much electricity through your body that whoever came and discovered you would surely think that you was one of the people who got killed on death row in the electric chair."

"Jay and Bee is dead. Somebody shot them. I don't know who, nor do the police," Miya blurted out, covering everything. The stun gun and the man in front of her had her going.

Picasso knew that he would get all the information he wanted out of her in no time. "So, who is this Dee Dee person that I'm hearing about?" he asked, still fiddling with the stun gun.

Miya didn't understand why he was asking questions about Dee Dee, but thought it was best to answer him.

"Dee Dee is Jay and Bee's sister."

"Sister, huh?" Picasso tapped his fingers on the table. "Well, where can I find this sister that you speak of?"

"I have no idea. I haven't seen her since she bought me this house—"

The sudden noise made by his balled-up fist crashing down on the table made Miya's eyes pop wide open. Picasso wasn't going for that answer.

"I swear, I don't know where Dee Dee is staying. The only time I see her is when she just pops up and walks in the front door." *Why is this man in my house with a stun gun? Why is he asking all these questions?* A million and one questions popped into her head, but unlike his questions, she found herself not having any answers to her own questions.

"If I heard right from other sources, Jay was your boyfriend, correct?"

"Yes, he was," Miya said honestly, hoping to garner some sympathy from her captor. "I miss him so much."

"So, if he was your boyfriend, and the girl is his sister, then you should have some kind of phone number to contact her." Picasso pulled the trigger on the stun gun once again.

When Miya saw the bright light and she heard that clicking and cracking noise, she got scared. The thought of not seeing her two kids anymore haunted her soul. She couldn't see herself not being there for them. "The phone number to her cell phone is in my pocketbook over there in my purse, and that's the only number I have to get in contact with her, I swear."

Picasso raised out of his chair and walked over to where Miya was indicating. He picked up her purse off the couch and opened it, dumping all the contents inside of it on the table. He picked up the black pocketbook. "This it?"

"Yes."

Picasso opened up the pocketbook and flipped though the pages. He found a number with Dee Dee's name written above it. "Is this her number?" He held the book up in front of Miya's face.

She nodded her head.

"Are you positive . . . 'cuz I don't want to have to come back and find the three people in this photo?"

"Yes, I'm sure. I wouldn't lie." Miya had tears in her eyes. She knew deep down inside that the man in front of her was going to harm Dee Dee in some type of way and was afraid that she'd endangered her sister-in-law.

Picasso walked behind Miya to the sink and pushed the chrome handle to the stopper, to prevent the water from draining out. Then he cut both faucets on, so water would fill up the sink faster.

Miya was trying frantically to look behind, but the restraining tape had her locked tight in one position. She knew the water was a bad sign, even though she didn't know what it was for or what he was up to. The tears were rushing out of her eyes just as quickly as the water was filling up the sink. "You not going to kill me, are you? I told you everything I know." Miya's words were muffled, due to her fright and all the crying she was doing.

"Now, did I say I was gonna kill you? All I wanted was a glass of water. But since you brung that up, I'm going to leave this water running, so you can drown in it. I'm sure you won't have any problem getting free before the water could possibly get high enough to do that."

Picasso knew damn well that letting the water run over

from the sink or tub couldn't drown anyone, and so did Miya. That's why she felt that she wouldn't be a victim of death, but was she ever wrong in thinking like that.

Picasso grabbed the toaster and set the timer for the longest duration on it. Five minutes was more than enough time for him to do what he needed it to do. He placed the toaster on the floor just a little bit behind where Miya was restrained in the chair.

She wondered about the odor she was smelling. The breadcrumbs left in the toaster were being burnt each second, and the water was now starting to overflow out of the sink and pour onto the floor.

Picasso planned to electrocute Miya. Once the water made its way to the toaster, the fiery red coils inside of it would do the job.

When Miya saw Picasso standing in front of her with his serious face, she panicked. She started hopping around, trying to get free, but wound up tilting the chair over. There, she saw the toaster on the floor and the water from the sink headed toward her and it. With the toaster lying on its side, Miya knew what awaited her and began to scream loudly. But the sound coming out of her mouth stopped when she saw the big black handgun staring her down in the face.

"You can easily take one of these bullets in the head and have your kids see their momma's brains scattered all over the floor."

Miya thought about what he said for a second. She knew she was about to die, and there was nothing that was gonna stop that from happening. Her babies were her life, and to her, Picasso was right about what he said. She wished that she'd never told him anything about Dee Dee.

She now lay quietly, her eyes closed, and began to pray to God to watch over her kids and her soul, and to protect Dee Dee from the evil man doing this to her.

Picasso noticed the water getting seconds away from making contact with the toaster and quickly grabbed his belongings.

Miya was so far into her prayers that when the water made contact with the toaster and then herself she didn't notice anything.

Picasso just watched as her eyes started bleeding and smoke coiled from her body, which started twisting and twitching from the volts jolting through her small-framed body.

Chapter Fourteen

Perkins sat at his desk pondering how America got to be one of the most powerful nations in all the world. He had some words doodled on the tablet that lay in front of him on his desk. Everything seemed to be going wrong for him. At age forty-seven, Perkins knew he was no spring chicken. The streets weren't the same anymore, and neither was crime or crime fighting, for that matter. Robbers were smoother. Stealing cars without anybody being inside them had turned into a person sticking a gun in someone's face and forcing them to get out and run for their life. Selling crack had made its way into the white neighborhoods. The number of police who were becoming crooks was uncountable. Now the Feds were taking over cases that they wouldn't have touched back in the day.

Perkins was ready to retire. He and his wife Emily could no doubt live off his pension and her teacher's pension comfortably, so money wasn't an issue.

Perkins had too many bad dreams haunting him in his sleep, and being stuck on the case involving Dee Dee was taking its toll on his personal life. He was finding himself always thinking about whether he was doing the right thing. Gary, on the other hand, didn't seem to care about the case at all, as long as he got the collar to stick.

Perkins didn't like wondering if someone was innocent or not. He felt as if he was judging people, something only God could do. Of course, when he was a wet-behind-the-ear rookie, he thought he could make a change by fighting crime. But as he got older and became a veteran in the field, he learned that fighting crime was a myth, because no officer could get help from the public, and the detectives who had rank couldn't do any detecting if they didn't have clues to go on. Hell, he felt that informants did more detective work than any detective in all of the fifty states in America.

"Ugggggh!" Perkins yelled out loud and started scribbling all over the paper in front of him.

The whole department became quiet. Every officer and criminal stood still where they were and looked on.

Perkins raised his head and caught the onlookers' eyes. He stood up and yanked his jacket off the back of his chair. As he walked by the people he worked with, he noticed all eyes silently saying the same thing, "What the heck is eating him?"

"Nothing is eating me," he said out loud, answering their question.

Perkins walked out of the police station and just stood on the steps for a second, looking around at the officers bringing in lawbreaker after lawbreaker. He grabbed his hair and just felt like pulling his shit right the fuck out.

"Get it together, Perkins," he said to himself, as he released the grip on his already short hair.

"Hey, guy, you all right? You lookin' kind of pale, Perkins." The tall, thin, white man dressed in blue jeans and a red Ohio State University sweatshirt rested his hand on Perkins's shoulder.

Perkins turned around to see who was touching him. "Oh, hey there, Jim."

"Oh, hey there yourself," Jim said in a sarcastic voice. "My question was, Are you all right?"

"Yeah, sure. Hell, to tell you the truth, Jim, I don't know if I'm coming or going. Fighting crime just isn't the same for me anymore."

"First of all, take one of these, and secondly, walk with me." Jim offered Perkins one of his generic cigarettes.

They walked down the sidewalk in front of the police station, passing more co-workers and people who were handcuffed and headed to be booked for something or the other.

"Have a seat. The fresh air will do you some good, seeing as you're having a crisis and all." Jim sat on the hood of his grey Crown Victoria.

"I'm not having a fuckin' crisis."

"Hold up, *kemosabe*! I didn't mean no harm by stating that, but if you ain't having a freaking crisis, then why did you just use profanity, when I haven't heard you cuss in years?" Jim lit his cigarette then extended his arm to give Perkins a light.

"I'm sorry about snapping just then. This job is really getting to me. The chief got us working constantly on this one case, and it seems like we aren't getting anywhere. Hell, I don't even think the girl killed the guy now." Perkins wasn't much of a smoker, but the cigarette was doing the job, calming his nerves.

"It's quite all right. Besides, I never took it serious. Now tell me what's eating you."

Perkins leaned back against the passenger door and crossed his ankles. He raised the cigarette up to his lips, took a drag, and immediately started coughing.

Jim patted him on the back, to give him a helping hand of some sort.

"I'm all right. It's just been a while, that's all," Perkins said, trying to act like he had the smoking thing under control.

"Oh, I forgot. Everything with you is always all right." Jim blew smoke out in front of him. "Now save the bull and tell me what's on your mind."

Perkins thought about whether he wanted to go any further with the personal conversation that he wasn't even sure he understood. He felt that if he didn't understand what was going on with him, then how could anyone else help him out? Jim was like everybody else, always wanting to offer advice, but never wanting to listen to the problem. People had a way of doing the backwards shit, when it came time to listening to someone else's problems.

After a while of thinking and smoking, Perkins opened up and told Jim that he believed he and his partner Gary would soon have to part ways.

Jim knew all too well what it was like when partners felt the need to split up and go their own separate ways. He, himself, had two partners in his career whom he had to part ways with. One was his first partner, Ronny, who he called Young Ronny because he was a wild and eager rookie. Jim felt responsible for the youngster, seeing he was the kid's trainer. They parted ways when Ronny moved on a 211 (law enforcement code for a robbery in progress) by himself, without backup.

Jim had just gone into the convenience store before the call came across the police car radio. He was trying to pay for his donuts and coffee. While he was carrying on a conversation with the night clerk, a call had come over his car radio. Jim had his portable radio on his waist with the volume turned up too loud. He quickly turned it off when he heard that the call didn't concern him. That's why he wasn't able to hear the second call when it came across the radio.

Ronny, eager to prove himself as a crime fighter, did. When Ronny heard the call, he radioed back, knowing that it could be his first collar. He thought he could make the arrest by himself. When Ronny radioed back in and found out the address where the 211 was taking place, he couldn't believe his luck. The address was a sporting goods store only two blocks away from where he was.

Ronny got out of the police cruiser ready for battle with the lawbreaker.

Jim spotted Ronny getting out of the car, but he didn't know that anything was up because Ronny never signaled him.

Ronny wanted to prove to Jim that he could do the job just as well as any veteran who had been on the force for many years. Ronny just waved at Jim, and Jim waved back.

When Jim made it back to the cruiser with his donuts and the hot, steaming coffee, he was shocked to see that Ronny was nowhere in sight. The thought that he went to go take a leak around the building popped into his head. That all changed when he got inside the car and saw the note that Ronny had left:

Hey, Old-Timer!
By the time you finish reading this note, I will have made my first arrest. The call that came over the radio for the 211 is two blocks down and I should be there already. Hell, I should have the perp in custody by the time you get there. I'll be waiting for you, so get ready to celebrate my first arrest as a rookie.
                                    The #1 Rookie, Ronny.

"God, no!" Jim yelled. He quickly dropped the note and called the dispatcher to get the address where the 211 was going down. He felt like time was going as slow as molasses, as he waited for the dispatcher to come back on the radio with the information. Jim stood outside the car, looking all around, not knowing which way Ronny went.

The call finally came back. Jim unlocked the riot pump that was locked onto the steel cage in the car. He didn't even bother to close the door as he bolted off running like he was a world-class sprinter. The only thing on his mind was seeing Ronny alive and well.

He cursed Ronny for being so young and dumb. He cursed himself for not hearing the 211 call in the first place. He immediately turned his radio back on to call for backup. Jim could now see the sporting goods store.

Perkins listened carefully to the story that Jim had never talked about before since the Department Review Board hearing years ago. "What happened then?"

It was hard for Jim to talk about this particular subject. He was like the man who'd been to Viet Nam and had seen too much to ever talk about it. He gathered his thoughts, so he could follow through with the story.

Jim reached the building perimeter and cocked the shotgun once to make sure it was ready to fire if need be. His back was sliding against the brick wall as he scooted alongside it, making his way to the storefront window. This would be a time when his veteran's skills would come into play. By being careful, he was able to go home every night to his wife and kids.

Jim took a quick peek at the window to see if he could see anything. There he saw a body flash across the inside of the store. He quickly leaned back against the wall of the building, hoping that he wasn't spotted by the break-in artist. Jim knew the perp had to have gained entrance to the building from some other area of the store, because neither the storefront window nor glass doors were shattered.

Jim backed up real slowly, until he was sure that he was out of the storefront window's view then took off for the back of the building. While he headed to the back in the alley, he passed the side door where the fire escape was. Something told him to turn around and go check that particular door out first. When he did, he saw that the lock on the door had been broken.

Jim placed the riot pump on the ground, so he could check his handgun. He pulled it out of his holster then popped the clip out. He saw that he had a full clip of bullets. He slammed the clip in and pulled the chamber back. Then he holstered the handgun and picked back up the riot pump.

Jim's heart was beating fast as hell as he reached his arm out and took hold of the doorknob, not knowing what was waiting inside for him. All he wanted to know was that the kid was okay. He'd tried radioing the kid, but there was no response. Which meant one of two things. Either the kid had his radio off, or he was hurt. Or worse.

He made his way into the dark place, where there was only little specks of light here and there throughout the closed store, mostly from the reserve box lights mounted on the wall up above the doors throughout the store, along with light coming through from the windows.

As Jim walked carefully through the store, he had the riot pump ready and aimed to start booming away if need be. He swung the gun back and forth very slowly with every step that he took. His black combat boots made a tapping sound every time his feet made contact with the glossy, well-kept waxed floor. Jim kept both eyes open as he crept through the store.

The sudden noise that he heard made him duck down and take cover between the clothes rack that rested on the carpeted section of the floor. He motioned from side to side, repeatedly looking for whatever made the noise. Now Jim had one eye closed. The other one was looking down the sight of the gun, to make sure he could no doubt hit his target.

Suddenly, Jim heard a noise similar to what he heard when he was walking, like shoes on a waxed floor. He kept fingering the trigger, beads of sweat forming on the tip of his nose. His heart was now beating at a rate that could cause an elderly person a heart attack. The sound got closer with every step, which told Jim that the person was headed in his direction. Jim gave a silent prayer to the Lord, asking him to let him make it out of there safely. He knew his wife wasn't ready to be a widow at the age of thirty-four, and he wasn't ready to die at that age either.

As the sound was directly up on him, Jim decided to move on his veteran skills and jump out, hoping to catch the perp off guard. With the shotgun butt braced tightly up against his shoulder, he raised himself as quickly as he could, hoping to surprise whoever it was. "Don't move!" Jim recognized who it was, even though Ronny was frozen dead in his tracks, his back toward Jim. "Ronny, is that you?"

Ronny turned around, glad that the person who'd caught him with his pants down wasn't the one he'd been having the gunfight with in the store.

"Jim, there's one suspe—" was all Ronny got to say before the sound of someone else's gun started firing.

Pop! Pop! Pop!

Jim took cover by hitting the ground, never letting go of his shotgun.

Ronny hit the floor also, but he wasn't as fast as Jim. Ronny lay on the ground twitching and squirming. The third shot struck Ronny in the side of his throat and exited on the opposite side.

Jim crawled over to his rookie partner to see how bad the damage really was. Blood was squirting and pouring out of where the bullet entered and exited, and Ronny's eyes were dilated. Jim placed his hand over the wound, hoping to slow the bleeding down. With the blood flowing so quickly and escaping through the cracks between his fingers, Jim tore his shirt off to try to staunch the wound.

Jim could remember himself telling the kid to hold on and don't give up, as if it happened yesterday.

"Rollins to dispatch, I have an officer down! I repeat, I have an officer down! Send a paramedic, and where the fuck is backup?" Jim yelled into his hand-held radio. The backup he could use, but the paramedic wasn't going to be any help at all, as Ronny gurgled his last breath and drowned in his own blood.

As Ronny's eyes stayed open and his grip on Jim's hand loosened, Jim shouted, "Noooo!" and rocked him back and forth in his arms.

The word *no* echoed throughout the store, spooking the break-in artist. He couldn't tell which direction the yell was coming from, so he took off for the exit he came through.

Jim quickly picked up on the sound of shoes hitting the waxed floor and figured it had to be the perp who'd shot and killed Ronny.

Jim laid Ronny's body gently on the ground and closed his eyes with his hand. Then he covered his face with the bloody shirt. Now set for vengeance, he yanked the shotgun off the ground and went in search of the cop killer.

Jim ran after the assailant. He spotted a shadowy figure and felt that he could catch up with the guy, and he did. "Freeze, you cop-killing asshole!" Jim shouted, the perp in his target range.

The guy kept running and never looked back, but he did raise his handgun and let off three more shots.

Jim ducked out of range, as one of the bullets whistled by his head, barely missing him. Jim saw the guy headed for the door they both came in through. He knew he had to shoot now, if he wanted to have any type of chance of

catching Ronny's killer, because once the perp got outside, Jim knew the chances of catching up to him would
be as slim as milk.

Jim stopped in his tracks, raised the shotgun, and let it
sing.

B-O-O-O-O-M!

The guy hollered from one of the shotgun pellets hitting him in the leg, but that still didn't stop him from
moving.

Jim fired again. He saw the guy make it to the door. He
knew the cop killer was gone. Jim stood there thinking
about how he let Ronny's killer get away, but then hope
was renewed when he heard the oh-so-familiar, "Freeze!
Stop where you are and put down the weapon!" a cop said
through a bullhorn.

The cop killer ran smack dab into Jim's backup.

The one thing about cops, whenever they got a call that
an officer was down, all of them dropped whatever they
were doing and went to give aid, because they knew that it
could one day be them needing the same help.

Jim's call for backup brought out about a hundred
cops, who had the whole store and the block radius surrounded. He moved quickly to the door.

The young black cat stood there bleeding from his leg,
his hopes of getting away having disappeared into thin air.
The thought that he would spend his life behind bars didn't
even enter his mind, as he knew the cop was dead, from
what Jim had shouted out to him. The electric chair had
his name written all over it, and he knew it. And, by killing
a cop, which was a capital offense, he knew his date with
the hot chair would come in less than a year's time.

The young black thug decided to go for broke, even

though he had about two hundred guns already pointed at him. "It's better to have my sentencing here than to let some honkies fuck me over in court," he shouted, before going out like a *G*. He raised his arm up as quickly as he could to get off two quick pops, one hitting the officer on the bullhorn.

In response, bullet after bullet flew out of each and every last one of the cops' guns.

Jim stopped just short of the door when he heard all of the shooting. He wasn't that eager to see the guy, because he knew all too well that bullets didn't have eyes and didn't care who the fuck they plugged.

The cop killer took about four bullets in various parts of his body, out of all the bullets that were flying, but none managed to stop his heart from beating, or stop his leg from moving as he made his way back inside the sporting goods store.

It was Jim's lucky day. When he looked out from his hiding spot and saw the thug moving slowly down the aisle, leaving about five different blood trails, Jim crept up slowly behind the guy, then stopped, cocked the shotgun to let him know that somebody wanted to talk to him, the somebody being the riot pump that he held in his hands and pointed dead ahead.

"Fuck you, honky! You might as well shoot me, bitch, 'cuz if I turn around, I'm gonna shove this gun in my hand up your ass and let the bullets fuck the shit outta you!"

That's all that needed to be said. Jim squeezed the trigger.

B-O-O-O-M!

The perp's head went in every direction, decorating the

hunting clothes section with blood, bone, and brain fragments. The body stood there for about ten seconds before falling forward.

"Damn, Jim!" Perkins said. 'I'm sorry about all of that. Are you all right?"

"Look, I only told you that story because I hope you get something out of it. So, if you did, it was worth reliving that unforgettable moment in my life." Jim patted Perkins on the shoulder and told him to take it easy as he walked off.

Perkins was left there to soak that up. He didn't want to leave his partner any more. The thought of Gary getting killed and him not being there to know who did it would kill him.

Chapter Fifteen

Lil' Man was sitting in the same park in the same un-marked five-O ride, talking to Gary, Perkins's partner. He was tired of Lil' Man laying the same bullshit on him since they'd made the arrangement to have him work to-ward helping them bring down Dee Dee.

"Look, you little piece of shit, if it was up to me, I would lock your little black ass up right now, but it's not up to me. But you can bet your little young black ass that I do have the power to tell the boys downstate that you ain't co-operating, and you know what that will do for your snitch-ing career. Hell, I can even put the word out on the street that you been workin' with us. Now I'm sure you don't need me to tell you what that will do to your health." Gary was pouring the you-better-get-with-the-program-or-else shit on really heavy. He was dead serious, and that meant that he wanted "intel" right then and there.

Lil' Man knew that the cracker wasn't going for the bullshit anymore.

Gary looked over at Lil' Man with a look that said, "I'm waiting to hear something come outta your mouth."

"All right, man. Check, the word on the street is that she's looking for the fool or fools who killed Jay and Bee."

"You mean Bret and James Davis, right?"

"Yea, man, that's them."

"Now we're getting somewhere," Gary told him. "Please feel free to continue."

"Well, like I said, she lookin' for the muthafucka who killed her brothers, and she got a reward an' shit out for whoever come to her with the info. I don't know who killed those cats, but she ain't playin' about finding out who did it. And with the reward that she's offering, trust me, it won't be too long before somebody is a done deal."

Gary was taping everything that Lil' Man was saying with the little hand-held Sony tape recorder.

Lil' Man knew that Gary was the type of cracker who would blow his name up in the hood as a snitch just for GP, so he was keeping everything as real as he could.

"So, you think that she will put a hit out on the person or persons who killed her brothers?"

"I don't know, man. I do know that she got it in her to do it herself. Dee Dee a fine muthafucka, but believe me, the bitch know how to handle up and get shit taken care of. Niggas know not to fuck with her money or her product."

"When you say *product*, you mean drugs?" Gary asked, just for the record.

"Yeah, man," Lil' Man replied with an attitude, tired of

the honky acting like he didn't understand muthafuckin' English.

"And you have no idea who the person is who shot her brothers?"

"Man, how many times I gotta tell you? Hell, fuck no!" Lil' Man felt like the cracker was trying to play on his emotions with all the stupid shit he was asking.

"So, it's fair to say that Deondra Davis is planning on killing someone or having someone killed, right?"

"Listen, all I know is that she got a reward out for anybody that got info that will lead her to the nigga who killed Jay and Bee."

Gary's mind started racing. He wanted to know who she was looking for. If he could solve this case, he knew he had a job waiting for him at the DEA office in Memphis. This was a chance for him to let his partner get three murders solved in one shot, and by doing so, it would make his departure, breaking up his and Perkins' partnership, a little easier. He didn't know how to tell Perkins that he was trying to leave the force to become a DEA agent.

"You said that you're close to Deondra, right?" Gary looked closely at Lil' Man's face.

"Yeah, we tight."

"Good then. That'll make it all the easier for you to start wearing a wire."

"What? A wire? Man, have you lost your fuckin' mind? I ain't wearin' no fuckin' wire!"

"C'mon, girl, why you trippin'? Ain't nobody gonna bust us." TJ tried to ease Jackie's head back down to his dick. He didn't know why she was trying to stunt on him now. It wasn't like she wasn't used to doing that type of thing, anyways.

Jackie was the neighborhood ho. Most niggas in his hood either hit the ass or got their dick sucked by her already, and some was still getting both on a regular, like TJ. Granted, it wasn't all the way dark yet, but it was damn near there, as the sun was about a second from disappearing from sight.

"Uh-uh. I gave you a sample, and that should be good enough for right now. Besides, you ain't gotta wait too much longer till it's completely dark outside."

Jackie tried to raise her head up, but TJ was keeping her head pinned to his crotch. He didn't want her to stop because her head skills were off the hook.

"Look, ain't nobody even walking in this park, and on top of that, it's only two cars parked out here, anyways. So who gonna bust us?"

"You sure ain't nobody out there?"

TJ turned his head to check again, even though he already knew the answer.

"All right, we goin' to hook you up this Thursday, so make sure that you spend as much time with Deondra as you can, and get her to talk about what she got planned." Gary reached across Lil' Man's body to open the passenger door. He wanted Lil' Man to hurry up and get out so he could be on his way to set things up with Dee Dee. Gary had a hard-on for Dee Dee. He wanted her to fry, and it didn't matter which way she went in the skillet, so long as he got that DEA job.

* * *

As TJ looked around, he spotted the unmarked detective car. He didn't think the car was out there for him, but the thought did pop into his head because it was strange for a detective car to be in the park. "Is the car out here for me?" he asked himself.

"TJ, do it look cool or what?" Jackie held TJ's dick in her hand, ready to get the party started, since it was almost dark. "TJ, you hear me?"

TJ saw the car door open, and legs plant themselves on the ground, but what fucked TJ up even more was who he saw getting out of the car. TJ couldn't believe it. "Naw, fuck naw, it can't be!" he said out loud.

"What can't be? Somebody comin'?" Jackie raised her head up to look at whatever it was TJ was looking so hard at. "That's Lil' Man over there?" Jackie wasn't up on game about niggas workin' for the police, so she didn't understand. All she knew was that she was ready to get her freak on, and she didn't want TJ to offer Lil' Man a lift and spoil her groove. She loved kicking it with TJ because, afterwards, they would go smoke that good weed that he had for hours.

Lil' Man fuckin' with five-O! That bitch-ass nigga. Wait till everybody hear about this shit. Hell, wait till Dee Dee hear about this. She gonna flip the fuck out, TJ thought to himself.

As Lil' Man started to walk off, TJ noticed the driver's door of the detective car open, and Gary got out and called out to Lil' Man. Lil' Man stopped in his tracks and turned around.

Gary propped himself up against the car, his hands resting on the roof. "Hey, Lawrence, let's make sure to play this cool. I don't want no fuck-ups, okay?"

The wink that Gary gave with his right eye after he was done speaking made Lil' Man's blood boil. He wondered just how he could have let himself fall into a bullshit-ass situation like fucking around with the police. As Lil' Man turned around and continued stepping, he heard Gary slam the car door and start the engine.

Lil' Man nodded his head as Gary rolled by and honked his horn. When Gary was almost out of the park, Lil' Man cocked his arm up and gave Gary the middle finger. "Fuck you, honky!"

TJ couldn't believe it. He started his ride up and put it into drive. He had to hurry back to the hood and let everybody know what was up. TJ rolled right by Lil' Man just as he started to walk on the grass to take the shortcut out of the park. TJ decided to fuck with him a little bit, since he was in a crackhead's ride that was actually a really nice newer car model, and honked the horn like Gary did.

Lil' Man turned his head to see who was honking at him. Lil' Man didn't recognize the car, nor could he see who was inside the ride because of the dark tint covering the windows. He raised his fist to his chest as if to say, "What's up?" to whoever did the honking inside the ride.

"Since we leavin', you coulda gave Lil' Man a lift, TJ." Jackie brushed some lint off the shoulder area of his shirt.

"I'm gonna give his ass a lift all right, as soon as he get back to the hood." TJ stared hard at the road ahead.

As TJ cruised down the road, he reached in his pocket and pulled out about a half ounce of that new green "kill-kill" that he had with him to trick off with Jackie. He then handed it over to her so she could begin to roll a couple up to smoke.

When she raised the open bag up to her nose and smelled how strong the green shit was, she threw any other questions out of her head. Weed to Jackie was like crack to a fiend. When she had it, she became quieter than a church mouse on Sunday morning service.

After she was finished rolling up, she lit the blunt and started chiefin' real big as she reclined in her seat, exposing only part of her head to any onlookers outside. After feeling the one-hitter-quitter stimulate her lungs, she passed the blunt to TJ, who was still in a daze. She held the blunt out so long waiting for him to take it that she had to nudge his arm to get his attention.

TJ finally broke out of his daze and took the blunt. Lil' Man and what he saw was weighing heavy on his mind. He puffed on the weed with one hand and pimped the steering wheel with the other, like a real *G*. He puffed on the blunt for so long that he had a long stream of ashes hanging from the tip of the cigar by the hair of its chinnie chin chin. "Hand me the ashtray," he demanded, trying to not let the ashes fall on him.

Just as he was about to take the ashtray, he noticed that the streetlight up ahead was on yellow. He wanted to take his chances and run the yellow, but then he said, "Fuck it", and stopped like a law-abiding citizen. Besides, he was chillin', smoking.

TJ reached for the ashtray, and that's when he saw how filled up the muthafucka was. There had to have been about a hundred cigarette butts in it. The owner of the ride was certainly a heavy cigarette smoker. TJ thought about rolling down the window and tossing them out, but he remembered in the past how he had played himself by doing that. Unless the air was still outside, it wasn't a wise idea to toss ashes out of the window, if you knew what was good for you, and TJ knew what was good for him, fo' sho'.

He opened his driver's door, which cut the interior light on, and made the tinted windows on the car useless. As TJ was dumping the ashes underneath the car so as not to have the wind whisk it right back up in his eyes, a brown, old-school Chevy Caprice with tint on the windows pulled up alongside him and honked its horn. TJ raised his head up to take a look at who was honking in the ride next to him. He nodded his head in acknowledgment, just to be cool, even though he hadn't the slightest idea who was in the ride. All he could make out was the silhouette of a few people behind the dark-tinted windows, which helped to camouflage their identities from everyone, including TJ and Jackie.

Jackie was trying to be nosy when she heard the horn honking. She raised up out of her slouched position in the seat to look. But, the look she should've been peeping out was to look the other way as she ran for her life because, right then and there, both passenger doors to the Chevy swung open, and two niggas stepped out wearing leather jackets with hooded sweatshirts pulled over their heads. What they had in their hands made Jackie scream crazy loud, as she frantically tried to pull TJ up and back inside the car, as if he had enough time to drive off.

It all happened so quickly that TJ was only able to raise up off the ground and sit in an upright position. Both carrying nines, the two guys started letting off shot after shot. TJ took one right in the head, sending him slouched over in Jackie's lap, who was still screaming, and trying her best to push a bloody TJ off of her. Her screams were quickly silenced when about five bullets meant for TJ's already dead body sank into hers.

The first bullet sank into Jackie's left arm in the biceps area and then hit the bone, snapping it in half. The second one pierced her side and exited straight through her, but managed to miss vital organs. The third, fourth, and fifth bullets hit their marks, piercing her heart and silencing her for good.

The way TJ and Jackie lay dead in that ride was going to be a fucked-up photo, plastered on the front page of the *Sentinel*, come morning.

"Yo, Craig, Seth, let's peel. That fool and his trick-ass bitch is knocked out for the count." Drew sat behind the wheel of the Chevy Caprice, his right arm resting across the front seat headrest.

Seth and Craig turned around then hopped back in the ride like they were told to do. As both doors slammed, Drew floored the Chevy right on out of there as if they were never there in the first place.

"Yo, I'm glad you peeped that buster-ass nigga out, 'cuz I damn sure couldn't tell who that nigga was," Craig said.

"I can peep that bitch-ass nigga out anywhere," Seth said. "Shit! Me, Jay, Terry Tee, and that fake-ass nigga ran together back in the days, so it's no way that I can't peep that nigga out, come rain, sleet, or snow, or nighttime for that matter,"

"It serve that bitch-ass nigga right. I bet he won't bump his gums again about what he gonna do to somebody, ol' ho-ass nigga," Drew busted in as he blazed up a freshly rolled blunt.

THE BADDEST CHICK

As they rolled on, cruising down Popular Avenue, they smoked and chopped it up about what they were going to do for the night. Once Craig put it out there that he felt like kicking it at a club, they all became game for the same adventure.

Chapter Sixteen

Dee Dee was laying on the couch, her head in Prat's lap. As she looked up into his eyes, listening to him talk, she had her feet propped up on the armrest and wiggled her red painted toes around. Dee Dee felt good knowing that her feelings hadn't changed for Prat in all the time they hadn't seen each other.

As Prat leaned his head down to give Dee Dee a kiss on her soft lips, their lovey-dovey session was interrupted by the sudden ringing of Dee Dee's cell. She was making an effort to get up, but Prat halted her in the process. He wanted that kiss that he was just about to receive, and he got it because Dee Dee wanted it also. Lips locked and tongues dancing, the ringing of the phone wasn't barring none of the shit that they was off into.

It kept ringing, and once again, Dee Dee felt like somebody's timing was definitely fucked up. Dee Dee knew that Prat wasn't trying to let her answer the phone and spoil the groove he was trying to get set, both of them butt-naked, doing the nasty on the couch, so she had to be slick. Without any notice, she broke their kiss as she rolled right off the couch and landed on the floor. "I gotta answer that, you know that, Prat." Dee Dee pulled her Loony Toons cotton nightgown down, which had risen up when she rolled onto the floor, exposing her pink panties and thick creamy thighs.

"Go 'head, see if the other person calling you loves you," Prat shot back, being funny.

Dee Dee laughed and told him to quit his pouting as she reached inside of her purse to retrieve her cell. Once she had it in her hand, she quickly glanced at the screen. The number wasn't registering as one that she was familiar with, so she flipped it open. "This Dee Dee. What's up?"

Lil' Man's voice blared into the phone, "Somebody murked TJ and Jackie!"

Dee Dee knew her ears weren't playing tricks on her. She was now looking dead at Prat, shocked at what she'd just heard. "Lil' Man, what the fuck did you just say?"

"Yo, I said somebody killed TJ and Jackie over on Popular Avenue. We don't know who did it, but it gotta be those punk-ass niggas, the Robinson boys, 'cuz TJ or us wasn't beefing with anybody else."

"C'mon, Lil' Man, tell a bitch you just fuckin' with me," Dee Dee shot back, not wanting to believe that sad-ass news flash.

"Yo, straight up. Both of them is fucked up in that crackhead Paula's ride. They even plugged my man in the head. It's all bad, Dee Dee. I'm tellin' you."

"Where you at?"

"I'm over here in the hood. Why? What's up?"

"Is everybody over there with you?"

Lil' Man looked around to see who was out there with him and who wasn't. "Yeah, at least most of everybody is here."

"Good. I need all of y'all to come to the drop-off spot. I'll be there in a minute, so hurry up and tell them to be strapped, but be careful, 'cuz we don't need no five-O stopping nobody and taking them to jail, not tonight. Got it?"

Dee Dee closed her phone back up and sat there in puzzlement for a moment. The news was a serious blow, but she knew what had to be done. The Robinson boys had been asking for somebody to put them out of their misery for a while now. Dee Dee got up and paced back and forth, trying to come up with something. She was a leader now, with people working underneath her belt, so she knew that she had to step her game up.

"What was that all about, Dee Dee?" Prat asked, knowing something was dead wrong.

"Prat, look, I gotta take care of something right now. Why don't you give me a call tomorrow and we can pick back up where we left off at, okay?" Dee Dee kept pacing, trying to plot something out.

"You want me to bounce? You trippin'. Here we are, chillin', and just because the phone call you just got unnerved you, you want me to leave. Damn! If it's another nigga, then just tell me and I'm cool." Prat was really thinking that Dee Dee had somebody else coming over, but he didn't know just how far off he was from the truth, nor did he know that Dee Dee was pushing weight and had people working for her. Hell, Prat didn't know just how ill Dee Dee had gotten since she entered the game.

"Prat, I ain't got time for this shit right now. I said just give me a call tomorrow, all right." Dee Dee opened the door.

Prat grabbed his shoes and slipped them on. Then he yanked his royal blue and white leather Rocawear jacket off the back of the chair and headed for the door that Dee Dee was still holding open.

As he walked out of the apartment and into the hallway, Dee Dee told him that he shouldn't be bugging out, because the matter surely wasn't over any other dude. That lifted his spirits somewhat, but the part about having to bounce was still weighing heavy on his mind. Prat didn't have time for the bullshit, so he bounced.

Once Dee Dee saw the outside door to the building close, she closed her own door. She walked into her bedroom to get dressed. As she slipped on her sweatpants, her slightly pudgy stomach caught her attention. She rubbed her belly. "What the fuck do you think you're doing, Dee Dee?"

She had gotten confirmation from the doctor that she was indeed pregnant, not just with one baby, but triplets. Three babies. When the doctor told her, she tripped out, recalling that Alastair had told her that he had three people in his family who had triplets and one with quads. Hearing the news that she had three babies inside her stomach made her decision not to have an abortion easier. If it were one, maybe, but having three inside of her, there was no way she would go that route. She didn't know their genders, nor did she care to find out. Hell, she had more than enough money to buy everything in one day after their birth. The one question she had for the doctor when he broke the news was, "How the hell could I be pregnant and not really be showing?" He simply told her that some women, because of their genes and metabolism, didn't show like everybody else.

Dee Dee pulled the matching sweatshirt down over her head then bounced out of the apartment and up the stairs to the drop-off spot. None of the fellas knew that she had moved into the apartment building, and that's just how she wanted to keep it.

It wasn't long after she'd made it inside the apartment that everybody started arriving. They all had the same thing on their minds, as heaters of all sorts were displayed in the open, resting in their hands. No one was able to get a word in since everybody was talking at once. Feelings and emotions were running high at the moment. Dee Dee couldn't blame them, because she too felt the same.

Jesse saw Dee Dee raise her hands to try to get everybody's attention. "Yo, everybody, Dee Dee's trying to speak. Yo, go 'head, Dee Dee, spit what's on your mind."

"Look, I know that was a hard-ass blow. I feel what y'all feel, but TJ's death ain't nobody's fault but our own." Dee Dee paused to gather her thoughts.

"Bitch, how the fuck you figure that whack-ass shit out?" Breeze erupted.

Breeze was a wild and crazy nigga. No one could stop him from saying what he wanted to, but at that moment, everybody was prepared to blow a hole in his cool, wild ass when they saw the look on Dee Dee's face, the word *bitch* catching her off guard.

"Breeze, that was a good one. But you know what . . . I'll be that bitch, but remember this from now on—When you refer to me as a bitch, make it the *baddest* bitch, or else that fly-ass shit you just let slip out of your mouth won't be taken so lightly next time. Believe dat, homie!" Dee Dee truly had Jay and Bee in her, and it was noticed by all who were present in the apartment. She just needed to work on setting it off quick, off the jump, like her brothers would have done.

"I ain't mean it like that, Dee Dee," Breeze responded. "We cool."

"Cool then. But like I was saying, we let those niggas come in our hood and cause havoc not once, but twice. I know ain't none of y'all no hoes, but we got to hit these bitches up, and hit them up now, before they come back and hit us up again. Now, if y'all got some suggestions, then go 'head and take the floor, 'cuz I don't know about y'all, but I'm already on a murder beef, and I ain't trying to hang myself by doing some dumb shit and get caught up and not have a prayer in the world of getting off."

Just then, Jesse's cell rang. "Yo, what's poppin', play-boy?" he said to Tweeky and Toone, who weren't on the scene when the news flashed. "For real?" Jesse spoke with excitement in his voice, which caught everybody else's attention in the room. "Naw, man. Just be cool and post up right there, 'cuz we got something for their slippin' ass! Yo, fo' real, don't let those niggas out your sight!" Jesse said before hanging up.

Jesse let it rip about what he'd just heard from Tweeky and Toone, who were driving, headed over to where everybody else was, when they spotted about five of the Robinson boys and a couple of their coattail dick-riders getting out of rides, chopping it up in a parking lot, look-ing as if they were about to go into Club Pure Passion to kick it.

Instantly, Dee Dee's mind got to turning, thinking of what Diamond's little ass could persuade a nigga to do.

"Yo, what was that all about?" Breeze asked, sensing that something was up. He'd overheard part of Jesse's phone conversation.

"Tweeky and Toone said those niggas is over at the Pure Passion club right now."

"Who? Those Robinson faggots? Awww! Let's go ride on those fools then!" Lil' Man slapped his hands together and grit his teeth.

"Look, y'all, just slow your roll. I told y'all already that I ain't trying to have none of us doing something irate and wind up in jail crying about you can't get out. We need a plan." Dee Dee walked over to the front of the big-screen TV.

"A plan? Come on now, Dee Dee. This ain't no TV show where that plan shit works. This here is the ghetto, the real world where anything goes, and right now, their punk asses gotta go. And the longer we wait, gives them niggas a chance to split before we get there to put some hot ones in their ass." Breeze gripped his heater tight.

"Hey, hey! Now look, I don't know about y'all," Dee Dee said, "but that sitting in the county jail shit on a murder charge ain't nothing nice. I know, 'cuz I been there. Y'all trying to play this shit the wrong way, and somebody gonna wind up sitting in that bitch like I was. Shit! You need to listen, 'cuz if something goes wrong, then the police will no doubt try and get you to tell on me and everybody else, from murders to selling dope."

When she said that, Lil' Man bowed his head, feeling guilty like a straight buster, because he was already in that position, speaking on Dee Dee to the police.

"I'm not saying that any of y'all is a snitch. All I'm saying is that pressure bust pipes, no matter how strong you are."

"Pressure don't bust no pipes right here," Duke shouted, tilting his black and grey Spurs hat down.

"Yo, y'all, Dee Dee's right. She's facing a 187 rap right now, which is something that we ain't never been through. Yeah, some of us been down for other shit, but I know from being y'all's homie that y'all ain't never caught no 187 case. So let's just hear her out." Jesse tried to get everybody to calm down and be quiet, because he knew that they were too amped up for their own good.

Rascal, a short, stocky nigga who just got out of the joint for shooting a nigga, asked, "So what it be like then, Dee Dee? What you got on your mind?"

Dee Dee looked around the apartment checking out their mugs. No one was speaking. She didn't know whether it was from their wanting to hear what she had to say, or if it was because Rascal had just spoken. Rascal didn't speak a lot. Hell, he rarely spoke at all, which is what stunned everybody. All Rascal did was react and attack. When he attacked, it would usually be with his fist when he stole on somebody and rocked their jaw loose, or that trigger-happy hand of his would squeeze the trigger and let the bullets do the talking for him.

Dee Dee was now finally convinced that she had the floor. She reached her hand out and grabbed hold of Jesse's cell out of his hand. She quickly dialed a number to someone who answered on the second ring. She walked into the hallway to get a little privacy while she talked, and when she was done, she flipped the phone closed and walked back into the living room.

"So, what's up, Dee Dee?" Duke asked her.

"Jesse, I need you to call Tweeky and Toone back and see what's up with those niggas in the club. Tell them not to leave for nothing in the world, and for some reason if the Robinson boys do leave, then tell them that they should follow them and call you immediately. Now, I need one of y'all to go pick up Shanetta and Biscuit, 'cuz I got something for them to handle."

"What the hell you got bitches in this mix for, Dee Dee, when we trying to handle business?" Breeze probably used the word *bitch* about fifteen hundred times a day.

"Breeze, my nigga, y'all men think with y'all dicks. Y'all don't even use the big head when the pussy is around. Pussy runs everything, if you don't know. And the finer the bitch is, as you so happily choose to label us females, the more the pussy make y'all dumb. So just follow my lead, and let the two *bitches* that one of y'all is about to go pick up handle shit, okay?" Dee Dee patted him on his baldhead.

Fifty-two minutes had passed since they all left the apartment building. Dee Dee, Biscuit, and Shanetta sat in Dee Dee's Excursion smoking a blunt as they talked about what Dee Dee needed from them.

Shanetta was a hood chick who had four kids, and with four kids, sometimes she had to do what she had to do to make a dollar. Back in the days, she used to fight all the time. Even though she was "hood cute," looking good never stopped her from getting ill. Shanetta's body was also banging. She was one of those females who possessed a black chick's "ba-dunk-a-dunk' that just made a nigga wanna holla and squeeze his dick. Still, she was always trying to get her hustle on.

Dee Dee remembered that Jay and Bee used to holla at her from time to time when they needed her to handle something for them. And sometimes they used Biscuit to tag along.

Biscuit was a duplicate of Diamond. They both resembled one another in so many ways. That's why when Dee Dee thought of Diamond at the apartment, she thought of Biscuit. Then Shanetta popped into her head. Dee Dee needed females to get the Robinson boys out of the club, for them to follow the females to their wake-up call and goodnight dreams.

After talking, Dee Dee handed the females twenty *G*'s apiece, which they pocketed. The payment was for whatever they wanted to do with it, but they knew what they had to do to keep it.

The car door opened on both passenger sides of the Excursion, then Biscuit and Shanetta got out. They didn't even look back as they headed for the club to do their jobs.

Shanetta was draped in red spandex, which showed off everything, including the fact that she didn't have on any underwear, and a white T-shirt that was two sizes too small and tied in front draped her top half, highlighting her big titties and an okay stomach. She also sported a red and white red Reebok classic cross-trainers. Big hoop earrings and about ten matching silver hoop bracelets dropped on her wrist, and her hair was pulled back in a long ponytail, which everybody could tell was fake. But, all in all, she looked hood-sexy and ghetto-fabulous.

Biscuit had on a Lakers long-sleeve dress, with matching Pro-Keds kicks.

Even though it was chilly outside, they chose to leave

their coats in Dee Dee's ride, just so they could show off what they were working with. Besides, it was common in the South to wear summer shit in the winter.

When Biscuit and Shanetta walked into the club, they were tripping because the club only had about fifty people at the most in it for a Sunday. That would work to their advantage, because if it was crowded, they would have to work extra hard to get the attention of one of the Robinson boys.

They strolled over toward the bar to catch a seat. Once there, they placed an order for drinks with the male bartender. No sooner than they placed their order, Shanetta felt the palm of a hand on her ass. She quickly turned around, shaking the hand off her ass, and saw who it was. "Is you crazy or something, nigga?" Shanetta said loudly. She knew Craig, one of the Robinson boys, was one of the people she was looking for. Even though she had twenty *G*'s, she still felt the nigga was out of line for putting his hand on her ass.

Biscuit just looked on, sipping her newly acquired Long Island Iced Tea that the bartender had just brought her.

"Girl, quit trippin'. All I'm trying to do is get to know you like that," Craig said, hinting at both of them knocking boots after the club in some motel room somewhere in town.

"Look, fella, I don't mind us talking and everything, but just keep your hands off the booty, okay?" Shanetta reached her hand up to his face and squeezed his right cheek.

"Yo, who we got here?" Seth asked, appearing out of nowhere.

"Hi," Biscuit said, knowing that Shanetta had Craig on lock.

"So, what's your name, Miss Sexy?" he asked as he crowded her on her free side.

"Everybody calls me Biscuit."

Seth said, "Biscuit, huh? Well, peep, I'm sure you taste good as fuck with some gravy on you, if you know what I mean."

"Whatever's clever." Biscuit gave him a sexy wink.

Seth patted Biscuit on the ass, trying to see just how game she really was, as he excused himself and raised his hand to signal his brother Craig for a word in private for a second. Craig then leaned into Shanetta and whispered into her ear, telling her not to move an inch of her fineness from where she was. Before walking off, he reached into his pocket and peeled off a fifty from his large knot of cash, and Shanetta gave him a smile and told him in a seductive voice to hurry back.

Seth walked over to his brother, giving him a pound as he came into hearing distance.

"What's poppin'?" Craig asked.

Seth glanced over at the two females posted up at the bar. "Yo, man, those hoes got back, especially that one you got."

"Yeah, she do, don't she? I'm tryin' to slam that pussy tonight."

"You think she gonna give it up?"

"Shit! She better, after I just handed that bitch a fifty spot to get something to drink."

"I ain't trying to give that other bitch shit but some dick, so she better not even fix her trap to say some slick shit about some cash action. The bitch is fine, but pussy ain't that important to a baller like that cash is."

"Seth, you be trippin' too much. The hoes should get

something for giving any nigga some pussy. Hell, if all the hoes put that pussy on strike, niggas would be payin' out their asses like a muthafucka, right?"

"Maybe so, but that ain't the case, and until then, ain't no bitch gettin' shit or none of this, feel me?" Seth played with the big-faced bankroll in his hand.

"So, you rollin' if these hoes is 'bout it?" Craig already knew that his brother wasn't going to miss out on a piece of ass. He may not stay long after he hit it, but he surely wouldn't miss out on a chance at getting some new pussy. Old pussy that he was used to hitting, yeah, but new pussy, he was on it like white on rice.

"Yo, Seth, you hear me man?" Craig asked, trying to break his brother out of whatever trance he was in.

Seth was looking over at the girls again. It wasn't the sexy fineness that he was peeping out this time, but more like trying to figure out from where he knew the bitch his brother Craig had on line.

"Seth, man, you trippin'." Craig shook his brother's arm.

"What's up, playa?" Seth asked, when he realized his brother was talking to him.

"Man, what the fuck got you trippin'? I been talkin' to you for the past two minutes, and here you are in a fuckin' daze. That pussy got you goin' to where you wanna buy the store up on her ass." Craig looked over at the females, who were looking at them and waving their fingers in a sexy manner.

"Yo, man, I know that bitch that you talkin' to from somewhere. I don't know where, but I'm telling' you that I know the ho."

"Nigga, you mean you wanna know the ho like how I'm

about to know her at the end of the night." Craig playfully pushed his brother in his chest.

"Yo, nigga, I'm serious! I don't know where, but I'm tellin' you that I do know the bitch. I just can't place her ass right now."

Seth was right. He did know the bitch. The name and the face had rung a bell inside of his head.

Two years ago, Shanetta had a nigga named Bab, a "jack boy" who would hit any- and everybody up. In Bab's last three jack moves, he had teamed up with a female who was down for the action as long as she was getting paid right. That female was Shanetta. Bab and Seth was cool with each other, at least cool in the sense that they didn't have a problem with each other, and said, "What's up," whenever they crossed paths.

Bab's last attempt to jack this nigga named Big Rob, a heavy roller from Chi-town who had hoes all through Memphis, went haywire. Shanetta was the setup artist. Her role was to act interested in the big fella and lure him to some place. The only problem, Big Rob wanted to go to one of his hoes' crib to have a threesome, freak party. Shanetta wasn't into that freaky shit. Hell, she didn't even plan on fuckin' the nigga. All she was doing was going along for the sake of getting twenty grand out of the move, which was what Bab promised her.

When they got to Big Rob's bisexual bitch's crib, everything seemed like a go. Shanetta went into the bathroom, acting like she was getting cleaned up, but all along, she was calling Bab, telling him to get to the crib and everything would work out smoothly, as she would have Big Rob slipping, with his pants down, literally, while he was thinking he was gonna get some of what she had.

Big Rob's plans changed again. He wanted the two to get busy while he watched. That was the turning point.

Ol' girl was already in something sexy, a lacy red see-through negligee. She was looking good enough to eat, but not for Shanetta to go that route. The sum of twenty thousand kept rolling around in her head, and she figured it would be over in a minute if she went through with it.

As she began to undress, Bab picked the window lock located on the side of the house. He slipped into the house and landed on the couch. He then crept down the hallway, heater in hand.

Bab was one of those niggas who didn't use a mask or anything to disguise his identity. He was raw with his shit and ready for combat if a nigga wanted to ever try to get his back. Most niggas didn't wanna try because they knew he was crazy as fuck.

Bab made it to the bedroom door and just stood there for a second, listening to the noises. On the count of three, after hearing Big Rob's voice and knowing that he was on the left side of the door, he went for broke. The door swung open quickly, catching everybody off guard, including Shanetta, who was just about to come up out of everything. Bab went straight for Big Rob, pistol-whipping the shit out of his two-hundred-and-sixty-pound ass in the chair he was sitting in.

The female dressed in the lacy negligee jumped on the bed, scared as hell, or so Shanetta and Bab thought. Little did they know, ol' girl was just as 'bout it for Big Rob as Shanetta was for the twenty thousand she had in her possession. She reached under the big, long pillows resting at the head of the bed and pulled out the big chrome .45-caliber Smith & Wesson crime stopper. One blast caught Bab dead center in his back, tearing his spine into pieces. He fell on top of Big Rob who was still sitting in the chair.

Shanetta knew that she was next. She put her "hood speed" to work and bolted for the front door. The sound of two loud booms made her duck for cover behind the wall in the living room. That spot was temporary, as she knew she had to get ghost.

She spotted the same open window that Bab had come through and decided, *Fuck the door*. She didn't want to take a slug dead center in the spine like Bab. It was time for a window escape.

The word had gotten around that Bab got killed for trying to jack Big Rob. When Seth got word and heard that there was a female involved, he had an idea that it was Shanetta. He didn't know where she stayed or what side of town she was from. Matter of fact, he only saw Shanetta two times with Bab, but he was sure it was her.

Two years had gone by, and that was the main reason he couldn't place her sexy, ghetto-fabulous ass right away.

Once he and Craig were done talking, they headed back over to the girls to get it poppin'. Once again, as they got closer, the thickness captivated their eyes. Both Shanetta and Biscuit were grinning and looking devilish.

While Seth and Craig were talking, the girls were carrying on their own conversation about getting up out of the spot, since they had what they came in for.

"What took y'all so long?" Biscuit asked.

"Shit! Girl, they was talkin' about which one of us they wanted," Shanetta cracked.

"Shit! There's no doubt about who I want." Craig placed his arm around Shanetta and pulled her close to his body.

"Now that's what I'm talkin' about," Shanetta looked up and placed her lips on his, giving him a quick kiss.

"So, what y'all say, we break out of this place and get it poppin' at a motel or something?" Seth grabbed a hold of Biscuit's hand, basically telling her, "Let's go."

Biscuit grabbed her purse and cell phone off the counter, and Shanetta followed her lead. They made their way to the door.

Just when they stepped into the cold fall wind, Shanetta reached into her purse for a blunt. That was the cue for Dee Dee to know that the plan was on and poppin'. Shanetta lit the blunt and puffed like it wasn't anything to smoke in the cold.

That should've been a sign for the two Robinson boys that something was up, because hoes would usually try to get the fuck out of the cold as quickly as they could, even leaving their niggas when not dressed properly for the weather. But they didn't pick up on it, nor did they tell their other brothers and boys in the club that they were breaking camp.

"Y'all rollin' with us or takin' your own shit?" Seth asked.

Biscuit smiled. "We can roll with y'all, if that ain't no problem."

Dee Dee peeped them all getting into an old-school Chevy, the same one that they used to roll up on TJ. She then started her ride and followed them as they rolled out.

Shanetta and Biscuit rode in the back seat, while the two brothers sat in front, all smoking on something good.

As they drove by the gas station that was up the road from the club, Dee Dee flashed her brights twice as she pulled into the lot. She spoke quickly into her cell, saying they were in the brown Chevy ride. Two cars packed with heavily strapped fellas pulled off and followed the ride Dee Dee had just informed them about. Now, there were four sets of headlights trailing the brown Chevy. Shit was about to stink the place up in a little bit, and it would no doubt start a war that Dee Dee had already planned on ending with the second wave. Bee and Jay would have been proud of her, if they knew just how clever she really was.

Dee Dee drove off and headed back to the crib, where she would wait to hear from Jesse about how the job went down.

Seth was at the helm, steering for the nearest motel. He was ready to bang something and get the fuck on. His brother, on the other hand, was ready to lay up with Shanetta's ass all fucking night.

Seth spotted the Days Inn up the street and decided that would be the spot. He pulled into the parking lot and parked in one of the available parking spaces. He peeled off a big, "Y'all don't mind going in and getting the room, since I'm paying for it?"

"Naw, it's all good," Biscuit said. "Upstairs or down-stairs?"

"Upstairs," Seth responded before his brother had a chance to fix his lips.

The girls got out of the car, and Shanetta reached in to get the cash from Seth, who was holding it in his hand. When she placed her hand on it to take it, Seth held on. "Yo, where I know you from?" he asked as he puffed on the blunt, the fire on the tip of the blunt lighting up his face.

"You think you know me?" she asked in stunned response.

"Shit! Your face is in my head from somewhere. I just can't place from where, though."

"I don't know. I do get around, but not in that type of way, though." Shanetta took hold of the money again. "Now, when you do find out, let me know."

As the two females walked off, they saw who they were supposed to see pulling into the parking lot.

Seth was really brainstorming, as Craig puffed on the blunt. Then it hit him. "Yo, I knew I knew that bitch. That's the bitch who was jackin' niggas with Bab's crazy ass."

"What? You think the bitch is tryin' to jack us?"

"Shit! Let the bitch just try." Seth pulled his 9mm chrome dome from under the driver's seat and placed it on his lap, clutching it tightly.

Craig chuckled. "Now, that's what I'm talkin' 'bout."

Seth accepted the blunt from his brother's outstretched hand and started to puff. Then he turned back around and reclined in his seat, waiting for the girls to get back with the room key.

Craig started flipping through the CD case to see which ones he wanted to fuck and grind to. When he finally saw the Menace II Society soundtrack, he realized his favorite fuck jam was on there, "On Top of the World." Feeling good that he had that jam, he began wondering how good Shanetta's pussy would be. Thinking hard about pussy, he turned his head to stare out of the window to see if the girls were on their way. What he saw when he looked out the window made him reach out and grab his brother's arm tightly, without even glancing in his direction.

"Yo" was all he was able to get out, before slightly ducking from the pointed guns.

All the fellas that had trailed them to the motel stood outside, a car-length away from the Chevy, with masks on and guns aimed.

Boom! Pop! Pop! Rat-a-tat-tat! The noise filled the cold night air. Paint chips from the car flew off as the bullets pierced the metal frame and shattered the windows. Two tires popped loudly from bullets hitting them.

It was mayhem at the Days Inn. Payback time with Jesse and the boys was going down, all eight of them blasting away.

"Open the fuckin' door!" Craig bent over, trying to get out of harm's way.

"I'm tryin'! I'm tryin'!" Seth shouted back over the noise of the booming guns as he fiddled with the door handle. He finally got the door open and slid out onto the pavement in the parking lot, his butt on the ground and his back against the tattered car.

Craig slid out next, unharmed, and scooted carefully to the other tire so as to have a shield like his brother's to protect him from the flying bullets. They both knew that they were in a fucked-up position, especially without their brothers and crew.

As both clutched their gats and sat in a crouched position, keeping true to the little protection behind the wheels of the car, Craig became unnerved. He knew time was short, and that hiding-behind-the-car shit would only allow himself to take one in the head when the shooters decided to close in. Craig wasn't having that. He decided to make a dash for it. "I'm out." He hastily looked over at his brother then quickly made his move. He raised his arm with the gat in it first and started busting wild shots off, one after the other, letting his black .44 Desert Eagle sing.

Jesse ducked as one of the bullets whisked by his head, barely missing his skull. The fellas all spread out when they saw the bright flash coming from the other side of the car.

Craig raised up all the way, exposing his body, fully blasting away as he ran backwards still busting.

"Craig, get down!" Seth shouted.

Craig turned around and ran as fast as he could, but a bullet plugged him in the back of the neck in mid-stride. His hand went to the back of his neck, and he fell face forward to the ground.

"Craig! No-o-o!" Seth shouted, as his brother twisted and convulsed, blood gushing out of the hole in his neck. "I'll kill all you punk bitches!" Seth raised up and started firing his chrome 9mm. No more shield protecting him, it was him against the world, or more like him against his enemies who shot his brother. His bloodshot eyes pierced the bodies that were shooting back. It didn't matter that he was drastically outnumbered. All he knew was, if he was to die, he was going to take as many bitches with him as he could. Seth started walking toward all of them, busting like crazy.

Tightwad was the first to get plugged by one of his bullets, which crashed into his right shoulder and swung him all the way around, sending him to the ground. The hollow point bullet with a crosscut at the head shattered Tightwad's shoulder on impact, and he lay in pain without the slightest bit of blood dripping from where the bullet entered.

Seth homed in as he walked slowly toward Tightwad, who lay on the ground moaning and clutching his damaged shoulder. Seth didn't know that his brother, who was losing blood by the bulk load with every passing second as he gasped for air, was still alive. At least for now.

Tightwad realized that Seth had targeted him. As he got closer, the look in his eyes seemed to scream, "Die, muthafucka, die!"

The bullets that Jesse and them were firing didn't mean a damn thing to Seth at that moment. Why should it, when he saw his little brother get plugged in the neck? Seth wanted somebody to pay instantly, and right now he had his man. "Bitch-ass nigga, you shot my brother in the neck! You dead muthafucka!" Seth stood over Tightwad and aimed the gun barrel downward. "Take this, muthafucka!" Seth discharged one from the chamber. *Pow!*

Tightwad's head exploded as the bullet smacked his shit from east to west, and blood oozed out of his head, along with bits and pieces of his brain.

As Seth stood there admiring his work, a hail of bullets tagged his cool ass. His body jolted from left to right as the impact from the bullets forced him to take backward steps, until he was no longer able to stand up. Seth fell backward and squeezed off his last shots. Each body part made a thumping sound as he hit the pavement and lay on the ground helpless.

As Craig choked on his own blood, Seth felt his eyes closing for the rest of his life. They both died looking at the niggas they were at war with.

"This one is out for the count," Lil' Man shouted to the other fellas standing over Seth.

Jesse looked down at Craig's open eyes. "This one is too."

Breeze looked down at his dead homie. "Yo, what we gonna do 'bout Tightwad?"

"Hell! What can we do? He dead," Jesse stated. "Now, let's break before five-O get here. Mission accomplished, but there's more that needs to be done."

Chapter Seventeen

Dee Dee couldn't believe that Miya was gone. She blamed herself for Miya's death. She kept asking herself, "Why didn't I go by the house earlier?" Normally, she would have, but her newfound happiness with Prat and dealing with the business was taking up so much of her time, not to mention the Robinson boys had been causing havoc around the way. There was just too much shit happening in Dee Dee's world, and not enough time to lend to anyone who wasn't part of what she had to do, even though Miya was all that she had left. No Bee, no Jay, no Ronshay, no RBM Clique, no relationship with her mom, and now, no Miya.

Dee Dee was losing her sanity, with all the shit that was taking place around her. She cursed herself as she looked into the mirror. What she saw looking back at her was a person who had gone through all kind of changes, both physically and mentally. Her world went from calm and peaceful to turbulent. Now she was a killa, a dope dealer, and a boss in control of everything and everyone. She was alone, doing everything by herself. The only thing going good for her was the three babies inside her, and the nigga that she cared about very much, who was standing by her side.

She knew that she'd been treating Prat unfairly lately, so she planned on making it all up to him later on and to show him that he was number one in her world. But right now, she wanted to know who killed Miya, just like she planned on finding out who killed her brothers.

Dee Dee decided to give Lil' Man a call to see if he could find out anything. She didn't understand why anyone would want to kill poor, sweet, little Miya. It wasn't like she was a troublemaker or in the game. Hell, Miya was the sweetest person in the world, who was still going through some things just by losing the man of her life, Jay, one of the reasons why Dee Dee purchased the crib in the good, upscale neighborhood for her and the kids anyway.

Dee Dee paged Lil' Man's beeper, but got no answer. She was getting tired of Lil' Man and his antics. She grabbed her purse and car keys and decided to head over to his house, since she wanted to talk to him in person and not over the phone anyway. Especially since she was going back and forth to court for some serious shit that the white folks wanted to hang on her.

As she drove down Jackson Road, a store sign caught her attention. The sign read in big red letters, "TREATS 2 READ." Dee Dee suddenly remembered that Chills had asked her to send something to read. *Better late than never.* Dee Dee smiled at the good memories of her homegirls. She waited for the traffic on the street to clear, before smashing down on the gas pedal and speeding across the street and into the bookstore parking lot.

Dee Dee grabbed her purse and stepped across the parking lot, headed for the store. She stood there in the doorway amazed at what she was looking at. Never had she been in a bookstore before. The place was as packed as a mall would be on Friday, but it was like a library, except for the instrumental music that flowed from hidden speakers at a comfortable volume.

A young white girl with shoulder-length blonde hair greeted her, "May I be of any assistance?"

Dee Dee broke out of her trance. "I'm sorry. I was just tripping on this place." Dee Dee walked toward the back to look around.

"First time, huh?" The white girl flipped her hair back over her shoulder.

"Huh? Oh, yeah, first time."

"Well, do you have anything in particular in mind that you want?"

Dee Dee looked around the huge store and wondered how anybody could find anything they wanted. Hell, it was big enough to throw a block party in. "Well, it is something particular that I need. My friend from outta the country wanted me to get this one book for her and send it to her." Dee Dee tried to cover up the truth about her friends being locked up, but what she didn't know was that bookstores all across the country mailed books to people in prison.

"You got the title of the book?"

Dee Dee went blank for a moment. She didn't have the piece of paper with the title.

The white girl saw that Dee Dee was lost for an answer,

so she went into phase two of customer service help, which was to ask her, "Do you know the name of the author?" Still seeing Dee Dee struggling to remember any sort of info that her friend had given her about the book, she asked Dee Dee, "What's the book about?"

When Dee Dee explained to the white girl that the novel was a street book, the white girl said, "Follow me." She led Dee Dee to a section where she saw nothing but books with hip covers, looking like they were CD hip-hop covers. Just by looking at the covers alone, Dee Dee finally got why Chills was saying that the book was good.

"Now, from the look on your face, I would say that you're in the right section, right?" The girl smiled.

Dee Dee smiled in return, but she still didn't know what book Chills wanted her to get. She cursed herself once again for being so forgetful.

"I hope you find what your friend needs. If there is anything else I can help you with, just call, okay? My name is Elizabeth."

"It's gonna be a task finding what she wants, but thanks anyways."

"Look, if my uncle gets done with the new inventory quicker than I think, then I'll be back to help you."

The word *uncle* clicked in Dee Dee's head. She ran down everything in her head. Then it hit her. "Uncle Al's classic joint," Dee Dee said out loud to herself. "That's it, Uncle Al. He's the author my friend was telling me about."

The white girl turned around and headed back toward Dee Dee, stopping just short of reaching where she stood. She scanned through a section of the books on shelves, until she spotted what she was looking for. "Over here."

The girl pointed one of her small cute fingers at some books.

"You found 'em." Dee Dee took one of the many Uncle Al classic novels into her hand. She scanned the cover with her eyes. The saying 'Don't judge a book by its cover' may be true, but Dee Dee was judging the book she was holding because never before had she seen a book cover that looked like the cover for an urban movie on DVD. The cover had her sold, lock, stock, and barrel.

"He's a good author. I like his writing technique."

Dee Dee looked at the white girl in astonishment. "You read these types of books?"

"At first I didn't. I didn't even know what they were, until people started coming in here asking about street stories. There's been such a big demand for these books this past year that we had to start stocking them. People come in here regularly and buy these type of books, if not for themselves, for someone they know in prison or over in the war. I gotta admit, curiosity finally got the better of me, and I read one of Uncle Al's novels. He paints such a beautiful picture with his words."

"No shit!" Dee Dee looked crazy at the white girl. "You really read these type of books?"

"Look at it this way, I listen to hip-hop, and it taught a white girl like myself a lot, and the songs are only three minutes long at the most. A book is a couple of days, at least, of being in another world, and if it's that good, then you gotta get the next one. I like this type of storytelling. These books are another form of hip-hop to me, and I'm proud as a white girl to read it."

Dee Dee was fucked up at the white girl's elaboration on the subject.

"Elizabeth Strausbaugh, can you please come to the storage room? Elizabeth, can you please come to the storage room?" a male voice said gently over the loudspeaker.

"That's my dad this time. I guess he can't do anything without his angel there to help him out. I hope you find everything you're looking for." Elizabeth extended her hand for Dee Dee to shake.

"Oh yeah, I think I found everything, thanks to you and your kindness," Dee Dee said, shaking her hand.

"Maybe we will see each other again, you know, discuss the books over a cup of cappuccino or latte."

"That sounds good." Dee Dee was like, *Cappuccino? Latte? What the fuck! Black people don't drink that shit.* Now she could have said something like, "Get a soda, or smoke a blunt, and talk about the book," but, naw, the white girl was in another zone. Dee Dee waved bye to the helpful but dense girl, who headed to wherever her daddy was.

Dee Dee collected about four of Uncle Al's titles and headed for the checkout line. As she waited her turn in line, another book caught her attention. It was the most powerful street book a person could ever buy—*The Holy Bible.*

Dee Dee placed the books on the checkout counter and picked up one of the big, expensive-looking bibles, the kind that people would give you props on when they spotted it. There was something about the book as she held onto it. She didn't know what it was. All she knew was that strange vibes surged through her body. She quickly gave the checkout girl, dressed in a green smock, the money for the books.

Dee Dee hopped in her ride and placed the bag of books in the passenger seat. She looked through her rearview mirror before backing out then placed the ride in reverse. Just as she was backing up, she had to slam her foot down on the brake pedal, sending her whole body jerking forward as she clutched the steering wheel. Her heart was beating fast as she sat there in her seat looking crazy at the bitch in the car that came out of nowhere and almost caused a wreck.

Dee Dee started honking her horn. "What, bitch!" Dee Dee shouted, anger in her voice and her hands up in the air.

The black middle-aged woman sat there in her car looking puzzled at Dee Dee, waiting for her to move the massive SUV. The lady knew she was in the wrong, but she went on and acted like Dee Dee was the one in the wrong.

Dee Dee was still mad about the lady scaring the bejesus out of her. For some reason, the *Bible* that was in the bag was now out in the open and resting on the passenger seat. Apparently, the sudden slamming on the brakes made the book slide out of the bag. As Dee Dee was about to shout some more at the lady who was eyeballing her heavily, her eyes caught sight of the *Bible,* and something came over her. What it was, she didn't know, but she placed the *Bible* back into the bag and took off.

Dee Dee rode all the way over to Lil' Man's crib, rubbing her stomach filled with her little ones. The thought of Alastair came into her head. She was pregnant with a nigga's babies—not baby—and when the time came, she would have to erase him from the earth and from her kids' lives. It was a dirty game, but there is something called, Blood is thicker than water, and the oath that she'd made to her brothers was written in blood, their blood, when the nigga pulled the trigger and killed them.

Dee Dee pulled her Excursion alongside the curb and parked in front of Lil' Man's mamma's crib. With the ride still running, she looked out of the window, hoping that Lil' Man would feel that she was outside waiting. She decided to page his beeper again, when she saw no sign of him. As she flipped her phone closed after placing the page, she nestled into her seat and plucked one of the Uncle Al books out of the bag. She glanced at the back cover, which gave a brief description of what it was about.

Dee Dee was no avid reader. Hell, she wasn't even a reader, but there was something about the cover of these books that she'd seen in the "Street Lit" section of the bookstore that just caught her attention, as if to tell her that this would be some shit she could get into reading. She glanced back over at her phone on the dashboard. Still no return call from Lil' Man's funky ass.

Dee Dee placed the book down on the seat, opened the door, and stepped out, closing the door behind her. Kids were outside, draped in different coats and tossing a football. Once again, she thought about her soon-to-be-born babies. Dee Dee walked up the sidewalk to Lil' Man's house, which was neither super nice nor straight-up ghetto. It was your basic neighborhood with trees, fenced-in yards, broken-down cars along spots in the street and, of course, the smell of soul food permeating the air.

Lil' Man's crib is a one story wooden house painted white with red shutters encasing each window. There was a nice flowerbed decorating each side of the steps. Dee Dee knew that someone in the house had a green thumb to keep it looking so nicely taken care of.

Dee Dee knocked twice just below the Christmas wreath hanging on the door. Even though Thanksgiving was in a couple of weeks, someone in Lil' Man's crib was getting prepared for the jolly season.

Just as Dee Dee was about to knock again, she heard someone yell out, "Who is it?"

It was the voice of a woman. No doubt, it had to be Lil' Man's momma. Dee was reluctant to say anything, for fear of too many questions being asked about what she wanted with her son, who was only sixteen, and Dee Dee being the age she was.

"It's Dee—I mean, it's Deondra. Deondra Davis, ma'am."

"It's who?" the voice asked.

"Deondra Davis, ma'am. I'm a friend of your son, Lil'— Lawrence." Dee Dee was fucking up big time with the name shit. She didn't want to use any nicknames, knowing a parent didn't like that type of shit, when it wasn't the name their child was given at birth.

The front door lock suddenly made a sound, and the door slowly opened. Lil' Man's moms was beautiful, but you could see the ghetto sass in her looks. Her complexion was that of brown sugar, and her size was that of Miya's and Ronshay's, petite. Her hair was wrapped in one of those paisley satin scarves, and her eyelashes were visible beneath her recently done eyebrows.

"You lookin' for my son?" she asked, dressed in a white robe and wearing thick, white, fluffy house shoes.

"Yes, ma'am. I'm Deondra Davis, a friend of Lil'—I mean, Lawrence," Dee Dee said, stumbling again with her words.

"I know everybody calls that boy Lil' Man. Why? Only God knows, 'cuz his daddy was six-six and I ain't short either, as you can see. Heck, the boy only sixteen. It ain't like he's through growing yet." Lil' Man's mom looked at Dee Dee's cute face. "With a name like Deondra, you wouldn't go by the nickname Dee Dee, would you?"

Dee Dee wondered where that came from. *Never let 'em see you sweat*, Dee Dee thought, in case Lil' Man's momma was hinting at something.

"Yes, ma'am, that's what everybody calls me. Except my momma."

"I know that's right." Lil' Man's momma grinned and then began to cough so heavily that she collapsed to the ground on one knee, holding her chest, with what seemed like serious pain to Dee Dee.

Dee Dee dropped down to where Lil' Man's momma rested on her knees and placed one hand on her back, the other on her shoulder. "Ma'am, are you all right?" Dee Dee asked, trying to see her face.

"Just help me up, child," she gasped. "I'll be okay in a sec."

Dee Dee could sense that she wasn't really okay, from the pain etched on her face, and by the way she clutched her stomach. "Ma'am, you sure you all right 'cuz, if not, I can take you to the hospital." Dee Dee helped the lady up from the floor.

"Baby, this stuff come and go. I'll be okay. Now just help me over to the couch so I can sit my butt down.

Dee Dee helped her over to the brown-and-beige couch then eased her down gently. "Would you like for me to get you some water?" Dee Dee rubbed her back.

As Dee Dee waited for an answer, Lil' Man's momma

began coughing all over again. It was so bad this go-round that Dee Dee stepped back, fearing that the couch was contagious or something. When she saw the woman point toward the kitchen like she really wanted something, Dee Dee had to play charades for a second to find out just what she wanted. "You want something from outta the kitchen?"

The lady shook her head and kept pointing, unable to speak due to the nonstop coughing.

The light bulb finally went off in Dee Dee's head. "You want some water?"

Lil' Man's mom nodded yes.

Dee Dee spotted some clean dishes in one of the dollar store dish racks on the kitchen counter. She picked out the biggest glass in the rack and filled it up with water from the faucet. She quickly rushed back into the living room and handed it to the lady, who then took quick sips until she was breathing easier.

"You work just as quick as Lil' Man do when he's around," she stated as she reclined back on the couch, getting comfortable.

Dee Dee looked at the couch then took a seat.

"I don't mean to pry, ma'am, but that cough don't sound too healthy, nor do it sound like it just came about the other day." Dee Dee was fishing, but only because she was concerned for the lady's health.

Lil' Man's mom turned sideways on the couch and scooted all the way to the end of it, with the glass of water in her hand. Then she kicked her feet up onto the other end of the couch and stared at Dee Dee.

Dee Dee sat at the edge of the couch, her forearms rest-ing on her thighs, legs slightly spread, hands clasped together, and fingers locked. Her back was arched, as her frame leaned forward. She wanted to just spit it out and ask Lil' Man's momma what the deal was, but she knew it wasn't her place.

"How old are you, girl?"

"Ma'am?"

"Now, don't tell me your ears is full of wax like that boy of mines is." Lil' Man's mom cracked a smile then took another sip of water.

"I'm twenty-six, ma'am."

"You know, Lawrence's sister would have been your age if she was . . . I'm sorry, I just get a little caught up when I think about my baby, Tiarra."

"She's not dead, is she?"

"Eight years next month. Some jackass ran into Lawrence's father's car while he was teaching her how to drive. They both died at the scene. That was a sad day for the family, but I think that's why Lawrence is the way he is now. The boy took losing his big sister and father hard. God knows, I try to keep him outta them streets and from around bad people."

Dee Dee sat upright when she heard those words, because she knew damn well that she was acting like a bad person, with the streets dictating what she had to do to maintain.

"But I just don't know what else to do. I ain't gonna be around forever to take care of him, and he ain't but a child."

Dee Dee looked strangely at Lil' Man's momma when she made that comment. "You gonna be around to see him grow up and be a handsome, successful man, if you get rid of that ugly cough that you got going on inside of you," Dee Dee joked, but all she saw from the lady's face was a slight smile that wasn't going any further. "Besides, you look too good to be a momma. I just hope I'm looking as good as you when I have my babies and get to be your age, and they get to be Lawrence's age."

"What you mean, when you have your babies? That little pudge I see don't have a baby in it, do it?" she asked, looking shocked.

"Yes, ma'am. Only, it's three in there, not one."

"Good gracious God Almighty! You mean to tell me that you gonna have triplets?" she asked, sitting up for this one.

"That's what the doctor told me."

"You and that boy who got you pregnant must've been goin' at it like rabbits." She chuckled. "I hope he's still around, 'cuz you gonna need some serious help to raise those three at the same age."

Dee Dee became quiet as she tilted her head to look at the carpeted floor. That alone told Lil' Man's mom all she needed to know. Dee Dee was going to bring another black child into this world by herself.

"Look, child. I don't know what planet you think you on, but let me hip you to something. I had hell raising Lawrence by myself when his father was killed in that car accident with my baby girl. Kids need their parents in their life. If not, they gonna rebel, and it's gonna be hell on you to pay the cost as a parent. I don't know what happened with you and the kids' father, but if he ain't dead, then you need to fix things between y'all. You gonna need him in your life, and that ain't no lie. I know who you is. I just never met you. Lawrence talks about you all the time like you're his big sister or something, so I know he ain't the baby daddy."

They both laughed.

"I also know what you do in those streets. What I'm surprised at is that you're a female who's doing those things, and you're cute at that. Them there streets out there belong to them thugs and killers. Now, do you want your kids to idolize people like you, or people in the same line of work that you're in? I heard about what happened to your brothers. Lawrence was crying a whole week 'cuz he looked up to them two boys. I'm sorry about your loss, but if you don't want your kids to be looking up to somebody else and try to fill a void that you gonna cause yourself to be in, then I suggest you leave them mean ghetto streets alone and let the dummies who think they are smarter than the police have 'em."

Dee Dee sat there looking stupid, like the preacher at her momma's church had put her out there on Front Street for the whole congregation to see. She didn't have anything to say, and looked away from the woman who'd just given her a lecture on life and its consequences.

"It's something I would like to share with you, and I hope you think real hard about what I'm about to tell you." She paused for a second to take a sip of water. "I don't have much time to live. That cough that you heard and the way it makes me weak all over is all due to cancer. Breast cancer." Lil' Man's mom looked into Dee Dee's eyes the whole time she talked. "That's right, I'm dying, Deondra, from breast cancer. It done made its way past my breast, and there is nothing that can save me except for a miracle from Our Father Himself."

"Do Lil' Man know?" Dee Dee blurted out, still shocked.

"He don't know nothing. See, as a parent, you try and protect your babies from all bad things, but what could be worse than him losing me, or your kids losing you, whether you go to jail or it be that God calls you home? He's not ready to hear something like this, even though he knows I'm sick. He do everything I ask, but I know he can feel something wrong. That's why he stays gone all the time."

Now, Dee Dee was beginning to understand why Lil' Man was always MIA when she needed him. Dealing with issues like what he and his momma were going through, it was obvious that he would act strangely and disappear to get time alone by himself.

"What's gonna happen to Lil' Man . . . I mean, if God don't send a miracle? 'cuz I know he didn't send me one, letting my brothers get killed and all, like they did."

"I don't know, child. I just don't know. God is taking me, and I don't have the slightest clue as to where my baby gonna live or who's going to take care of him. That's the type of stuff that pains a parent to death. Not the disease, but what I'm gonna do to protect my baby's future existence on this planet. Oh God! Help me, Lord Jesus!" Lil' Man's mom shouted with her hands raised in the air, waving back and forth, tears dripping down her cheeks.

The thought of Lil' Man's momma dying at an age when she looked so young didn't make sense, but Dee Dee was all too aware of the dreaded disease that was killing women fast, next to HIV.

Dee Dee walked over to Lil' Man's momma to console her, and tears began to fall from her eyes now. Lil' Man's momma gripped Dee Dee and held her tight, burying the right side of her face into Dee Dee's chest, as she held her tightly in a warm hug.

The words *God help us . . . give me strength* echoed through Dee Dee's body, and she felt the vibe flow through her body as the two embraced in a comforting hug.

Lil' Man's momma finally broke their embrace and wiped the tears from her eyes. "Deondra, can I ask you a question?"

"Yes, ma'am," Dee Dee said, wiping away any signs that she was also shedding tears.

Lil' Man's momma got up off of the couch with all the power she could muster. She then crept over toward the kitchen table and picked up something off of it.

Dee Dee knew what it was right off the bat from seeing it in her hands, but what did it have to do with what she had to ask Dee Dee?

"Do you know what this is, baby?" she asked as she sat back down.

Dee Dee looked at her. "Yes, ma'am, that's a *Bible*."

"Do you believe in the Word?"

Dee Dee didn't give a response right away. Eventually she said, "I don't know, ma'am. I was raised in the church, but I ain't seen what good He's been doing for me. It seems like everybody I let into my life dies or gets killed. Now what should make me want to believe in the Word, or God, when, no, especially when He let my brothers get killed?" Dee Dee was heated all over again because she needed to get with Alastair and make him pay for what he did. She believed that if he was gonna get revenge for his cousin, then he should have got her, not her brothers.

Lil' Man's momma was now the one left in awe. Coming from a youngster, Dee Dee's words weren't that uncommon to her ears. She knew that Dee Dee and Lawrence just didn't "get their roll-out yet," an expression that she'd heard from her mother and all the other elders around her way while she was growing up.

She reached under the pillow on the couch and pulled out yet another *Bible* and flipped through it. After a moment of silence, she told Dee Dee to turn to a specific page.

Dee Dee turned to Psalms and read the verses that Lil' Man's mom had instructed her to do. Nothing was making sense to Dee Dee at the time, but that's how God works at times. Nothing is supposed to work until he delivers the understanding for the person to grasp.

As they got into a discussion, they heard the knob to the front door turning. It was Lil' Man, sporting his purple-and-gold Lakers Starter jacket with the matching gold and purple skullcap. His black Girbaud jeans were sagging almost off his ass, which is what made his momma scold him before greeting him physically with a hug.

"Boy, if you don't raise up those pants up on your behind, then I know something." She gestured to him with her hand to pull them up.

Lil' Man did as he was told and struggled to pull his pants up the whole time as he headed toward her. He looked at Dee Dee and wondered what the fuck was going on. He knew that Dee Dee was trying to contact him for the last two hours, but he didn't think it was so important that she had to come by his crib and converse with his "mom dukes."

"Now, that's better."

Lil' Man gave her a warm, loving hug and a kiss on the cheek. "What's up, Dee Dee?" He raised up from his momma and looked at Dee Dee, *Bible* in hand and sitting opposite from his mother on the couch.

"Nothing. Just chillin' with your moms. That's okay, ain't it?" she asked, looking in the face for any resentment.

"Naw, everything cool. Besides, I see she got you hooked up in the Word, so that means you gonna be around for a minute," he said with a slick smile on his face. "Mom, I'll be upstairs if you want something." Before bouncing, he extended his arm toward Dee Dee and waited for her to press her closed fist up against his.

"Lil' Man, please don't break camp 'cuz I need to holla at you, all right?" Dee Dee told him before they disconnected fists.

"It's on and poppin', just go 'head and get your lesson by the best," he stated with a smirk on his face.

After Lil' Man got ghosted from the living room, Dee Dee looked over to his moms, who had her hands over her eyes. "You all right?"

"It just kills me that he don't know what's going on. Those streets got my baby and I know it. He really looks up to you, Deondra. I don't know what it is, but whatever it is, let me tell you this." She paused and took a deep breath. "When someone looks up to someone else, that means that they look at that person as a role model. You have the chance to change my boy's life from nothing to something. You are the person that he looks up to right now. Now, I'ma ask you what you gonna do about it 'cuz, remember, he's only a child, not a grown-up like you and me."

Those words hit Dee Dee like a ton of bricks. Why was this shit happening to her? She didn't ask to be a mother, nor a role model to anyone. Yet, she couldn't reject Lil' Man's momma's words. Dee Dee sat there looking confused and dazed. She placed her hands on her thighs and rubbed them, wiping the sweat away on her jeans. She glanced toward the steps where Lil' Man had vanished. She could now see what she couldn't see before. Lil' Man did look up to Dee Dee, just like he looked up to Jay and Bee before their tragic deaths.

After talking to Lil' Man's momma for a little while longer, Dee Dee chose to leave without even hollering at Lil' Man like she'd intended. The reason for breaking camp and not talking to him was part guilt and part respect. Guilt, because of what Lil' Man's momma had laid on her about being a role model and a big sister to him. Respect, because Lil' Man's momma knew what she did for a living and might figure out what she wanted to holla at Lil' Man about.

All in all, Dee Dee enjoyed her conversation with the lady. As she walked down the sidewalk heading for her ride, she looked back and saw Lil' Man's momma standing in the doorway. She wondered just where she was gathering her strength from to move and get around, considering she was dying. Dee Dee waved to her as she reached her ride.

When she saw the house door close, she hopped in her ride and just sat there in her seat for a few minutes, gripping the steering wheel. She was lost in thought, not knowing what to make of all that had gone on. She broke herself out of the trance and started the engine, putting it in gear and driving off.

She had something that she needed to do, so she wheeled her brother's Excursion through the Memphis traffic and headed to a special place she often visited when she was feeling the way she was feeling now. She pulled her ride into the Drexler Cemetery. The tall, black, steel gates were wide open as she drove through the wide cement maze. Different-sized and model tombstones lined each side of the road, and the grass was so well manicured, it looked fake.

Dee Dee went around the curve, covered by the tall, bare oak trees, and saw a funeral in progress. She drove slowly by and said a silent prayer for the family and their lost one, hoping it did them some good. She knew all too well what it was like to lose loved ones.

She finally made it to the section number twenty-seven and parked. She stepped out of her ride and closed the door, fastening up her jacket to protect her from the cold, forceful breeze. Dee Dee didn't know where the wind came from, because it wasn't as strong when she left Lil' Man's crib. The pine trees were swaying back and forth, letting Dee Dee know that snow would be coming soon.

She walked through the grass and came to where Jay and Bee were laid to rest. Instantly, tears flooded her eyes. It was very hard for her to be without the two niggas who basically raised her. She dropped to her knees, placing her hands on their charcoal-colored marble tombstones with black chips in them. As her tears dripped from her eyes down onto their graves, Dee Dee felt a stronger breeze whip through the air, sending chills up her spine. She instantly raised her head and looked around. It was a spooky and eerie feeling. She wrapped her arms around her body, then stood up and looked at her brothers' tombstones one at a time, their names inscribed on the marble, along with their birth dates, dates of death, and a special note: "For the Love of Family. Oh God, Watch Over Us."

Right then and there, Dee Dee knew that the strong breeze was a sign from her brothers, telling her to handle up. Or that's how she chose to interpret it. Then she walked off and headed back to her ride, ready to put her plan into action.

Chapter Eighteen

Picasso trailed Dee Dee as she left the cemetery. In fact he'd been following her since daybreak. He wanted to know her every move before he put the hit down and headed back to Cali.

Dee Dee cruised through the streets as if they were her own personal maze she had created. As she made each turn down a block, the beige Chrysler LSE rental Picasso was driving did the same.

Picasso followed Dee Dee back to the apartment building, where he'd staked her out umpteen times. It didn't take him long to figure out that she was living in one of the apartments in the building. After all, seeing her going in and out of the building constantly, and staying inside until the next morning, made it obvious that one of the apartments was where she called home.

Picasso slowed his roll, letting Dee Dee park and get out of her ride. He pulled to the left side of the street and parked undetected, leaving the car running as he watched her every move. The last thing he saw was Dee Dee pull the big door to the building open and disappear inside. He pulled his phone out of his suit coat pocket and placed a call. He spoke in Spanish for a few minutes, then flipped the phone closed. Whatever Picasso told the person on the other end had to be serious, because the caller told him that he would be on time.

Before pulling off, Picasso lit a cigarette from his stainless steel silver case. As he took a couple of puffs, he noticed through his rearview mirror a green Nissan Xterra SUV coming down the street, the bass thumping loudly and shaking his rearview mirror. Picasso hated loud music. As a matter of fact, Picasso only liked classical music, Bach and Beethoven being his favorites. It brought peace to his soul, when so much blood and death surrounded his thoughts.

Picasso eyed the vehicle like a hawk. When it made its way to the right side of his car, it slowed down. He was able to see five male figures inside. The men in the car were all looking to their right, which made Picasso suspect something. Then he saw one of the guys in the passenger seats extend his arm out of the window with a handgun in it. Picasso quickly raised up out of his laid-back mode and reached for his own weapon in his shoulder strap. The part that got him the most was that the guy brandishing the weapon was only playing, as the car kept rolling without a shot being fired. Whoever they were in the SUV, they seemed to be targeting someone in the same apartment building Dee Dee lived in. *Could they be looking for her?*

Picasso followed the SUV. He couldn't take a chance on the guys fucking things up for him and his reputation, especially now that he was about to accomplish the mission he'd accepted from Don Ruiz. He trailed the vehicle all the way over to the North side of town to a dead-end street that had about ten one-story houses. He observed the five men step out of the ride and head to a red house trimmed in white on the left side of the street as you entered the dead end. He quickly labeled all five men as thugs because of the way they were dressed: pants sagging, unlaced Timberlands, and hats cocked to either the left or right side, or just worn backwards. One of the men had a forty-ounce bottle clutched in his hand as he walked. Picasso knew all too well that something was up with these guys, and that they had a purpose for driving by the apartment building the way they did.

Picasso drove out, headed for his hotel suite. He'd seen enough. Now it was time for him to get some rest so he could handle his business in the morning, the early morning, that is, before most people would be up and moving about. Picasso's plan was to put on one of his disguises and go up to the door of Dee Dee's crib and knock, which would catch Dee Dee totally off guard, because she would still be partially asleep. Once she opened the door to see who it was, he would then place his gun with silencer attached to her head and give her one kill shot to the dome, dropping her dead to the ground and disappearing back into the early-morning rush hour. Picasso was no joke, and that's why he was so heavily recruited from top echelon people.

Picasso made his way into the hotel lobby and to the elevator. It instantly opened when he pressed the button with the black arrow pointing up. He stepped in and pressed the button for his floor. He watched as the door closed, then he leaned up against the back of the elevator and waited for it to come to a stop. When it did, he stepped out of the door and headed for his room.

Once inside, he went to the bathroom and brushed his teeth, to prepare for bed. To be on time for handling his business and concluding the line of work that he was good for, he needed his sleep.

The morning came, and his alarm buzzed, waking him at four-thirty. He was up and about, getting his face together with his makeup kit. While doing so, he had to pause at the knocking on his hotel room door. He already knew who it was. While outside Dee Dee's apartment building the night before, he'd placed a call to his chauffeur, telling him to bring a certain uniform to complete his disguise.

Picasso placed the stencil brush back in the kit and raised out of his seat. He grabbed his handgun off the already made bed, just in case. He opened the door quickly, basically to catch whoever off guard. He didn't bother even asking who it was, in Spanish or English. If he was going to die, then he would accept that, but if the person wasn't as smart as him, he would enjoy putting a bullet in their body and watching them die right before his eyes.

"Señor Picasso, I have a package for you," the chauffeur quickly blurted out, knowing that Picasso would be upset if he didn't see what he was asked to bring.

Picasso grabbed the brown envelope out of his hand, then made the handgun noticeable for the first time as he shooed him away before closing the door. Picasso walked over to the bed and placed his gun between his belt and pants. Then he spilled the contents of the envelope on the bed without even looking inside it. His eyes stared at the gray and black portable pocket Sony tape recorder. He also noticed the yellow tab stuck to it with something written on it. Picasso didn't waste any time, as he read the few words on the piece of paper. He knew where the envelope had come from, and that meant that whatever was on the tape had to be serious.

Picasso sat down on his bed and pressed the red play button on the tape recorder. First there was nothing but static, then an older, stern, groggy-sounding voice began speaking. Picasso knew the voice very well. He sat and listened to the entire message, which was music to his ears. A smirk came across his face. Just like he'd planned, he had to do just one killing, and then he'd be free from doing another one for anybody.

Picasso took the tape player and placed it in the briefcase with his other belongings. It was now time for him to handle business and head back to see Don Ruiz, which would be the last time they'd ever see each other again in life.

Picasso examined the weapon of choice secured to his belt. He held it, ejected the clip, looked at the bullets, then placed the clip back into the gun, and pulled the chamber back once. He sat down and took care of the final touches to his face then left the hotel room with everything he'd arrived there with.

Dee Dee was sitting on the toilet pissing when she heard her cell phone ringing. She had earlier placed a call to someone, and hoped that it was him calling her back. She took some toilet paper off the roll and wiped herself quickly. Her pants weren't even all the way up around her waist and fastened, but she hopped and bounced into the living room, where she grabbed her phone off its charger and flipped it open. "Hello!"

The caller at the other end didn't utter one word as he heard the Dee Dee's voice, which caused him conflicting emotions.

"Hello! Well, is you gonna say something or not?" she said, irritated.

He was now ready to speak, after all, things had gone on for too long without him being able to ask the question that had been plaguing his thoughts. "Dee Dee, it's me."

"ALASTAIR! Why didn't you say anything? I'm sorry. You're not supposed to answer something as stupid as that." Dee Dee was overexcited about him calling her back, hearing the voice of the man that she really loved.

"So, what's up? Why you callin' me after all this time?"

"I wanted to talk to you."

"Talk about what? 'Cuz, if I remember right, the last time we talked wasn't such a pleasant thing to hear what was coming outta your mouth."

Dee Dee wanted to yell right back into the phone and ask the nigga why he took his anger out on her brothers like he did, and not her instead. She took four deep breaths to catch herself before she said something stupid and blew her plans. "Look, I'm very sorry about what happened to your cousin. You think I wasn't serious about apologizing about having a part in taking another life? Hell, Alastair, my life has been a living hell. The dreams been killin' me, not to mention how I been lost without you and not having my brothers around."

"Look, I'm sorry about your brothers."

Dee Dee damn near threw up on that one.

"But please don't put me in the same category as them

'cuz that's your flesh and blood, and I ain't nothin' but a nigga that you got over and went on living your life without.

"Alastair, you are such an ungrateful bastard. You think it was easy for me to just pick up a phone and call you after all this time?"

"You think it was easy for me to let you get away with what you did to my cousin? Hell, if you was any other bitch or nigga I know, I would have been done had your ass slumped over in a ditch somewhere."

Dee Dee was quiet for a moment. She'd finally heard it out of his mouth about what he wanted to do to her, but she would have rather he did it to her instead of taking his anger out on her brothers and killing them.

"You don't have to do me no favors 'cuz I'm ready to leave this world anyway. At least I'll be with the two people who really cared about me," she said, feeling unhappy and heated at the same time.

"You really want to be with your brothers? That's bad. Damn! The rumors I heard about them are true then."

"Don't worry about what you heard about them 'cuz they ain't here to defend themselves. If you want to clear your cousin's death, then come on over and kill all four of us, 'cuz we ready to die!"

"You trippin', girl. I'm not about to kill you or whoever the other three people you're talkin' about. I made peace with God on that subject. Yeah, it hurts thinking about my cousin, but what would I get out of it by doing wrong for wrong? I think you're already paying a big enough price."

One thing that Dee Dee said stuck in Alastair's thoughts, so he asked, "Yo, Dee Dee, what you mean, come on, 'cuz all four of y'all is ready to die? You got somebody over there waiting to take me out 'cuz you think I want to hurt you?"

"I don't . . ." Dee Dee's words were muffled as the tears started dripping from her eyes and running down her cheeks. The phone call had done more than she anticipated. The tears were a dead giveaway to just how much she still loved Alastair. How could she still love this nigga this fuckin' much after all this time? After all, when two people know what's right for them, nothing or no one can stand in the way of true love, not even death.

Dee Dee gathered herself together and got her words straight in her mind.

Alastair heard the sniffling on the other end of the line. "Yo, I'm waiting to hear an answer, 'cuz if someone is over there wanting to cause me harm, then that's fucked up, Dee Dee."

"There's no one over here waiting to do anything to you."

"Then why you said something about the four of y'all are ready to die and leave this world?"

"I'M PREGNANT. Pregnant with triplets. Pregnant by you!" Dee Dee was more relieved than she ever thought she could be.

The surprising news had Alastair all fucked up. "Pregnant?" he asked, dumbfounded. "But how?"

"HOW? How the hell do you think? After we split up, I found out, you know, by the morning sickness and shit. And to top it off, you couldn't have just put one in me, no, you had to put your family genes in me and give me three of them!"

He knew the babies were his after hearing that, because he'd told Dee Dee about twins, triplets and quads running in his family. That alone was proof enough for him not to say something stupid like, "How you know they're mine?" He couldn't believe he was going to be a father of three. Joy leapt into his body. God had answered his prayers, showing him what he should do, as far as loving the woman who'd done something so wrong that he didn't think he could forgive her.

The truth of the matter was, Alastair couldn't get his thoughts off Dee Dee. In the morning when he woke, in the evening when he would be chilling, and at nighttime when he would be sleeping, Dee Dee was on his mind.

"Look, this is great news, Dee Dee," he said, holding the phone closely to his mouth to get her to hear what he was saying.

"Huh!? It is?"

"Hell yeah, it is! You havin' my babies. Look, we really need to talk in person about all of this."

"Huh. We do." Dee Dee was stunned, happy, and upset all in one. "Well, I been tryin' to talk to you for the longest, and now you wanna talk to me 'cuz you're ready, or only 'cuz you know I'm pregnant now. Okay, where you wanna meet at?"

"Ummm . . . okay, how about over here at my place?"

"What? Why we gotta meet at your place? Why we can't meet at mine?"

Dee Dee thought about what she was saying, but it was too late because she'd already let the words out of her mouth. For him to come over to her house meant that when she handled her business, she would be leaving a paper trail to the cops on who killed Alastair. She could have slapped herself if her hand would allow her to do so.

"Look, your place is just as cool as any."

That was perfect. Now Dee Dee saw an opening to put the invite back in Alastair's corner, and then she would accept it.

"I'm sorry. It's just this pregnancy has had me jumping in and out of mood swings. Your place is cool for us to meet. Besides, I ain't seen that place in a while, and I kinda miss it, to tell the truth."

"All right, cool then. I'll see you here in a little bit. Drive carefully, all right, Dee Dee?"

"I will. Just be there when I get there, okay?"

Alastair felt good knowing that Dee Dee was still the same after all the months of separation they'd gone through. All he wanted to do was see her and that stomach of hers that was filled with his bloodline.

Chapter Nineteen

Lil' Man was walking down the street, heading home. The fall sky was gloomy, and the wind was blowing hard, swirling leaves around in circles and blowing them away. Lil' Man loved the fall. Then, he could get funky with his dress code and wear shit like his leathers, hoody sweatshirts, and skullcaps, that he couldn't wear in the summer. Actually, he loved the winter snow more than the cold wind and rainy weather of the fall, which he was walking in right now.

Lil' Man reached his house then walked up the walkway to his front door. When he reached the door and was about to place his hand on the knob, he heard his name being called out.

"Lawrence, come here, boy," nosy Ms. Jean said. She lived next door to him in a brown, one-story house. Dressed in house shoes and thick winter socks raised all the way up her legs and disappearing under her long, buttoned-up cotton nightgown, she waved him over. Her hands were crossed over her chest, fighting off the cold wind, as she stood on her porch. "Come inside for a minute," she said to him, as he made his way to her.

"You need me to help you with something, Ms. Jean?"

"Have a seat, Lawrence."

He did as he was told out of respect to his elder.

"Boy, do you know God is good?" Ms. Jean looked into his eyes and held his hands as she sat next to him.

"Yea, Ms. Jean, God did a lot for me and momma," he replied, feeling a little vibe floating through her hands and into his.

"Baby, I don't know how to tell you this, and maybe it's not my place to even bring this up." She paused as a tear dripped out of her eye and rolled down her cheek. "Lawrence, while you were out, your mom—"

The expression on her face wasn't looking too good to Lil' Man. "Ms. Jean, I don't know what you got to tell me, but you're starting to scare a brother." He let go of her hand then stood up and looked down at her.

"Baby, I'm sorry about scaring you. It's just that telling somebody something like what I have to say ain't easy to just speak on."

"Well, just tell me. I can handle it, all right."

She bowed her head and gathered her words, then she looked at the boy who she watched grow up. All of a sudden, Lil' Man didn't look so small and young to her anymore. "Lawrence, your mother is gone. It happened about two hours ago."

Lil' Man's mouth dropped, and his stomach sank.

"Before she passed, she said to tell you to listen to Dee Dee, 'cuz Dee Dee was gonna take care of you. I don't know who this Dee Dee person is, but your momma's dying words were that you grow up to do the right things in life."

"Nooooo!" Lil' Man yelled, before bursting out of Ms. Jean's crib and bolting to his own. "That lying, old, nosy-ass bitch don't know what she's talking about. My momma ain't dead!" he shouted as he leapt up the five steps, holding onto the banisters and yanking himself forward. "Mommie! Mommie!" he yelled out twice.

There was nothing but silence in the air.

When Lil' Man got inside, he ran up the stairs, hoping to see his momma laying in the bed asleep or something, but when he opened her bedroom door, she wasn't anywhere to be seen. He turned around and sat down on his mother's bed. He clutched his fists tightly together and started pounding one into the other hand as pain and rage filled his body. "God, why you playin' with me like this? She ain't dead, is she?" He looked up, tears blurring his vision.

He ran downstairs into the living room and plucked the keys to the newly purchased, cherry red Pontiac Sunfire coupe that he'd surprised his mom with not too long ago. Then he rushed outside to go over to his girl's house. He needed to be with someone who would understand and console him.

Ms. Jean watched through her window as Lil' Man sped off. "Lord, please watch over that child for his momma's sake." She looked up to the sky. "After all, Lord, he is only a young'un."

Lil' Man arrived at Montreya's crib and parked the car. Deep in thought about what he'd just learned, he didn't immediately get out.

After a couple minutes of reflection, he finally pulled himself together and wiped his face and eyes free of tears. He opened the door of his mother's ride, which she'd never driven due to her illness, and got out. When he bought the car, he just knew that she would drive it as soon as she got over what he thought was food poisoning, like she'd told him.

The cold wind and rain pounded on his body, which he didn't give a fuck about. Hell, he really didn't feel it either, being numb now. He reached the front door and knocked very hard three times. The knock was so hard that he got a loud reply back from the person coming to answer the door. "I know whoever the fuck is knocking at my door like they're crazy or something better chill now!" the female voice shouted through the house.

When Montreya swung the door open, she saw the fucked-up look on Lil' Man's face. "Baby, what's wrong?" He looked like he'd been crying. He may have wiped the tears away, but his red, glossy eyes gave him away.

Lil' Man didn't answer. All he did was bow his head and rush into her open arms, burying his head in her chest and letting it all out.

Montreya didn't have the slightest idea what was eating him, but she knew it had to be bad because Lil' Man was never one to cry. Montreya just held him tightly as if he was taking his last breath. With all the crying that Lil' Man was doing, she couldn't help from tearing up in sympathy. "It's gonna be all right, baby. Whatever's bothering you, it's gonna be all right, I promise." She rubbed her hands up and down his back.

After eating a grilled ham and cheese sandwich topped off with lettuce and tomato, Lil' Man was in a calmer state as he lay on Montreya's bed, his shoes off. He told her everything that Ms. Jean told him.

Montreya didn't want to believe that Lil' Man's momma was gone either. To make sure that Ms. Jean knew what she was talking about, Montreya took it upon herself to call the hospital and find out the facts, since Lil' Man didn't do it himself. It was confirmed when she talked to the doctor who took the call.

Not knowing what else to do, Montreya let him lay on the bed without saying a word, keeping her arms wrapped around him, showing him that she was there for a nigga.

Lil' Man felt so much at ease, resting on the bed, and secure in his girl's arms, he drifted off into la-la land.

After a couple of hours of rest, Lil' Man woke up in a place he really didn't remember coming to and falling asleep in. After surveying the room for a moment, drool on his cheek and sleep in his eyes, he realized exactly where he was. The problem he had before he fell asleep was now back in full effect, and his girl Montreya wasn't anywhere in the room.

Lil' Man rolled off the bed and walked toward the bedroom door to relieve himself of the piss, his bladder ready to burst open. If it wasn't for him having to piss, he would never have awoken, at least not this soon. He opened the door and was hit with the aroma of home-cooked food pounding his nose. The shit smelled good as fuck to him.

On his way to the bathroom, he noticed the door to his girl's sister's room was cracked open slightly. As he passed it, he heard talking and wanted to stop to talk to his girl, but the pissing sensation had to be attended to, like now. Lil' Man flipped the toilet seat up quick as fuck and raised his shirt up. He had forgotten all about what he had strapped to his body. He looked around the bathroom, paranoid, as if somebody was watching him, the feeling that someone got when they knew they were doing something that just wasn't right.

He quickly locked the bathroom door and turned around, placing his back against the door. He couldn't believe that he let himself get into a position where he had to snitch someone out to keep his freedom. And this little episode had to go a couple of steps farther. He would have to get Dee Dee to talk about shit so he could get it on tape.

He cursed himself for being such a sucker, such a weak-ass nigga, for going that route. He wished he'd told the Feds, "Y'all can go suck a dick," instead of being in the predicament he was in now.

Lil' Man traced the wire up from his belly, where the tape recorder was attached to his waist, to the center of his bird chest, where the tiny mic rested. Lil' Man let his shirt drop back down, feeling frustrated about what "whitey an' 'em" wanted him to do. He banged the back of his head against the door three times. Then he went ahead and relieved himself.

With more stuff on his poor mind than the law allowed, Lil' Man headed back down the hallway. When he got to Montreya's sister's bedroom door, which was still slightly cracked open, he paused.

Lil' Man would have walked away and headed for the kitchen, where he knew his girl had to be, but what he was now hearing caught his attention like a bum spotting a half-full bottle of Thunderbird on the ground. Hearing of Jay and Bee sparked his interest, seeing as how Jay and Bee had been dead for a minute now.

He looked carefully down the hallway just to make sure Montreya wasn't coming to bust him eavesdropping. And he didn't want her to ask him, "What the heck is you doing?" with no way to explain that it ain't how it really looked.

The words, "I didn't want to shoot the niggas, but I had to," made Lil' Man reach frantically underneath his shirt so he could push record on the tape recorder and get the words on tape. Lil' Man had no doubt that the cat inside the room with Montreya's sister was the nigga who'd killed Dee Dee's brothers. He listened closely as the nigga kept talking and the recorder kept taping. The only thing that flowed through Lil' Man's head now was telling Dee Dee about what he was now hearing. After listening to all that the nigga was saying in the room, Lil' Man finally made his move away from the door and back to Montreya's room.

Once inside, he closed the door and sat on the bed. He pushed rewind on the recorder and waited for it to stop. Once he heard the snap indicating that the tape was ready to be heard, he quickly pressed play. The words coming out of the small Sony recorder made Lil' Man clench his fist and yank it down, like Serena Williams does when she aces one of those white girls that battle her so tough in a match. He then quickly placed the recorder and wire in the deep pocket of his baggy jeans.

Without even thinking of anything else, he threw his body on the bed and snatched the phone off its base. Pressing the numbers on the phone pad, and now hearing the cell phone ringing, he prayed for her to answer. "Come on, Dee Dee. Answer the fuckin' phone girl," he said quietly.

* * *

Dee Dee looked on at a sound-asleep Alastair. She knew it was either now or never. Alastair had to be put to rest. She slipped out of bed, careful not to wake him. The sex was as good as ever to her just an hour earlier. He took such good care of being gentle to her and her big-ass stomach, concealing their unborn. She'd never anticipated Alastair making her feeling so good, re-sparking the light in her heart, admitting how lonely and miserable he was since they'd split apart.

Now, she had to go there. Tears flowed from her eyes as she reached into her purse and pulled it out the chrome .380. She was about to lose the best thing that ever happened to her. Love is a bitch.

Dee Dee stood on the side of the bed, butt-ass naked. She pressed the gun against the pillow, which she had in her other hand. Her heart was racing so fast, she could hear it thumping against her ribcage. She didn't want to kill Alastair, but what else could she do? As she eased both the pillow and the gun down toward his head, she jumped, startled by the sound of a vibration coming from her purse. She had to act quick or else get busted. She bent her head down near her purse and was able to hear her phone buzzing like bees. She quickly plucked it out of her purse, hoping it wouldn't wake Alastair.

She rushed into the bathroom, looking back once at Alastair, making sure everything was cool. She closed and locked the door, and placed her nice, firm, bare ass down on the toilet seat. She noticed the emergency code on the screen that only she and Lil' Man used.

She tripped out, for him calling her when he thought something was serious, but when shit was turned the other way, she couldn't pay the nigga to call her back. Anyways, she'd been looking at Lil' Man in a different light lately, even telling his mom she would look after him. "What you want, boy?" she whispered.

"Dee Dee, you ain't gonna believe this shit," he whispered back.

"What?"

"I know who killed Jay and Bee. I swear, I know who did."

"I do too. Now leave me alone, so I can take care of business."

"You do? How long you known Prat was the one, and why you haven't done nothing to the nigga yet?"

"What the fuck you mean, Prat? He ain't the one that killed my brothers. It was Alastair."

"Alastair? Where you get that from? He ain't the one, trust me. 'Cuz I just stood beside my girl's sister's door and heard the nigga confess the shit to her not even ten minutes ago!"

Dee Dee realized that her voice was raised, so she got off the toilet and opened the door back up. She looked at Alastair still sound asleep and was relieved that she didn't have to go through with what she had planned. "Thank you, dear Father. I owe you one," she whispered, realizing that she would have made the greatest mistake in the world by killing the true love of her life and the father of her unborn three.

She then asked herself how Alastair could put aside his difference about the pain that she had caused him and his family. "How can I make it up to him?" she asked herself, knowing that she would have to make a great effort to do so if she wanted to keep her babies' father and mother together. The only way she figured that could happen was by praying and talking things out with Alastair, so that he really understood just how sorry she was for the pain she'd caused him.

Lost in thought watching a sleeping Alastair, Dee Dee jumped at the voice of Lil' Man yelling her name through the phone, loud as heck, considering there was no other noise to be heard at such a late time at night, except for the music playing low in the other room.

She quickly rushed back into the bathroom and closed the door again. "Lil' Man, my bad. Now, slow everything down and let me know what's up, from beginning to end, all right?"

This time Lil' Man replayed Prat's whole story, holding up the recorder to the phone so she could hear for herself:

Bee and Jay hopped in the Excursion and rolled out, headed for the block where all the fellas were. Shit had been going smoothly for them since being back on the streets. The ride over to the hood was being spent smoking on some good-ass greenery that they copped from TJ that was from around the way.

As they made it to the hood, they saw that everybody was doing their thang on various blocks in the hood. Some niggas were hitting licks, some politicking with one another, others in groups just chillin'. Females were around too, looking good and showing what they were working with in the body department. Seeing so much activity, Jay parked the ride and sat there for a moment, still chiefin' on the blunt with his brother, getting higher than a kite.

As they smoked, they talked about the niggas they saw down a couple of blocks, shooting dice. Jay, feeling lucky, asked his brother what he wanted to do now. Bee placed the question back in his brother's lap, seeing as he was down for whatever Jay was up to, just like always.

Once out of the ride, they stood rapping to some of the fellas. They asked who was down the block shooting dice, and when they got the answer, Jay and Bee made up their minds to give the young niggas a chance to make a come-up. But, in Jay's mind, he knew that would never happen, because he know all too well that big bank always took little bank. The rule of the dice games was that if a nigga's cash flow wasn't long, then he would be bankrupt in no time, fuckin' around with niggas who had cash.

Rock pulled up to Montreya's sister, Tiffany's house and parked. He leaned over in his seat and gave Mieka a rough kiss on her nice, soft, dick-sucking lips. Rock then leaned over across Mieka's lap and opened the door to his BMW to let her out. Mieka, like always, did what she did best, held her hand out for that cash before she went anywhere. Rock gave a slight chuckle then reached in his pocket and pulled out his wallet. He opened it and let her do the picking of one of his many credit cards resting in it. VISA was her choice.

"Don't be buyin' up the damn store with my shit this time, girl, you hear me, Mieka?" He grabbed her hand.

"Rock, you need to cut that shit out, especially after how I be treatin' you like a king and shit. I tell you what, Why don't you take this back?"—She held out the credit card to him—"And drop me off back at home. Oh! Before you do that, why don't you think about how that bitch you married don't make you feel like how I be makin' you feel . . . in bed and out of bed."

Rock was no fool. He knew his wife couldn't fuck with Mieka in the bedroom department, but he also knew that Mieka was no classy broad like his wife was. Mieka and Rock's wife were as different as night and day. Mieka was that ride-or-die bitch who was in love with him, and his wife was that stay-at-home bitch who had his best interests in mind. But still, he knew Mieka was right about what she said about treating him like a king, because she made sure to keep her "money bank" happy and pleased, by any means necessary.

"Girl, quit trippin' and go get my lil' cousin for me." He pinched her on the ass as she was getting out of the car.

"Quit, Rock! You play too fuckin' much," she fired back, rubbing the hurt through her tight-ass jeans that practically suffocated her phat ass to make that shit look banging.

"Just go on and do what I said, and I'll get with you later on tonight," he said as he watched her shake her phat ass all the way up to the front door.

Just when she was about to knock, the door opened and out stepped Lil' Man and Montreya, sporting the same outfit, looking like twins. Rock let out a silent chuckle as he thought back to those days, thinking that the youngster didn't know that that shit would be setting him up for failure in the future if he ever started to become a playa. "He'll learn, that's for damn sure," Rock said out loud to himself.

Not long after Mieka walked into the house, Prat came out pulling on his shirt. Rock automatically knew that was an indicator that Prat just got through fucking Mieka's cousin, Tiffany.

"What's up, cuz?" Prat hopped into the clean BMW.

"Nothing much. But check this out. I need you to follow me in your girl's ride so I can drop my ride off at the detail shop so I can get my shit hooked up."

Prat got back out and headed for Tiffany's Blazer. He didn't need to go get the keys from her, he already had his own set of keys to her ride on his key ring. She also had a set of his keys on her key ring. That's just the way they rolled.

As Rock turned into Playa's Detail Shop, Prat did the same.

He watched Rock talk to one of the cats that worked there for a few minutes, then Rock made his way to the Blazer and hopped in on the passenger side.

"Where to now?" Prat asked as they rolled out.

Rock told him, "Head on over to the spot, 'cuz I gotta collect this money from this nigga I bonded out last week."

Jay's turn came around to roll the dice. He winked at his brother, then dropped five hundred strong down on the ground and picked up the dice. Feeling the hot hand, Jay let the dice roll and hit seven. It was his lucky day.

"Break these fools, bro, like they askin' you to do," Bee urged on, laughing. "Word to the wise, y'all little niggas better quit now, 'cuz it looks like my brother is gonna be down there for a while taking y'all niggas' shit."

"Tell them niggas again, Bee, 'cuz I don't think they heard you." Jay let the dice ride again. "Booyah! I told y'all niggas I'm feelin' the hot hand." He collected more cash for hitting eleven this time on the dice.

As Prat made the corner, he spotted some niggas shooting dice by a tall, four-story brick building. Prat took his attention off the cats shooting dice and focused back on the road.

It was Rock who peeped the scene out and spotted Jay and Bee. It was a shock to him, because he didn't even know the niggas was out of jail yet. "Yo, cousin, look who's out and sitting pretty for the plucking, like the ducks that they are." Rock pointed to Jay and Bee.

Prat's heart started thumping like a muthafucka when he saw them. Maybe if Rock wasn't with him he would have kept driving by, but since he was and Rock knew the whole story about how they had beat his ass, he knew he had to handle his business. He *had told himself a long time ago that the streets would be where his revenge would take place, and now was the moment.*

He remembered what he had in Tiffany's glove box. He'd placed his piece in there the night before, because she would always trip on him about bringing a gun into her house. Prat opened up the glove box and pulled out the gun and a black ski cap with eye and nose holes, and rested both in his lap. He drove around the block and parked.

Rock saw the worry in his cousin's eyes, so he talked him up on how those niggas fucked him up over their stank-ass sister. Prat didn't need any geeking up. But little did he know that Rock had his own agenda on why he was geeking him on to handle those fools. Rock hadn't forgotten about the nigga Jay and him having that stare down at Mieka's apartment the day that Dee Dee and Mieka got into it.

Heart beating fast and sweat making his hands wet, Prat was nervous as a muthafucka. He looked over at his cousin and saw Rock motioning him to go ahead and handle up. He put on the ski cap and pulled it down over his face, got out of the ride and peeked around the corner and saw that everybody was still in place and engrossed in the dice game they had going on. Right then and there, and after taking a couple of deep breaths, Prat made his move. He couldn't believe that the niggas weren't looking his way. Now, up close and undetected, Prat raised his pistol and broke the game up. Buck-buck! The sounds of the 9mm exploded, echoing throughout the hood.

Niggas didn't know what hit them, especially Jay and Bee. Prat watched all the niggas scatter like rats, sliding as they hit the jets trying to get away. He looked down at his handiwork, and saw Jay and Bee face down and not moving, blood streaming from their bodies.

Meanwhile, Rock knew that the shit had gone down, so he took

*it upon himself to hop in the driver's seat and drive around the
corner to pick Prat up. When he got there, he saw Prat just standing there like he was just waiting for the cops to come and book his
dumb ass. Then he broke out of his trance when he heard Rock
yelling for him to get his ass back in the car.*

Dee Dee heard the whole tape. The day she got the letter from her mother at mail call was as vivid in her mind as
the day when Prat got his ass whupped by her brothers.
She couldn't believe how she had been fucking the nigga
and thinking that she had found love with that fool. Now
she planned on putting that nigga to rest with her own
hands.

"Where he at now?" she asked loudly, not caring about
her tone of voice any more.

"Dee Dee, slow your roll," he said.

"This ain't no time to be playin' with me."

"Look, you're in your feelings right now. You ain't
thinking clearly. Just take some time and calm down and
plot on how you wanna handle this."

"Lil' Man, you gonna make me do something to your
little ass if you don't tell me what I want to know *now!*"

"You know what, Dee Dee, you don't care nothing
about nobody but yourself, so if you wanna go and get
yourself killed or put in jail, then go 'head. It ain't like I
need you in my life. Momma died on me today, so you go
on 'head and die on me too. Who needs to look at you
like a big sister?" Lil' Man proclaimed with tears running
out of his eyes.

Dee Dee couldn't believe what she'd just heard. She
just knew that he didn't say that his mom had died. She'd
just seen her at his house earlier today, getting her daily

Bible study on with his mother. "Did you say your mom died today, Lil' Man?"

"Yeah, she died and left me, and now you wanna do the same."

Dee Dee felt for Lil' Man, but the bottom line was, she had to handle Prat. "Look, why don't you meet me at my crib at the building in a hour, okay?"

"All right. In an hour."

After they hung up, Lil' Man came up with a plan on how to get out of giving Dee Dee up to the Feds. "My little friend, you're about to work a miracle," he said, talking to the tape recorder in his hand.

Chapter Twenty

Lil' Man pulled up in front of his crib and parked. With the car now off, he swung the driver's door open and ran to the front door. Once inside, he grabbed the phone and sat on the couch contemplating on how he should go about the urgent phone call he had to make.

Perkins sat in one of the chairs around the table in the break room eyeing the vending machine that was filled with junk food. "Aw, the heck with it," he said out loud to himself, making up his mind to cancel his diet for now. As he rose out of his chair, he caught the wary eyes of some of his uniformed co-workers in the break room. "A person has to eat," he shot back angrily, digging into his pockets for loose change. He placed a wrinkled five-dollar bill into the slot, and like a store that didn't accept food stamps, the machine spit the torn-up bill back out.

"Busted!" a voice yelled out loud.

Perkins knew without turning around that it was Gary. He hated being spotted putting money in that junk food machine when Gary knew he was on a diet. "It's not what it appears to look like, Gary," Perkins said, never bothering to turn around and look his partner in the face.

"It's not? Then explain to me why you're at the vending machine that's filled with nothing but junk food then," Gary said good-naturedly. He then took the exact same seat that Perkins just vacated and sat down.

"Okay, so what? You busted me." Perkins turned around to face his partner.

"Tsk, tsk, tsk, looks like somebody woke up on the wrong side of the bed this morning."

"No one woke up on the wrong side of the bed. Just got stuff on my mind, that's all," Perkins stated, as he retrieved something healthier out of the other vending machine.

"Then why all the attitude?" Gary looked Perkins in the face.

Perkins walked back and placed his garden salad on the table. As he began to peel the plastic security wrap off the top, he said, "Gary, why haven't you told me about this little move that you've been conducting by yourself?" Perkins didn't need to see the expression on his partner's face to know what was already on it. He kept his attention on his salad as he dressed it up with the two little packages of French dressing that came with it.

Gary was shocked to hear it. He stood up. "What little move have I been conducting? I'm not really following you, Perkins," he said, playing with Perkins like he was stupid or something.

"What a way to play dumb and stupid. Hell, for you to stand there and lie to me must mean that this is some serious stuff that you' re doing. But if it's so serious, why did the chief even let me in on what you've been up to?" Perkins wasn't stupid. The chief had seen him earlier and told him all about Gary working as a liaison for the Feds on a case involving Lawrence Parker, aka Lil' Man.

Both men were now looking at one another—Perkins, seated at the table with his salad in front of him, and Gary, who had his back pressed up against the soda vending machine.

"Okay, Perkins, look . . . I've been wanting to tell you this for the longest, but I just didn't know how."

"I don't see how you having to tell me that you've been working with the Feds is hard to spit out."

"That's not what I'm talking about, although that part does have a major role to play in it."

Perkins eyed Gary suspiciously.

"All right, here it goes. I want to leave the force and join the DEA," Gary said, feeling a whole lot better. But when he saw his partner raise up from the table with a hurt look on his face, he felt just as he did before he told him, which was low. "Perkins, look, you're my partner, but you're also my friend. I like the MPD and being a detective, but I've been propositioned by the Feds for a job opening that they say I can have if I can close this case."

Perkins turned his head away from his partner and walked away. He had wanted to hear the news from his partner's own mouth first. He headed through the detective squad, passing detective after detective in all types of civilian clothes.

He reached his desk and sat down. His eyes focused on

the wood-framed picture of him and his wife in their back-yard having a cookout, celebrating her forty-fifth birthday. With his thoughts divided on his partner and what he just heard, and looking at the picture on his desk, Perkins asked himself how could he get upset with the news that was making his partner Gary so happy. He knew he was being selfish and that he should be happy for him. After all, he himself was planning on retiring from the force and wondered how he would break that news to Gary.

Gary walked into the detective squad and spotted Perkins at his desk staring at the picture. He knew Perkins didn't take the news too well and had no clue what to say to him to smooth things out.

The phone on Gary's desk began ringing, but it didn't faze Perkins one bit. He could have easily reached across his own desk to answer it for Gary as he usually did, but his mind was elsewhere, and it seemed as if he didn't hear or notice anyone around him, not even Gary, who was standing at the door looking on.

"Perkins! You coulda picked up the phone." Gary said, trying to break the ice as he reached over to answer it.

"Hello. Detective Gary speaking."

"Yo, man, it's me. We need to meet up," the voice spoke.

"Lawrence, this you?" Gary asked, not really able to match the voice with the face.

"Yeah, it's me. Look, man, we gotta meet up. I got some-thing hot. So hot, it's gonna burn your fuckin' hands," Lil' Man informed him. Then he murmured to himself, "But I wish it would burn your ass to a fuckin' crisp, you pig," which is what he really wanted to say to Gary.

"All right, let's meet up at the usual spot."

"Nah, man. I got a better place to meet up." Lil' Man

ran down the address where he wanted Gary to meet him then he gave him the time of the meeting.

From the tone of Lil' Man's voice, Gary knew it was about to go down in a big way. A way that was about to get him a job he would retire from.

Lil' Man was getting ready to leave his crib and head over to check Dee Dee out when he spotted his mom's *Bible* on the coffee table with a piece of paper sticking out of it. Curiosity won him over, so he picked up the *Bible* and opened it. The piece of paper had something written on it, so he took it out and placed the *Bible* back on the coffee table. What he was looking at as he unfolded the paper was a letter from his mother intentionally left behind for him to find:

> *Dear Lawrence (or shall I call you Lil' Man like everyone else does);*
>
> *I must say that you have grown up to be a nice young man, one that I am so proud to call my own. You bring so much joy to my life. Watching you grow up has been a blessing . . .*

Lil' Man had to pause for a second as tears began to flood his eyes. He took a seat on the couch and prepared himself to be man enough to read the rest of the letter. After wiping his eyes clear of any tears, he was ready to continue.

> *Sometimes I wished that you would have never grown up. I guess that is selfish, huh? But you can't blame momma for wanting to always have her baby stay a baby, now can you?*

I know you're probably wondering where all of this is coming from and where it is heading. Well, son, I want you to brace yourself for what you are about to read. Now, ask yourself, are you man enough to handle what I have written? I said, **Are you man enough to handle what you are about to read?** *Now, that's my baby.*

Son, I have been going back and forth to the doctor, and Dee Dee has been accompanying me on my visits. She has been a great help through my whole ordeal of being sick. The doctor had diagnosed me with terminal breast cancer. **Stop crying right now! You promised me that you were man enough to be able to take this!**

Lil' Man paused for a second when he read that part. He wondered how his mother could know what he was feeling and doing when she wasn't even present. It was a strange feeling. He glanced back down at the letter.

Okay, that's much better. See, even with me gone, you are handling things just fine.

Well, son, I just want you to know that Dee Dee is going to be taking care of you. I need you to quit selling dope and hanging out late. I need you to start going back to school, and then head off to college. **Do you understand me, boy?** *I hope so, because if you don't, I will come through this paper and whup your behind (SMILE!).*

Lil' Man did exactly that. He smiled and smiled big too.

Son, I need you to listen to Dee Dee. I know things are going to seem hard without me there, but as long as you are strong, things will get easier from day to day and year to year. That I know. Keep your head up and stay focused, because if you stay focused, you will be able to see that God and me will send you a loving woman to be your wife who will help you grow on a day-to-day basis.

Now, keep your eyes open, so you can recognize a good woman when you meet her. And don't think she's going to be or act like me, because that would be wrong for you to look for that in any woman. She's going to be someone who fits you, someone that is herself.

I love you, son!
Love, Momma

Lil' Man let tears drip from his eyes as he threw his body back against the couch.

Gary convinced Perkins to come along with him on the ride to meet up with Lil' Man. As they drove, they talked about what they both had on their minds, not leaving anything out. Perkins was more understanding about why Gary wanted to leave, and Gary was shocked to find out that Perkins was thinking of retiring.

The two-tone maroon and gray Astro van rolled down the street, while the five guys inside all chatted about the mission they were about to embark on. Shit had to be handled. The sherm stick was being passed back and forth, along with the ounce of coke that was in the plastic sandwich bag. The fellas were getting blown as they were ready to get some payback, their destination—Dee Dee's building.

* * *

Dee Dee walked out of the bathroom and glanced at her wall clock. It was thirty minutes past the time that she'd told Lil' Man to meet her at her crib. She didn't understand that boy, but figured she had plenty of time to work with him.

She headed to the stash apartment. Once inside, she opened the wall and just stared at all the kilos of coke stacked on the shelves, and all the big-face bills stacked up from top to bottom. She knew the game wasn't for her anymore. There were just too many obstacles that came into play when trying to get big, not to mention, maintaining it once you were there.

The thought came across her mind on what would she do with all the dope. The money she knew what to do with, but the dope was another story. But knowing she was getting ahead of herself, Dee Dee put her mind back on the matter at hand—killing Prat softly with one, or maybe two bullets to the head.

She closed the wall back up and headed out of the apartment and down the stairs. She wondered what was keeping Lil' Man, so she went outside to check and see whether she could spot him coming.

Lil' Man was running late due to the call he broke down to Detective Gary when they'd talked. The letter he read and his emotions running wild took up some of the time also, but now he was back on point and was almost to the building where Dee Dee stood waiting.

Dee Dee kept looking from left to right down the street, hoping she would spot Lil' Man, but no such luck. "Damn, Lil' Man! Where are you?" She was just about to go back inside because the cold was too much to bear, but suddenly she stopped in her tracks when she saw headlights coming down the street. "That gots to be him." She played it cool because she knew it was better to be cautious than to set yourself up for the hoo-doo.

Dee Dee waited on the porch of the apartment building as she watched the red Sunfire pull up to the curb and park. She knew exactly who it was when she spotted the color and make of the car up close. He looked over at Dee Dee then held up the tape recorder. Dee Dee spotted the recorder, but didn't have the slightest clue as to what the fuck he was hinting at by showing it to her.

Perkins sat in the driver's seat thinking about all that he and Gary had talked about. He thought to himself that maybe it was really time for him to leave the force and collect his pension. A smile appeared on his face when he thought about how many years he had been on the force and was lucky enough not to have been shot, considering all the calls he'd responded to.

Gary spotted the smile on Perkins's face. "What's so funny, partner?"

"Huh? Oh, nothing."

"Oh, nothing, huh? Well, that big smile that I just saw didn't seem to be just nothing."

"Look, I said it was nothing. How far is this place where you're meeting up with this *C.I.* of yours anyway?"

"We're almost there," Gary told him. "Just three more blocks to go."

The two-toned Astro van turned onto Dee Dee's street. "Yo, y'all ready to handle this shit?" Drew, the oldest of the Robinson boys, passed the sherm stick.

"Man, Drew, we gonna put that bitch to sleep fo' sho'

tonight, and that's a fact, Jack." Timmy Robinson repeatedly slapped his .45 in the palm of his hand.

Everybody in the Astro Van was zooted, and with them being as high as they were, it meant that they were ready to take on an army. That sherm was a muthafucka. It made even the most scared nigga think he could wreck anybody.

"What was that you was holdin' up?" Dee Dee looked at Lil' Man.

"You mean this? Well, big sis, that's your proof on who killed Jay and Bee. But check, if we use this right, I'm sure we can get you off that case that they got you on." Lil' Man pushed the play button.

Gary turned onto Dee Dee's street, not knowing she lived there. All he knew was that Lil' Man told him to meet him at some address on that street.

Lil' Man wasn't a dummy to give up Dee Dee's address. All he wanted to do was have Dee Dee outside when Gary rolled up, and hoping that before he got there he would be able to put some spook into her. And then when Gary rolled by, he could add more fright to her by saying something like, "Is the police staking you out, 'cuz look how five-O is rolling, all slow and shit, by your crib?"

Lil' Man knew that Gary would be riding slow as hell down the street, looking for an address that didn't exist. He had the plan all worked out. Except the part about the Robinson boys riding in search of some get-back.

"Perkins, can you please be on the lookout on that side of the street for a 1728 address?" Gary was already driving slow as fuck, straining his eyes to see the numbers on every house they passed.

"Yo, Drew, look who's making our job easy as fuck." Jersey, one of their followers, patted Drew's arm as he was driving.

Drew spotted Dee Dee and Lil' Man standing in the front yard talking. "Oh, hell yeah! Tag that bitch right now."

"That's that little bitch-ass nigga, Lil' Man, with her. I heard he had something to do with that shit with your brothers an' 'em too."

"Tag his punk ass too. And I mean, lay those bitches out, cold out. And I mean that shit." Drew pounded his fist on the steering wheel, causing the tires to screech as the van swerved.

Dee Dee and Lil' Man both heard the screeching noise and looked up quickly, but what they saw now was the van in the middle of the street and Jersey's arm extended out of the passenger window with a .45 aimed at them. Their eyes got really big when the side door of the van slid all the way back and shit started happening. The street lights weren't the only things providing light that night.

"Perkins, you see that?" Gary shouted, stunned.

Perkins did more than see the bright flares coming from the automobile up ahead. He reached for his weapon and instinctively checked for his vest. "Stop this damn car, Gary, and call for backup!"

Lil' Man thought about Dee Dee not being able to get out of harm's way, so he threw his body in front of hers as a shield. "Get down, Dee—Awwww!" The first bullet sank into his lower back, and then a second, into his right calf.

Lil' Man was taking in bullet after bullet, protecting Dee Dee, who he really looked up to as his big sis.

Gary and Perkins had their car parked in the middle of the street with both doors open, using them as shields. Gary reached into the car and pulled out the detachable police light and placed it on top of the roof of the car, and Perkins grabbed the CB and placed it on loudspeaker.

"You ready, partner?" Gary asked.

Perkins gave him the thumbs-up signal. "As ready as I'll ever be."

"Okay, here we go." Gary flipped the switch to turn the light on.

The Robinson boys caught sight of the red and blue lights flashing from the opposite end of the street that they would have to drive down to get away. "Yo, the po-lice!" one of them shouted.

"THIS IS THE POLICE! PUT YOUR WEAPONS DOWN AND EXIT THE VEHICLE!" Perkins had the mic in one hand, and his black 9mm aimed at his target in the other.

"Man, what we gonna do?" one of the followers asked. "I ain't going to jail, man."

"Shut up, ol' bitch-ass nigga. Ain't nobody going to jail. If these muthafuckas wanna interrupt what we started, then let's make them part of the game too." Drew was dead serious about warring with the police. He slammed his foot down on the gas pedal and peeled off directly for Gary and Perkins. That sherm had his ass gone to where he was going all out. He had his arm out of the window, bucking left and right, trying to hit something.

Jersey was doing the same, and the niggas in the back was letting off shots out of the sliding back door.

The van was coming full speed, which shocked the shit

out of Gary and Perkins. By far, this was the most intense and most insane shit that they'd ever witnessed or been involved in. Gary and Perkins let off a couple of rounds before the ride reached them, and when they saw that their bullets weren't lucky enough to hit the driver and make the van either stop or swerve into the curb, they did the only thing they could do. They dove out of the way.

"Dive, Gary!" Perkins shouted, taking his own advice.

SMACK! was the sound of the van slamming into the unmarked cruiser, and the sliding door slammed shut, chopping off clean the two arms that held guns out of it. The force of the impact moved the police car completely out of the way.

Everybody in the van flew forward. Jersey's head slammed into the windshield, snapping his neck and damn near taking his head cold off his body. Drew was seriously hurt also, but the sherm had his ass so gone, he didn't even realize that he had a couple of broken ribs, or that his nose was broken and bleeding bad as fuck from his face smashing into the steering wheel.

Drew went on to try and start his ride back up, and it started as if it had a brand-new engine that had never been in a wreck.

"GARY! GARY!" Perkins shouted, scared and hoping that his partner made it away in time unhurt.

"I'm okay. How 'bout you?" Gary got off the ground, but was unable to see his partner, who lay on his stomach with the riot pump in his hands.

"I'm okay, but watch out, I can still see movement in the van."

Gary didn't think that anyone would be able to move from a wreck like that. After all, the van had to be going at least fifty or sixty miles an hour when it crashed into their car. He was just about to walk toward the van and check things out when all of the sudden, a loud bang from a .45 exploded into the air and sent him falling backwards.

"Perkins! I'm hit!" Gary shouted. The bullet clipped a major artery just beneath his armpit, and blood was coming out of his mouth.

"I'm coming, Gary! Just hold on! I'm coming!" Just as Perkins was about to get up off the ground, the van started driving off. Perkins wasn't going for that. He stood up and got into the middle of the street to meet the van head on. He aimed the shotgun and started letting off round after round. *Boom! Boom! Boom!*

The windshield shattered as one of the buckshots tagged it. Another ripped into the hood, bursting the radiator and making steam gush out.

Perkins remained steady and firm in his spot, as the van kept coming, ripping and roaring toward him. But without hitting his mark, Perkins had to do the wise thing and dive out of the way. As he hit the ground, the shotgun still in his hands, the van raced past him.

He leaned up and braced the shotgun against his shoulder and let off round after round. "Please God, don't let them get away." Perkins squeezed off another round that popped the back tire. He then let off another, which hit the gas tank.

KABOOOOMMM! The van sailed completely off the ground and landed on its nose, exploding into a ball of fire.

Perkins could hear the yells and screams coming from inside. He knew that for an automobile to be able to blow up like that from the impact of a bullet meant that they had to have a full tank of gas. He quickly said a silent prayer, then rushed off to his partner's aid.

"Dee Dee, use this. It will get you off that case." Lil' Man could barely speak, his head in Dee Dee's lap.

"How, Lil' Man?" she asked, her tears dripping like water.

Knowing that he was about to pass on and be with his mother, Lil' Man just simply said, "You the baddest bitch I know, so you should know what to do with it. Just don't go down if you don't have to . . ." Lil' Man didn't even get to finish what he was saying as his eyes closed shut for the very last time in his short life.

Dee Dee threw her bloody hands in the air and screamed to the top of her lungs, "Why-y-y-y?"

"Gary, hold on, you son of a bitch! You hold on!" Perkins shouted at Gary as he held him in his arms. Then he screamed into his radio, "Officer down! I repeat, officer down, godammit!"

Gary smiled as he heard his partner break his habit of not cursing.

"What are you laughing at?" Perkins found it strange that Gary, weak and unable to move, could manage a smile.

"You just used a bad word, Perk—" Gary took one last deep, desperate breath, then died with his eyes open.

"Gary! No, Lord. Garyyyy!" Perkins shook Gary's body up and down, hoping to some way bring him back to life.

As the firemen sprayed gallons of water on the burning van with its high-flaring flames, the paramedics tried to check Gary's vitals. But Perkins wasn't having it. He was in a rage, fighting them off and swinging his free arm around wildly like they were a pack of hungry wolves.

A black detective car pulled up to the scene, and a big, black, burly man, dressed in slacks and a sweater and his gun in back of him resting in a black holster, got out. He looked at Perkins fighting off the paramedics and the uniformed officers trying to assist them. He bowed his head, feeling Perkins's pain. He too had lost a good friend, since he was also Gary's supervisor. He couldn't believe one of his men was gone.

He caught the eye of one of the paramedics, and right away, without having to say anything, the paramedic shook his head, which told the sergeant that Gary was DOA. He now felt that he had to take control of the situation. He bent down. "Perkins, my friend," he said, placing his right hand on Perkins's left shoulder, "he's gone. Gary's gone now. Let these people do for him what we aren't able to do."

The sergeant's soft-spoken tone had somehow reached Perkins, who had now ceased his resistance. When Perkins looked up, the sergeant saw the tears in his eyes, and knew that the recovery process for him wasn't going to be easy.

Chapter Twenty-One

Three days later at the police station 9:00 A.M.

"Okay, so you now understand the terms of this agreement?" Ms. Cole held up her copy of the plea agreement that would grant Dee Dee immunity from the charges against her.

"The question is, do Agent Downs understand the terms? 'Cuz that's the only way I'm signing anything." Dee Dee held up her own copy, mocking Ms. Cole.

"Ms. Davis, the DEA understands that you're not the one who was bringing all of those drugs into Memphis, as we thought. Thanks to your tip, we had one of the biggest drug busts in this city. And with your testimony telling us about how Prattancense Collins found out you were at the hotel with Manuel Stevens, and then decided to take him out, you'll be in the clear," Agent Downs said.

Dee Dee turned her head to the left to look at her attorney.

"Everything's a go, Dee Dee." Mr. Cee slid his solid gold pen over to her so she could sign the paperwork.

Dee Dee took the pen, looked down at the paper lying in front of her on the solid black table, and gave a slight smile. She'd pulled off something that only the baddest bitch could've done.

After listening to the tape over and over again, she came up with a plan not to kill Prat, but to sink his ass. She'd hauled her entire stash of kilos over to Prat's garage and piled them up inside. Once the dope was in place, she called him and told him not to go anywhere, as she was on her way over.

Of course, that was a lie. Agent Downs, Perkins, and the DEA were the ones on their way. Dee Dee told them Prat was her boyfriend, and that she feared for her life because he was a killer. Of course, they'd soaked up every word, believing a female over a nigga any day of the week. Besides, Perkins never believed Dee Dee was a killer, so hearing her story made all the sense in the world.

Prat was going down, and going down big time, for the thirty-five hundred kilos that the DEA found in his garage, and Dee Dee wasn't about to lose any sleep over his bitch ass. The rest of the dope she distributed among the cats in her hood, so they wouldn't starve. All she asked in return was a hundred thousand to start up a charity in her brothers' names, to do functions around the way for the kids. She also expected for them to make contributions, as long as they were on and poppin', so that the charity could keep on keepin' on.

* * *

"Push, Deondra, push!" the doctor ordered.

Dee Dee felt like the inside of her pussy walls were on fire and breaking open. This was the last one out of the three cute babies to come out and see their family members. Dee Dee was grunting, puffing and pushing, all the while squeezing the shit out of Alastair's poor little hand as sweat trickled down her face.

"She's almost out. Just give me one last push. Now, push!" the doctor ordered again.

The sound of her baby girl erupted as Dee Dee pushed her out, then slammed her body back onto the hospital bed, exhausted.

"Two boys and one girl!" You're going to have heck on your hands, girl," her mother said. They had resolved their differences after Dee Dee and Alastair showed up at her mother's church and spent the whole day talking with her. "Child, what names have you got picked out?"

Dee Dee had been waiting to tell everybody since Alastair told her she could name them all. "Deosha, Jacob, and Braylin. Get it, Momma? Do y'all get it? Lil' Jay, Lil' Bee, and, of course, Lil' Dee Dee."

Everybody started laughing, except for Dee Dee's mother.

The coincidence of her daughter having two sons and one daughter, like she did, dawned on her. It should have been a proud moment, but it brought bad memories. She'd fought so hard to keep them from the street life. She thought she should tell her daughter why she was so into church and God now. She wondered whether her story would shine a light, break the curse that seemed to only leave the females in the family standing in the end.

She looked at her three grandbabies. *Maybe they would have a story to tell that would leave only Deosha standing at the end of it too.*

"Ms. Davis, before we conclude these proceedings and start closing arguments, would you please tell us what Prattancense Collins did for a living." Ms. Cole paced back and forth in front of the witness stand.

"He sold drugs. He supplied most of Memphis with cocaine. He had me so terrified to leave the house. He would beat me like a dog for nothing." Dee Dee played the role of a scared bitch, as if she were on the TV show NYPD Blue.

The jury was looking at Prat, seated next to his lawyer. The looks he was getting from the seven women out of the eleven jurors, well, it wasn't good.

Dee Dee may have been telling lies, but there was no doubt that they were some realistic ones. Good enough to sink Prat's cool ass.

"Okay, Ms. Davis. Here, take this handkerchief. I'm sorry you have to relive those horrible accounts. But, Ms. Davis, I need you to point out one more time whose voice is on this tape that you just heard so the jury will also know, okay?" She held up the tape recorder, Exhibit A.

"That's him right there." Dee Dee stood up and pointed Prat out. "He's the one who killed my brothers." Right then, Dee Dee wasn't acting.

"She's lying! She's lying! Man, do something!" Prat stood up looking around for someone, anyone, to believe him. His lawyer even.

Prat was as good as sunk, to at least get life in prison, all because he fucked with the wrong bitch. The baddest bitch!

Chapter Twenty-Two

The smoke gray, big-bodied S500 Benz made its way down the private road leading to Don Ruiz's estate. Picasso sat in the back seat as the driver wheeled the expensive automobile off the dirt road and onto a brick road. For the very first time, Picasso really paid close attention to everything around the ranch. Everything was so tranquil. He watched the birds flying around, the horses running and grazing in the fenced-in pasture, the ranch hands tending to the barn. Everything about the estate, Picasso realized he loved.

Don Ruiz wanted a head, and now he was about to get it, signed, sealed, and delivered in person by the man he'd sent on the mission.

The Benz pulled into a cul-de-sac driveway in front of the mansion and parked. Picasso saw the two bodyguards dressed in black combat gear, like S.W.A.T., standing on either side of the front door.

The butler was already awaiting Picasso's arrival, and so was Don Ruiz, who was inside.

Picasso got out of the car and into the cool breeze of the fall wind. The dark shades he was sporting protected his eyes from the bright sun above. Once again, he was sporting a silk suit, maroon this time, with the black turtleneck seeping through. The Italian boots he wore had an immaculate luster to them that screamed, "Expensive." His hair was slicked back, and his face had tiny sprouting beard hairs from not being shaven.

Picasso raised his arm up to brush back the sleeve of his left suit coat arm to check out the time on his sixty-thousand-dollar gold and platinum Movado watch. His gold and diamond ring sparkled as he angled his wrist to check the time.

"*Señor* Picasso, may I take your bag?"

Picasso waved the butler off and carried his briefcase himself, letting the butler lead the way as they walked into the mansion, followed by the two bodyguards.

Once inside, Picasso went back to observing what he'd paid so little attention to before. The expensive artwork on the walls was absolutely amazing to view. There were imported vases with all kinds of rare and exotic flowers in them that filled the house with their intoxicating aromas.

The butler escorted Picasso into the sitting room, and the two bodyguards stationed themselves at the door.

Don Ruiz was seated on a leather sofa, getting a pedicure from one of his playthings. He looked up and spotted Picasso standing there. "*Amigo, Picasso. Me da mucho gusto verte otra vez.*" Don Ruiz looked at his plaything. "*¿No te das cuenta que debo a hablar con mi amigo? ¡Vete de aquí!*" he said, basically telling her to get the fuck out, because he had important company to attend to business with.

The plaything quickly rose from the floor, grabbed her pedicure kit, and was out of there in no time.

Don Ruiz rose from the sofa and slid his feet into his leather slippers. He gave Picasso a hug then placed his hands on his face to kiss both of his cheeks. "*Por favor, mi amigo,* have a seat." He gestured toward another sofa next to Picasso. "Let me get us some drinks."

Don Ruiz summoned his butler, who came in pushing a glass cart lined with all sorts of expensive liquor. Don Ruiz selected bourbon for them to drink, and took the liberty of fixing the drinks himself, instead of having the butler do it for them.

"Here, *compadre*, drink up." Don Ruiz handed Picasso his glass. "So, my friend, I take it that your trip back was a pleasant one."

Picasso leaned back into a more comfortable position on the plush sofa he was sitting in and crossed his legs at the knee in a corporate American businessman way. He raised the drink to his lips and took a small sip of the bourbon. "My trip was a nice one."

"That's good, my friend, that's good. Now, my little matter in Memphis, tell me, was it painful for her to part with my possessions?" Don Ruiz had a sadistic grin on his face.

Picasso retrieved his suitcase sitting next to him on the floor and placed it on his lap and opened it. The next thing he did was pull out a potato sack and toss it over to Don Ruiz, who caught it out of pure instinct, because he wasn't prepared to catch anything.

Don Ruiz looked at the potato sack up and down in disgust then shifted his eyes back to Picasso. "*¿Qué es esta mierda?*" (What is this shit?)

Picasso raised his right hand up to his face and removed his shades. With his legs still crossed, he placed both his hands on his knee as if he was pimping something. He twisted his shades by one of the handles in a circle.

There was something about Picasso's beady eyes that was very uncomfortable for Don Ruiz to look upon. They were cold and blank, as if there was no life in them. They had seen more than most people had seen in ten life-times, stuff that would make a hard-core thug not want to act hard anymore.

"You toss a fuckin' bag over here at me and don't bother to explain yourself. My friend, I think you should start explaining yourself like pronto, 'cuz my patience is about this short." Don Ruiz used his thumb and forefinger to demonstrate.

"Don Ruiz, I'm sorry to inform you that your problem in Memphis is still your problem. You see, the strangest thing happened while I was—"

Don Ruiz jumped up. "*¡Chingada madre, pendejo!* You sitting in my home, drinking my bourbon, getting great hospitality, and you disrespect me by telling me I still have a problem. You know, *compadre*, you was once known as the best in what people in my line of work hired you for, but now you as worthless as the whores I got in the next room. It seems to me that you lost your *cojones*. Now, what shall I do to you for embarrassing me with such stupidity." He picked up his eagle-head cane by the handle and nudged Picasso on the chest, moving him all the way back on the sofa.

Picasso's facial expression didn't change one bit as he sat back like he was forced to do. His eyes were working overtime, giving off that eerie look. He didn't say one word when Don Ruiz threw the sack back to him and he caught it in midair.

Undetected by Don Ruiz, he then reached into his briefcase, placed something into the sack, and tossed it back to him.

Don Ruiz caught the sack again. Only, he caught it with his cane. He noticed there was something in it and slowly brought it in to check what was inside. "A tape recorder?" He pulled it out of the bag and laughed. He looked over at his two bodyguards then laughed even harder, making them laugh along with him as they held their automatic assault weapons in their hands.

Picasso was still cool and chill as when he'd first arrived. His legs were still crossed, and he was still doodling with his shades at his knee.

Don Ruiz's curiosity won the better of him, so he had to listen to what was on the tape. He pressed the red play button and waited. Then there was the voice that he was all too familiar with from back home in Costa Rica. The voice belonged to one of the Heads. As a matter of fact, it belonged to The Head of Heads, who ran all of the families.

Once he'd heard the whole tape, he shouted for his men to seize Picasso.

When he didn't see any action being taken from his command, he reiterated his words stronger this time, waving his cane wildly. "I'll do it myself, then I'll take care of you two for defying me, you *maricones!*"

Don Ruiz reached under the cushion on the sofa and grabbed his chrome, pearl-handled .45. When he went to whirl it toward Picasso, who was still calmly seated and didn't even flinch, the two bodyguards forcefully restrained him. The old man was struggling, shocked at what was going on. He managed to let off two shots, one hitting a flower vase and shattering it, the other slamming through the patio glass door and shattering it too.

The bodyguard on his left put the clamp down on Don Ruiz's wrist, damn near breaking his shit, with a force that knocked the gun out of his hand.

He looked up at both of them. "What's going on, men? What is all this about?"

"Don Ruiz, Don Ruiz, you know exactly what this is about." Picasso stood up slowly and removed his suit coat. "You touched someone in the family without permission. That's what this is about. Now it's time to pay the piper, as you heard on the tape."

Picasso walked off and began rolling up his sleeves. He reached the shattered patio glass and stepped on the shards as he made his way outside into the cool breeze. He threw his arms up in the air and stretched. "Men, let's conclude this business." He gave them the signal to bring Don Ruiz outside to him.

Don Ruiz wasn't budging.

The bodyguards didn't mind the resistance at all, no. All they did was pick up his two-hundred-and-forty-pound, five-seven frame straight up in the air, as if he weighed only twenty-five pounds.

Don Ruiz pleaded with them as he kicked and tussled. He wasn't sure whether he wanted to break free or convince them to let him go with bribes and threats, but there was nothing happening in that department, and he knew that time was running out.

"Place him on the stump," Picasso ordered as he stood next to them.

"Please, Picasso, I'll pay you twenty million to let me live. That's twenty million! Enough for you to retire on, *mi amigo!*"

Picasso shouted, "Mita!" and the butler came from out of the house.

Everything had all been pre-arranged. That's why the bodyguards didn't budge when Don Ruiz gave the command for them to seize Picasso. They all knew that there would be changes when Picasso arrived.

The bodyguards forced Don Ruiz to his knees as they held his arms stretched tightly behind him. The old man was no match for the two men, who held him down securely on a freshly cut tree stump.

Picasso accepted what the butler brought out to him. "Gracious."

"No, Picasso!" Don Ruiz pleaded one last time. "We can work something out! Please don't do this!"

Picasso wasn't paying attention to anything Don Ruiz was saying. He had accepted the proposition from the Heads, and once a person did that, there was no turning back.

Don Ruiz's pleading was soon drowned out by the loud noise of the chainsaw that Picasso had just started. It idled, keeping one constant sound, and as he pushed down full throttle on the power button, then got louder.

Picasso slowly lowered his arms, and the chainsaw made contact with Don Ruiz's neck, chipping away pieces of his flesh.

Once he let the chainsaw fully rip, the sound changed again, as it made its way through meat and bones. Don Ruiz's head fell straight to the ground, along with a gush of his blood squirting out of it.

He turned the chainsaw off and handed it to one of his newly acquired bodyguards, then grabbed the potato sack from the butler. "Your head is what goes in this bag, Don Ruiz." He spoke to the head then picked it up by the hair and placed it into the bag.

The Heads weren't called The Heads just because they were the big-shot callers of the families. They got the name because, to eliminate a problem, and to get proof that the problem had been taken care of, the head of the one creating the problem had to be chopped off and delivered in person.

Covered in blood, bone fragments and flesh, Picasso vowed that he would never commit another murder in his life, as he was now the new Don of California territory. But he would have to order that people be killed, because that was part of his new job description.

And to think that Dee Dee still owed their organization.